T0285467

Sawdust Joint

The *Emerson Moore* Adventures by Bob Adamov

- *Rainbow's End*   Released October 2002
- *Pierce the Veil*   Released May 2004
- *When Rainbows Walk*   Released June 2005
- *Promised Land*   Released July 2006
- *The Other Side of Hell*   Released June 2008
- *Tan Lines*   Released June 2010
- *Sandustee*   Released March 2013
- *Zenobia*   Released May 2014
- *Missing*   Released April 2015
- *Golden Torpedo*   Released July 2017
- *Chincoteague Calm*   Released April 2018
- *Flight*   Released May 2019
- *Assateague Dark*   Released May 2020
- *Sunset Blues*   Released May 2022
- *White Spider Night*   Released July 2022
- *Rainbow's End 20th
  Anniversary Edition*   Released October 2022

The *Zeke Layne* Adventure by Bob Adamov

Memory Layne   Released March 2021

Next *Emerson Moore* Adventure:

Holden's Promise

Sawdust Joint

Bob Adamov

Packard Island Publishing

Wooster, Ohio

2023

www.packardislandpublishing.com

www.bobadamov.com

www.BobAdamov.com

First edition • July 2023

ISBN: 979-8-9853593-3-6

Library of Congress Number: 2023907217

Printed and bound in the United States of America

Cover art by: Ryan Sigler
Blue River Digital
303 Towerview Dr.
Columbia City, IN 46725
www.blueriverd.com

Printed by:
Baker & Tayler Publisher Svcs
PO Box 388
Ashland, OH 44805
www.btpubservices.com

Layout design by: Ryan Sigler
Blue River Digital
303 Towerview Dr.
Columbia City, IN 46725
www.blueriverd.com

Published by:
Packard Island Publishing
3025 Evergreen Drive
Wooster, OH 44691
www.packardislandpublishing.com

Dedication

Sawdust Joint is dedicated to Steve Sitts, a friend of mine who passed away in the prime of his life. Whenever I stopped at my favorite car dealership, Don Sitts Auto, Steve greeted me warmly and helped me feel a part of the family. We always had great conversations about our mutual love of classic cars.

Sawdust Joint is also dedicated to Ed and Kathy Pickard. Ed was an avid fan and met me at a signing in Port Clinton years ago when he showed me a Kreigsmarine dagger similar to the one mentioned in my book *Golden Torpedo*. Ed, who recently passed away, introduced me to the team at the Liberty Aviation Museum where he worked on restoring a PT boat. He and Kathy met me there last October and we had lunch together. I miss you, my friend.

This is also dedicated to Paul and Norma Jean Pinnicks. When they traveled from Texas to visit family in Wooster, we would meet for breakfast and share life's adventures. Paul is a big fan of my books and has been very adept at making the very first buy on my website whenever a new book is released. Norma Jean passed away recently, and I so admired her warmth and Christian walk.

For more information, check these sites:
www.BobAdamov.com
www.VisitPut-in-Bay.com
www.MillerFerry.com
www.ianflemingfoundation.org

They that wait upon the Lord shall renew their strength;
they shall mount up with wings as eagles;
they shall run, and not be weary;
and they shall walk, and not faint.

– Isaiah 40:31

Mike VanBlaricum Acknowledgement

A few years ago, I presented at the Clive Cussler Collectors' Convention in Las Vegas where I met another presenter, Mike VanBlaricum. Mike, the co-founder and president of The Ian Fleming Foundation, had one of the most compelling presentations at the conference. Mike's knowledge level was incredible and I made a mental note to contact him in the future.

Over the past 40 years, Mike has amassed a world-renowned collection of Ian Fleming's literary works and associated James Bond materials including manuscripts, letters, books, art, recordings, and toys plus over 40 of the vehicles from the Bond films.

Last October, Mike and his wife, Pam, hosted a visit to the University of Illinois library to view several of the Ian Fleming documents from the 650 that he had donated from his collection of 10,000 items. It was just absolutely thrilling to hear Mike tell the story behind each document. He knows the Ian Fleming story very well!

The University collection includes a proof of Moonraker, edited in Fleming's own hand, rare scripts and screenplays like Warhead, an unfilmed Bond story with Sean Connery credited as co-author. The collection also features letters and telegrams related to the Casino Royale novel. Then there's the rarest and likely most valuable document Mike acquired: "A Poor Man Escapes," Fleming's first short story, written when he was 19-years old.

I am indebted to Mike for inspiring me to write a Bond-like adventure for Emerson Moore. Thank you, Mike.

Other Acknowledgements

When my treasure-finding friend, Ben Marich, relayed the spellbinding story about a diving incident in Grand Cayman, I decided to use it for the opening of this adventure. Tim Young, aka The Captain and the victim, and underwater videographer Roger Roth as well as my senior editor John Wisse helped in capturing this scene for the opening chapter.

Technical advice on the Catalina PBY and Sherp were provided by my friends at Port Clinton's Liberty Aviation Museum – Ed Patrick, Eric Paul and Todd Hackbarth.

I'd like to thank my amazing senior editor John Wisse and my team of editors: Cathy Adamov and Michelle Marchese.

The Ian Fleming Foundation

The Ian Fleming Foundation (IFF) was formed as a public benefit nonprofit U.S. 501(c)3 California corporation in July of 1992. The IFF is dedicated to the study and preservation of the history of Ian Fleming's literary works, the James Bond phenomena, and their impact on popular culture. One of the IFF's goals is procuring, restoring, preserving, archiving, and displaying the original works of Ian Fleming and all of the subsequent products of that original body of work. These include the films, as well as the merchandise and memorabilia spawned by the films. Another goal of The Ian Fleming Foundation is to establish scholarships or fellowships in studies related to the dedicated areas.

Presently, the IFF owns over forty vehicles used in the James Bond films. Over the years we have supported several of exhibitions such as the Fox Home Entertainment booth at Comic-Con in San Diego for the 50th Anniversary DVD release. In addition, we have supported exhibitions for other not for profit organizations by loaning, free of charge, our vehicles for their fundraisers and have leased our vehicles to several officially sanctioned EON Productions (the producers of the James Bond films) exhibitions such as Bond-In-Motion in Beaulieu and London, England, Brussels, Los Angeles, and Saratoga Springs, NY.

While we are primarily known for our collection of James Bond movie vehicles we are, as our charter says, interested in preserving the entire legacy of Ian Fleming's works. As such, the IFF collects documents, books, posters, and artwork related to this popular culture phenomenon. The IFF has endowed a collection, titled The Ian Fleming Foundation Collection, at the University of Illinois Rare Book and Manuscript Library so that the documents and art will be both properly preserved as well as made available to the general public in perpetuity. We are always looking to grow our collection of "paper-based" artifacts and encourage the public to donate or help us identify these unique items.

We have also established an endowed The Ian Fleming Foundation Undergraduate Research Scholarship in the College of Media at The University of Illinois at Urbana-Champaign. The scholarship recipients study the areas of film history or criticism, travel writing, or newspaper journalism which were all of great interest to Ian Fleming.

The IFF Board members and other associated IFF members are often called on for advice and consultation on Ian Fleming or James Bond matters. For the thirty years that the IFF has been in existence it has been run by totally volunteer help. The monies that come in are used to buy, store, and restore our James Bond legacy properties and to support the educational mission of the IFF.

To contact or to make a tax-deductible donation to The Ian Fleming Foundation please go to: www.ianflemingfoundation. org or write us at:

The Ian Fleming Foundation
P.O. Box 61908
Santa Barbara, Ca 93160

Sawdust Joint

CHAPTER 1

Late Afternoon
Montego Bay, Jamaica

On the surface, Montego Bay along Jamaica's north coast was relatively calm. A 40-foot dive boat (the *Mai Tai*) rocked gently in a slight, easterly breeze under mostly sunny skies. It was captained by Ben "Mongo" Marich, co-owner of the Veterans Dive Center, which was based out of the Ocho Rios area near the Ian Fleming International Airport.

The tough Serbian shipwreck finder had arranged a short dive vacation for his two friends who were taking in the last dive for the day. It had been two days of good diving, drinks and food in their rented beachfront villa. Marich was looking forward to another few rounds of rum before he grilled the four snappers he had caught while waiting for his diving friends below.

"Breeze is picking up," the helmsman called to Marich. Tim Young (aka "The Captain"), a gregarious Floridian who was a rascal like Marich, had been keeping an eye on the weather. There were reports of a storm soon heading in their direction.

Marich glanced around. "Sure does look like it."

Below the surface, the two divers had been cruising casually around Widowmaker's Cave, a popular recreational dive spot in the bay. One diver was Emerson Moore, a 42-year-old, tanned and lean *Washington Post* investigative reporter. The second diver was Roger Roth, famed underwater videographer and filmmaker turned author, who earlier had met up with the men at their villa.

Moore always enjoyed his recreational dive experiences. He

especially liked the feeling of near weightlessness while at depth. Observing the abundance of diverse sea life moving through the gorgonian corals that stretched upward from the sea floor was a special treat. There was a large barracuda on the prowl, and nearby Moore also noticed a large spiny lobster's long antennae poking out from under a rocky ledge.

Roth glanced at his air gauge and saw he was getting low on air. It was time for them to ascend. He motioned to Moore with a thumbs-up sign pointing to the surface. Moore answered with an okay sign. They looked up to locate the boat, then swam across the reef to be underneath it.

Both divers began to slowly ascend, being careful not to do so faster than their rising air bubbles. Once they reached a depth of 15 feet, they leveled off in neutral buoyancy to perform their safety stop for three minutes to off-gas excess nitrogen. Exiting the water with too much nitrogen in their tissues could lead to decompression sickness (aka "the bends," which often causes divers to bend over in excruciating pain) and death.

They continued to watch the underwater menagerie swim around them while a large green moray eel slithered across the ocean floor as they counted down the few minutes. Unfortunately, they hadn't realized that they had drifted about fifty feet away from under the boat. Everything about the dive and the safety stop had been routine. That would change when they broke the surface where an unseen, deadly danger awaited them.

Roth surfaced with no problem and looked for the boat as usual. Moore, however, surfaced among several dangerous, long tentacles of a Portuguese man-of-war that was floating on the surface. Several of its balloon-like tentacles had attached to the back of Moore's hands and one to his right cheek.

The tentacles, which can range from 30 to 165 feet long, are covered with nematocysts - microscopic capsules loaded with coiled barbed tubes that deliver venom capable of paralyzing and killing fish and other small creatures. The venom is not normally fatal for humans but can cause excruciating, painful welts. In some cases, they can send the victim into an allergic reaction, heart failure or anaphylactic shock.

In Moore's case, it sent him into anaphylactic shock. He passed out face down in the water. After seeing Moore face down with the purple "balloons" floating on the surface next to him, Roth carefully swam over to Moore, making sure to avoid the floating tentacles.

As Roth swam, he called to Marich in the boat for help. Marich saw the bright purple Portuguese man-of-wars and realized the severity of the situation. He had Young quickly bring the boat around.

As Roth reached Moore, his rescue diver training kicked in. He immediately grabbed Moore's head to turn it and keep it above water. He added air to Moore's buoyancy compensating device (BCD) to help keep him afloat. Roth and Marich then successfully brought Moore into the boat.

Marich grabbed a glove from a nearby tacklebox and went to the dive deck at the stern of the boat where he could disentangle the purple mess from Moore's hands and neck.

"He's out cold," Roth declared.

"Anaphylactic shock," Marich announced as he quickly stripped the dive gear off Moore before cutting off Moore's dive suit. "Anybody have any vinegar?"

"Not me," Young replied.

"I do," Roth answered as he quickly slipped out of his gear.

Marich was carefully peeling away the ends of the tentacles on Moore's skin, exposing several long, stringy red welts.

"Could you get it for me? I'll rinse the nematocysts with it. The vinegar will prevent any more of them firing," Marich explained.

Roth quickly found the vinegar in his dive bag and handed it to Marich. "We can use your tea water heater to warm up some saltwater and soak the area until we get back to the dock. If we can pull out some of the nematocysts on the way, that will help as well."

"I don't think he's breathing," Marich said as he bent close to Moore's face. "I'll give him CPR. Tim, take the helm and point us toward the dock closest to the hospital. Radio for help. Tell them what happened and ask them to have the hospital send an ambulance to that dock!"

Young did as instructed while Marich began giving Moore CPR. After a minute, Moore began breathing on his own.

"Hang in there, Emerson. You're going to be fine." Marich tried to be optimistic as he applied the vinegar to the swelling welts, but he didn't like what he was seeing. The color was rapidly fading from Moore's skin.

Marich stood for a moment and looked to see how close they were to the dock. When he glanced back, he saw that Moore had stopped breathing again. Marich dropped to the deck and began giving Moore CPR for a second time.

Marich was still administering CPR when he heard the boat motor cut back and felt the boat ease up to the dock. When he looked up, he saw three emergency medical technicians (EMTs) ready to jump aboard.

As they did, one said, "We'll take over." He began to treat Moore while the second attendant applauded the group for the use of the vinegar.

Marich made his way forward where Young and Roth were

watching as the EMTs quickly examined Moore, giving him an IV and oxygen. Carefully they lifted him out of the boat onto a gurney and began to wheel him toward the waiting ambulance.

"I'm going with him. You take the boat back to the marina," Marich, the tough former Marine, instructed Young and Roth as he followed the group off the boat.

"Got it," Young assured Marich.

Roth added, "Keep me in the loop, Mongo. I want to be sure he's okay. I will contact DAN to see about getting Emerson airlifted to a better hospital in Miami." (The Divers Alert Network is an insurance program set up specifically for divers and diving injuries.)

"Will do. We're not going to let "Hardhead" get away from us," Marich stated confidently as he climbed into the ambulance. "Let me know when a private jet will be ready for him."

As the ambulance headed the short distance to the hospital, Roth rummaged through his dive bag and grabbed a satellite phone to call DAN for arrangements for Moore's airlift. He then went into Moore's dive bag and removed his DAN card so that the correct policy number was provided to the doctor on call.

It only took a matter of about 10 minutes before everything was set with DAN. A small jet would be used to transport Moore to Miami. Roth headed to the airport to meet the plane, while Marich watched the doctors at the hospital as they prepped Moore for emergency air transport.

Once back in the ambulance on the way to the airport, Marich began giving Moore a hard time. "You really know how to ruin a good grilled snapper dinner!" He teased, "Not to mention the rum I could have downed by now!"

Moore wasn't in much of a joking mood and just grunted

a little as he moaned in pain. "Sorry for messing up our plans Mongo," he mumbled.

"Don't worry about that. You're more important. We're going to fly you to Miami for treatment," Marich replied in a positive, upbeat tone as he tried to cheer up his friend. He had come too close to losing him.

When they arrived at the airport, Roth was standing next to the plane. "I won't be able to fly with you. They only have room for you, Mongo," Roth commented, disappointed that he couldn't accompany them.

Marich nodded in understanding. "I'll give you a call with an update after we get to the hospital."

"Thanks." Roth turned to Moore. "You hang in there, my friend. You got this!"

Moore grinned weakly as he was lifted aboard. A flight physician also boarded the plane with Moore and Marich.

Within minutes, the plane departed on its emergency flight to Miami for advanced treatment at one of its premier hospitals.

Moore was very lucky to be alive, thanks to the quick thinking and reaction of his friends.

CHAPTER 2

One Day Later
Tulare, California

"Copy that. I'm on my way," Mike McMullen growled, angry that the dispatch had interrupted his donut break. He stuffed the last of the four jelly-filled donuts in his mouth and washed them down with a couple of swigs from his coffee cup.

He reached down and pulled the seatbelt across his bulging belly and clicked it in place before starting his truck. Putting it in gear, the Tulare County deputy sheriff pulled out of the parking lot. He drove past several dairy feed mills on his way out to the Boylen dairy farm. It was a wellness call. The Boylen's daughter in Spokane, Washington was worried that no one answered her phone calls to the residence over the past two days.

Probably didn't pay their phone bill, McMullen surmised as he wiped several beads of sweat from his brow. The truck's air conditioner had failed the day before and wouldn't be repaired for another day.

He knew the Boylens. Nice people, but tighter than a fiddle string when it came to handling money.

Thirty minutes later, he turned into the lane leading up to the barn and adjoining milking station. The Boylen house sat just east of the barn. As he drove, he noticed several deceased and bloated dairy cows on the ground.

He pulled the truck to a stop and exited the vehicle. Walking over to the fence, he hefted his bulky frame over it and tore his trousers as he dropped on the other side. Grimacing at the tear, he approached one of the dead cows. It smelled. His eyes then widened as he saw the underbelly of the cow, which was gaping open like something had been inside it and wanted to escape.

A shiver ran up McMullen's back as he quickly looked around for any danger. He didn't see anything but a pasture dotted with more dead cows. He walked over to a few of the other carcasses and saw their exploded bellies.

McMullen shook his head. He didn't like what he was seeing. He had been watching too many TV shows about aliens taking animal samples. This was freaking him out. Time to head to the farmhouse, he thought as he returned to the truck.

As he drove up to the ranch-style house, he eyed the milk parlor, milk tanks, hay barn, freestall barn and office for any activity. He didn't see any. It was like a ghost town. The property reeked of death and ominous inactivity.

McMullen continued to the main house. When he arrived, he parked by the front porch. "Hello? Anybody home?" he called as he left the truck and stepped on the front porch.

When no one responded, he tried the front door. It was locked, but he could hear either a TV or radio playing inside.

"Hello. Is anybody home? It's Deputy Sheriff McMullen."

His inquiry was met with silence. He then walked around the side of the house. Noticing the kitchen window open, he placed his face against the screen and called, "Wellness check. It's Deputy Sheriff McMullen."

He quickly pulled his face away as his nostrils were greeted by the overwhelming smell of death from within the house. Wrinkling his brow with concern, he placed his hand to shade his eyes from the sun so that he could better see through the screen. He held his breath as he moved back to the screen.

Inside, he saw the Boylens. Carl and Tammy were slumped on the floor next to the kitchen table with their chairs knocked over. They appeared to be dead. Stepping back, McMullen radioed the dispatcher, requesting backup and the coroner. He looked around the property for any signs of break-ins or strange vehicles. There were none.

Being impatient, he decided not to wait for his backup. He withdrew his weapon and headed for the kitchen door. It was unlocked. Carefully he pushed the door. It opened with a creak.

"Hello. Anybody here?" McMullen called as he cautiously entered the house. He walked into the kitchen, wrinkling his nose as the smell of death permeated the room. The Boylens had apparently been dead for several days.

McMullen knelt to examine Carl, whose eyes were wide open, staring vacantly in space. His face was contorted as if his death had been painful. Holstering his weapon, McMullen allowed his eyes to quickly scan the clothed body. He noticed a large stain of blood that had soaked through Carl's shirt over his belly.

The deputy next walked over to Tammy. She reflected the appearance of Carl and had the same blood-soaked stain over the belly area of her long nightgown.

McMullen stood and scrutinized the table for any clues. He noticed the unfinished meal of scrambled eggs, toast and bacon, which like the Boylens, were covered in an immense abundance of flies and gnats. Nothing unusual to McMullen. He decided to quickly check out the rest of the house for any clues. He started to walk away when he stopped and looked back at the table.

One of the chairs was pulled back as if someone had been sitting in it. Strange, McMullen thought as he made a mental note for future reference. An examination of the rest of the house didn't reveal anything suspicious. He left the house and explored the outbuildings for clues.

Finding none and hearing a vehicle drive up, he returned to

the house where he saw the coroner, Dr. Joni Sams, stepping out of her van.

"What do you have here, Mike?" she asked as the sheriff department chief detective, Joyce Doney, parked next to Sams and joined them.

"Homicide?" Doney asked before McMullen could answer.

"I don't know." McMullen quickly explained what he had found as the trio walked inside the house.

"Did you sit down there?" Doney asked as she observed the chair pushed away from the table.

"No. I noticed that, too," McMullen replied as the two others began to examine the crime scene. "Did you see the dead cows on your drive up?"

The two stopped their examination and turned to McMullen. "What?" Doney asked.

"I didn't notice. I was so focused on the farmhouse," Sams explained.

"There's a number of dead cows in the field. I checked on a few of them and it looked like their stomach had burst open."

"That's strange," Sams remarked as she set up her camera to film her examination.

"I'm calling in a vet to take a look at them," Doney said as she reached for her radio. Completing her call, she turned her attention to Sams who had finished examining Carl's corpse and now was inspecting Tammy's. "Find anything revealing?"

"Strange. They look like the cows that Mike described."

"How's that Joni?" Doney asked.

"Both of their stomachs burst open from the inside. I've never seen anything like it," Sams answered with awe.

"Could it be exit wounds?" Doney asked.

"No. I checked. One wound on each body, and it's the stomach bursting open," she affirmed.

CHAPTER 3

Several Days Later
Put-in-Bay, South Bass Island

South Bass Island's resort village of Put-in-Bay and the surrounding western basin of the Lake Erie Islands were known for being a summer tourist "hotspot". Each year, thousands of visitors find this to be a great getaway destination to swim, sail, boat, fish, jet ski, dine and party at the various attractions and venues. This "Key West of the Midwest" was a taste of paradise.

Moore was sitting comfortably as he enjoyed the late morning view from the porch of the East Point house overlooking Put-in-Bay Harbor. It was a sunny day with a promise of a warm weekend. He felt it was nice to be home from the recent dive misadventure in Jamaica and his brief stay at a Miami hospital.

"Thank you for the tour," Mike "Mad Dog" Adams called over his shoulder to Moore's Aunt Anne. He came out onto the porch after getting a personal tour of her rebuilt home, which previously was destroyed in an explosion. The perpetrators were Russian drug runners who kidnapped Anne and were after Moore. He and Adams had then led a team of associates to successfully locate and rescue her in the Florida Keys.

Turning to Moore as he plopped into a nearby porch chair, Adams remarked, "Roger Parker did a great job on rebuilding the house. It's amazing what he can do. I like this version, more modern."

Adams was the legendary island entertainer who had been singing while playing his guitar and cracking jokes at The Round House Bar for over forty years. The muscular singer was wearing a white ball cap, blue shorts and a pink T-shirt. The shirt was lettered with "I Work Harder Than An Ugly Stripper!" He had an earring in one ear and his hair was pulled back in a ponytail. His eyes twinkled and a warm smile emitted from his bearded face.

"She's very pleased with the results, and the old place needed serious work."

"A blessing in disguise," Adams suggested.

"Indeed. I think half of the island has been through the house for one of her tours," Moore smiled.

"She should start charging," Adams chuckled softly. Getting serious, he asked, "How do you feel, Emerson? You had a close call with death even though you pooh-poohed it when you told me about it. I know because my buddy Mongo called me from Miami and asked me to check in on your recovery." Adams had introduced Marich to Moore some time ago.

"I'm better. I was in the hospital for a couple of days, then flew back," Moore said lightly. "I'm fine. Really, I am."

"Man, you almost died from the shock you went into! Did you have any idea that you'd have that kind of reaction?"

"None whatsoever. I'm very lucky to be alive," Moore acknowledged to his concerned friend.

"How long until those welts disappear?" Adams asked as he looked at the back of Moore's hand and the side of his face.

"The doctor said it'd take about ten days or so. Shouldn't be too much longer." Moore shifted in his seat. "I'll tell you one thing."

"What?"

"I'm getting bored. I'm not used to sitting around like this. Doing the recovery from the shock thing for my body," Moore complained.

"Better take it easy."

"And I'm here to make sure of it," a voice spoke from the doorway as a gray-haired head popped into view. It was Moore's vivacious sixty-six-year-old aunt.

"I can't get away with anything with her here," Moore moaned good-naturedly.

"Darn tooting!" she remarked before disappearing into the house.

Moore's cell phone began to ring. "Hello," he answered.

"Feeling better, Emerson?"

Moore recognized the voice of his managing editor, John Sedler. He was calling from the newspaper office in Washington, D.C.

"Yes. Much better." Moore cut to the chase. "Anything for me to work on?"

Sedler chuckled. He imagined how antsy Moore must be feeling. "As a matter of fact, I do. Did you read about the two dairy farmers and the dairy cows that died in California a couple of days ago?"

"Yes. I saw it online. Did anyone figure out what happened?"

"No. Not yet. But I just got a report of another incident that involved cows dying in a similar fashion in your neck of the woods."

"I wasn't aware."

"It just broke on the wire. You feel up to taking a drive to Wooster, Ohio and see what you can uncover? May or may not be anything to it."

"Sure, Wooster is about a couple of hours southeast of here. I could use a change of pace. Did you know that area of Ohio is the largest dairy producing county in the state?"

"No, but I remember you had been to Wooster some time ago."

Moore nodded as he recalled his experience with memory loss and being a hitman for the mob. The hideout was a farm in the Wooster area.

"That I do remember," Moore commented.

"See if there's any possible linkage to the deaths in California and let me know."

"Will do," Moore said as they ended the call.

"That sounds interesting," Adams said as he stood.

"Want to come along for the ride?"

"Can't today. I have a show in a couple of hours," Adams said reluctantly. He always enjoyed tagging along with Moore on his adventures, and he usually ended up saving Moore's life.

After Adams left, Moore researched online what he could on the reports of the cow deaths. He then made a couple of phone calls and, two hours later, jumped into his red Ford Mustang convertible to catch the Miller Ferry at South Bass Island's Lime Kin Dock. After the short ferry ride to the mainland, Moore began his drive to the Wayne County dairy farm. It was a sunny day for a drive as he headed for Ohio Route 250.

Following his GPS, Moore turned off Smithville-Western Road two hours later onto the driveway leading to the Varns farm. He spotted several police vehicles near the barn and drove there. After he parked, he walked over to a group of people where it appeared that a law enforcement officer was giving a briefing.

"We're still investigating what caused the death of these dairy cows," Chief Hardman was explaining. "We don't believe it was vandalism or anything like that."

"Is it true that the cow stomachs exploded?" a person in the small crowd asked.

"Yes."

"Think it was aliens?" a reporter from a UFO publication asked.

"No," Hardman smiled at the question.

"Is this contagious? Any reason for humans to be concerned?" another reporter peppered Hardman.

"We've got the folks from the Ohio Agricultural Research and Development Center analyzing the cause of death. When we have the results, we will make it public," Hardman said as he referred to the Ohio State University operations in Wooster. It was the nation's leading Ag bio-science research institution.

"What does Mr. Varns have to say about the deaths?" Moore asked, referring to the owner of the dairy farm.

Hardman turned to the farmer who was standing nearby with his wife, Joyce. "Gene, are you willing to answer a couple of questions?"

"Sure, Charlie." The gray-mustached Varns stepped forward. "What can I answer for you?"

"How many dairy cows did you lose?" Moore asked.

"All of them. We had 100 of them."

"Were there any warning signs?" Moore followed up quickly.

"None. They were fine yesterday. This morning, we found them dead with their stomachs burst open. It was like they swallowed a bomb," he explained.

Several reporters fired off questions as Moore left the group. He walked around the barn where he found two of the Ohio State University technicians examining one of the cows. Another was taking pictures, while several others loaded one of the carcasses onto a flatbed truck to take back to the research center for further evaluation.

"Any ideas?" Moore asked when one of the technicians looked up.

"Not yet. It's the strangest thing."

Moore handed the man his business card. "If you find anything, could you give me a call?"

The technician glanced at the card and handed it back to Moore. "We're not allowed to talk to the press. There would be a press conference if we have anything to release."

Moore saw that he wasn't going to get anywhere with the technicians. He snapped off a few photos of the carcasses with the exploded stomachs as he walked around the dead cows. As he made his way back to the barn, he saw the dairy farmer and his wife.

"Excuse me, Mr. Varns."

"Yes?" the slightly-built man asked.

"Do you have any ideas as to what caused it?"

"That's the baffling mystery about all of this. Nothing unusual has happened here," Varns responded.

"How about the water?"

"We have the best well around," Joyce remarked as she smiled warmly at the handsome reporter. "It was tested a few weeks ago and passed with flying colors."

"Any change with feed or additives?" Moore asked.

"Nope. Like I said, nothing different," Varns replied.

Moore looked around the property. It didn't seem well-secured from his viewpoint. "Mr. Varns, would you know if anyone tampered with your dairy feed?"

Varns scratched his head for a moment as he thought before answering. "No one has in the past. I guess if someone wanted to sneak in and poison my feed, my well or pond, that they could. Stuff like that doesn't happen here in Wayne County. We're known for having good people here," he explained.

"That's right," Joyce chimed in.

"Thank you very much. Can I give you my card so you can call with any new developments?" Moore asked as he handed Varns his card.

Varns stared at the card in his hand. "I don't know," he said hesitantly.

Joyce snatched the card from her husband's hand. "Of course, we will," she smiled again at the handsome reporter. She'd welcome another visit with him.

"Thank you. I appreciate it and I'm so sorry about the loss of your cows," Moore said as he turned and walked away from the two.

He was frustrated as he returned to his car and drove off the property. He called Sedler and reported what little he had learned. Sedler asked him to catch a flight to Fresno, California and see what he could learn from the authorities in Tulare.

CHAPTER 4

Next Day
Tulare, California

Califarmia, as some would call it, is the nation's biggest milk producing state with a $7.5 billion in revenue per year. It is home to more than 1,100 family-owned dairy farms. The three largest milk-producing counties are Tulare, Merced and Kings counties. They were stocked with Holstein cows, each able to daily produce nine gallons of milk. The cows dined on grass, grains, silage and other feed ingredients. Tulare county in the Central Valley has the largest concentration of dairy cows in the state with more than 450,000 cows.

After landing in Fresno, Moore drove south along California Route 99 for the nearly hour-long drive to Tulare. He looked forward to meeting with the lead detective investigating the deaths of the Boylens and their cows. Shortly after entering the county administration building, Moore was ushered into Chief Detective Joyce Doney's office.

Doney introduced herself and the county coroner, Dr. Joni Sams, who was seated in Doney's office.

"How can we help you with your story, Emerson?" Doney asked as she sat.

"I was curious if you've made any progress on the cause of death to the cows or the Boylen couple?" Moore started.

"Like I told you on the phone, this is an active investigation and there's not too much that we can say yet," Doney cautioned. "I also said that I think you're wasting your time by coming out here."

Moore expected that type of response, but he was known

for digging deeper to get people to reveal more than they wanted to reveal. "Is there anything that you can tell me?" he pushed.

"You can tell him about the kitchen chair," Sams suggested.

Moore observed the disappointing look that Doney shot Sams. "What's this about a chair? Was there a fight?" Moore probed.

"No. Nothing like that. We noticed that a chair was pulled back from the kitchen table like someone had been sitting in it. May be nothing. Could have been from a visitor the previous day," Doney said, downplaying the information.

"From what I've learned thus far, it sounds like there's a strong connection between the deaths of the Boylens and their cows," Moore iterated. "Was there an issue with their well water? What about the livestock feed and any of its additives? If so, how would that have been consumed by the Boylens?" Moore was on his game but getting slim results.

"We are checking every possible avenue in our investigation. There have been no conclusions yet," Doney answered in a professional tone.

"Tell him about the sprinkles on the eggs," Sams suggested as she tried to be helpful.

"Sprinkles?" Moore asked as he looked from Sams to Doney.

"Like everything we found on the Boylen's kitchen table, we are analyzing the food for any evidence of poisoning. We don't have the toxicology report back," Doney confirmed.

Moore again turned to the more forthcoming Sams. "Was it something like wheat germ that a person would sprinkle on their food?"

Sams glanced at Doney who was slowly shaking her head from side to side. She did not want Sams to answer. "I've probably said too much. Like Joyce said, we're waiting for results from the tests."

"Are you aware that there was a report of cows dying in Ohio with their stomachs bursting open?" Moore asked.

"Yes. We saw that yesterday. We're actually in discussions with our counterparts in Wooster," Doney acknowledged.

"Charlie Hardman?" Moore asked.

"Yes," Doney replied, sensing that Moore had already talked to him.

Moore realized that he wasn't going to get anything else from the two and concluded his futile meeting with them. When he left the building, he drove to the Boylen farm. Seeing no cars in the drive, he drove up to the buildings and parked. He spent an hour walking around and snapping photos. But to his dismay, he didn't discover anything new that would help him with his investigation as the dead cows and the Boylens obviously were no longer present.

He climbed back into his car and drove to several nearby dairy farms where he asked the farmers various questions, but again with no interesting revelations. It did appear to be an isolated case, although he wondered how the cow deaths in Tulare connected to the ones in Wooster.

As he drove back to Fresno, he booked a flight home for the next morning and reported to Sedler what little he had learned. Moore was frustrated with his lack of progress on the story.

CHAPTER 5

Two Days Later
Put-in-Bay

Late that morning, Moore sat on his aunt's porch and was typing away on his laptop. He was researching the dairy industry and specifically focused on unusual cow deaths where their stomachs were found to have burst open. He found nothing, so he next researched livestock deaths related to feed and various additives used to increase milk production. Were any cow deaths directly related to human illness or death? Again, Moore came up empty.

"Can I freshen your coffee?" Aunt Anne asked as she entered the porch with a coffee pot in her hand.

"I really need to freshen my brain," Moore stated in frustration as he held up his coffee cup for her to fill.

"Tough morning?"

"I'll say," he answered as he sat back in his chair, sipping the hot liquid.

"Maybe this will cheer you up. You've got express mail from your buddy, Sam Duncan," she said as she handed him the envelope. "It just came in."

"Interesting," Moore said as he took the envelope and stared at it. He wondered why his friend would contact him by mail rather than email or by phone.

"I've got things to do," Aunt Anne said in a cheery tone as she walked away.

"Thank you," Moore called as he set down his coffee cup and opened the envelope. When he did, a plane ticket and wad of $100 bills fell out. He picked them up and saw that the ticket was for a nonstop flight from Detroit to Las Vegas for the next day. Wrinkling his brow with a lack of understanding, he unfolded the letter and began reading.

Emerson,

I know this will sound strange, but you're going to have to bear with me on this. I have to go off the grid, so don't try to contact me by phone, email or snail mail. I need you to catch that flight to Vegas with the enclosed ticket.

Do not bring your cell phone, laptop or any means of communication with you. This is very serious and dangerous.

Use the cash and take a taxi to the Cote d'Azur Casino. There's a room reserved for you under the name of Ian Bond. Sorry, couldn't help myself.

I then will contact you in your room.

Don't tell anyone what you are doing. I'll explain when I see you and you'll understand.

Thanks,

Sam

Moore's face had a concerned look as he wondered what kind of trouble Duncan was in. He stared blankly at the adjacent harbor as several thoughts ran through his mind. Duncan had come to his rescue several times previously, Moore noted, and this, perhaps, was a chance to pay him back.

Moore sent off a quick email to Sedler to let him know that he'd be taking a few days off due to an unexpected trip and could not be reached, then went upstairs to pack.

CHAPTER 6

The Next Afternoon
Cote d'Azur Casino

The flight to Las Vegas was uneventful, although Moore's mind was tormented with anxiety for his good friend, Sam Duncan. He felt uneasy at not having his cell phone or laptop with him as they were so essential to his work. He felt unarmed.

As he disembarked from his plane, Moore was greeted by the whirring and noisy sounds of the slot machines scattered throughout the airport corridors. The airport was teeming with people of all ages, eager to head for the casinos. Carrying his duffel bag, he headed for the taxi stands outside of baggage claim.

Moore caught a taxi for the short ride to the casino on the Strip. The taxi pulled to a stop under the large, covered entranceway where Moore paid the driver, grabbed his duffel bag and walked inside the opulent resort.

The Cote d'Azur Casino was the newest property on the famed strip of casino/hotel complexes. It was known for its extravagant décor and furnishings. Everything was first-class at this resort.

Moore strode to the reception desk where he checked in under the Ian Bond name. Picking up his room key and dismissing an eager porter who wanted to carry his duffel bag to his room, Moore walked over to a bank of elevators. Five minutes later, he was standing in front of his room.

Upon entering, Moore noted how dark the room was. Before the door had closed behind him, Moore became startled when a small desk lamp across the room turned on. Sitting there with a half-filled glass of rum was Sam Duncan, who laughed aloud and said, "Surprised you, didn't I?"

"You certainly did. What in the world is all this cloak and dagger stuff about, Sam? What kind of trouble have you gotten yourself in?" Moore fired off the questions quickly.

In response, Duncan countered good-naturedly as he indicated for Moore to take the chair across from him, "What? No hello, Sam? It's been a long time, Sam?"

"Not when you send me a letter like that. Something is up and it sounds pretty urgent and important! Especially the way you've gone about setting up this meeting," Moore replied with a bit of frustration as he sat.

"Rum?" the tough-looking blond asked.

Moore shook his head negatively. "Nope. I want to get down to business. I know you well enough to know that you didn't get me out here at the last minute for some Las Vegas getaway with your buddy. What's going on?" Moore pushed.

"It's a long story and I need your help with two issues."

"Get going with your story."

Duncan leaned forward as he began his tale. "You are the perfect fit for this mission. I saw that you were chasing down the cow deaths in California and Ohio."

"You don't miss much." Moore wondered how Duncan was aware and how it tied in with this Las Vegas trip but decided to let him continue.

"Did you know that Germany is the biggest dairy producer in Europe? They have about four million dairy cows. France is the second largest dairy producer in the EU with over three million dairy cows on more than 700,000 dairy farms."

"No, I didn't. What does all of this dairy cow stuff have to do with me being here?" Moore was becoming impatient.

"Did you know that a herd of cows each in Germany and France were found dead today with their stomachs burst open?" Duncan asked slyly.

"No. I've been away from any electronic communications as you instructed."

"I'm suspicious that the deaths are connected."

"There have been no more human deaths like at the Tulare farm, right?" Moore asked as he sat upright.

"That's partially correct, but I want to come back to the Boylen farm in a minute."

Before he could continue, Moore interrupted. "Did anyone find out what killed the cows in Germany or France?" He eyed his friend closely. "You know something that you're not telling me."

"Very perceptive, and I'll tell you in a second. To answer your question, no one has officially determined the cause of the cow deaths, but I believe I know who's behind it." Duncan's eyes narrowed as he resumed his explanation.

"I suspect his first stage is to create a growing global public panic. A continually spreading and unexplained death of dairy cows would tip an international dairy crisis. The second stage, I believe, may be to eliminate certain populaces around the world. His team probably tested their lethal approach on humans."

"The Boylens in Tulare," Moore suggested in a convincing tone.

"Right."

"Who's behind all of this and why?"

"Easy boy," assured Sam. "I'm coming to that. There's a very wealthy, international biotech CEO involved. He's a genius when it comes to breakthrough technology for human and animal pharmaceuticals. His name is Bjorn Hansen Lee. Chinese father and Norwegian mother."

"What's with this guy? Why is he doing this? To create a market for another one of his cures so he can expand his wealth?" The questions poured out of Moore's mouth.

"I don't think it's about the money. It's about revenge and ego."

"How's that?" Moore probed.

"Lee's father was a leading researcher and developer of formulas to help cows increase milk production. His reputation was tarnished when he was blamed for the death of a large dairy herd at a farm in England. It wasn't his fault. He was the patsy for his boss. He tried to clear his name, but he died a broken man."

"Why doesn't Lee go after his father's boss?"

"The boss died. A part of it was that Lee's father's name was dishonored, and his awards were stripped away. And that shame, that dishonoring and loss of face, play a big part in driving Lee."

"How's that?"

"With the Chinese culture dating back to Confucianism, when Chinese people do well, they share the honor. When people fail, they not only lose face, but they share their disgrace with their family and community. It's something that's buried deeply in their psyche."

"So that's really eating at Lee," Moore suggested. "Revenge!"

"That's part of it."

Moore nodded as he listened. "What about the ego issue you mentioned?"

"Lee is on a power trip. He's quirky, but cool and dangerous. At least until he loses his temper. Then watch out."

"Screaming match, right?"

"No. It's a deadly, controlled anger. Cool and controlled. That's Bjorn Lee," Duncan replied.

"I'm not sure where this all is going and how I fit in. You said in the beginning that there were two issues. What's the second?"

"I'm just coming to that. I am certain that we have a mole inside the agency where I work. We've been trying to get close to Lee and his operation so we can nail them, but everyone that we've sent in has been discovered and eliminated. The latest was an undercover agent named Tom Boylen," Duncan said as he looked straight into Moore's eyes.

Moore's head snapped back. "Related to the dead couple at the Tulare dairy farm?"

"His parents. We think Lee's people caught him snooping before he could let us know and then gave his parents whatever it is that's causing the cow bellies to explode open. Probably had him watch his parents die by remote broadcast before giving him some of the same stuff. Tom's body recently was found on a country lane in England. His stomach was exploded too, but we've managed to keep that out of the media."

"Oh my," Moore said with a sad tone. With a wary eye, he looked at Duncan. "Is Lee in England? Is that where he manufactures whatever is killing cows and humans?"

"He's a high roller. Has several estates around the world. Likes to gamble. High-stakes stuff. We haven't determined where he's making the bad stuff yet."

"And how do I fit into all of this?"

"I need you to help me. I'll be off the grid and providing cover. We need someone who has no apparent connection to us. Someone outside of the intelligence circle. You'd fit the bill and could get in his organization. I can't trust anyone at the agency because I don't know who the mole is."

"How am I supposed to help?" Moore asked.

"Get close to Lee. Get him to like you. Let him beat you at gambling."

"That would be easy. I never win at gambling as little as I do," Moore commented.

"Come on. You gamble your life quite a bit on your investigating misadventures," Duncan countered.

Moore nodded with a slight smile. "And why should I get close to him?"

"I'd like him to get so comfortable with you that he might open up and tell you what he's planning. The best thing would be for him to reveal where he's developing his stuff so it can be destroyed."

Moore nodded as he listened.

"And don't be surprised when you eventually meet Lee. He has one golden eye. The other is dark brown."

"What?"

"Yes. It's kind of weird-looking. He's got an Asian girlfriend, too. Quite the looker. It appears that he has some strange hold over her. Not sure what it is. She runs hot and cold on him but doesn't leave him. Her mental stability is questionable. Contrary to Lee, she can be very unpredictable."

"What's her name?" Moore asked.

Duncan wrinkled his brow as he tried to recall it. "It's Yoki something. I've got too much data swirling in my brain today."

"Not important. I'll remember Yoki," Moore commented.

"You'll have to be careful. He has a tough bunch of Chinese henchmen, including one who isn't Chinese, Arsalan Mangan. Mangan is his lap dog. Lethal guy. Kills at the drop of a hat,"

Duncan explained. "You still working out?" Duncan asked as he eyed Moore's physique.

"Yes. I learned a lot from my training in Cedar Key with that Special Forces guy. Stuff that I don't use in my investigative work."

"Hand-to-hand combat and weapons expertise?" Duncan asked as he recalled Moore's training.

"Yes. A bit rusty."

"You're going to need all of that and more. You're going to have to stretch those skills if you want to survive this mission. I've lost too many agents on this one and I don't need you to be next," Duncan warned seriously.

"I'll be careful," Moore said in a confident tone.

"I've started putting together a team to work with you."

"Wait a second. I thought you just said that you couldn't trust anyone at the agency?" Moore was confused.

"That's correct. These are people I've worked with in the past. They are not connected. I'll set up introductions for you. The first one is Mitch Salimbeni. Mitch is with Canada's Royal Mounted Police as an inspector. Tough. Good to have next to you in a fight."

Duncan glanced down at his watch. "It's mid-afternoon. Let's head down to the pool for some drinks. I told Mitch to meet us there."

Moore allowed a smile to cross his face. "Some things don't change. I hear you say pool, but I know you mean girl-watching," Moore chuckled. "Of course, you'd pick a place like that for a meeting with Mitch."

"Nothing like a little eye candy, right?" Duncan teased as he stood.

"Did you tell Mitch about the mole?" Moore asked.

"No. That's between you and me. Be careful who you confide in. Don't trust anyone," Duncan cautioned.

The two men left the room and took the elevator to the first floor.

"We do work well together," Moore commented thoughtfully.

"We do," Duncan acknowledged. "I am thunder; you are lightning. Together, we are the storm," he cracked.

Moore grinned at the comment. "Are you staying here?" Moore asked.

"No. I'm staying off the Strip at a little run-down motel. Remember, I'm trying to be off the grid," Duncan answered as the elevator reached the first floor.

They walked through the noisy casino and to the pool area where Duncan stopped and looked around.

"We may be early. I don't see Mitch," he said as he looked around the crowded pool area. Spotting a couple of open chaise lounges in one of the rows of chairs around the large pool surrounded by towering palm trees, he suggested, "Let's get comfortable while we wait."

The two strode to the chairs with Duncan taking the aisle chair. Moore sat down next to an older blonde wearing dark sunglasses who flashed a big smile at him.

"Hello young man. Where's your swimming trunks?" the gregarious woman asked.

Moore grinned. "Just taking a quick moment in the sun before a meeting."

"I'm Amy Kocias," she said as she introduced herself. She leaned toward Moore as she looked over the top of her sunglasses. "My husband Dale said he had to go to the restroom. That was an hour ago. I think he's checking out the topless pool," she giggled.

Laughing, Moore responded, "I'm Emerson."

Before Moore could continue, she interrupted, "My friends and I are on our first Vegas trip." She pointed to the people sitting in the row of chairs. "That's Blonde Karen, Sharon and Dave Bubacsz, and Carol Lake. Hey everybody, say hello to my new friend, Emerson."

Her group of sunglass-wearing friends waved at Moore as they shouted a greeting.

"My Dale better get back here soon, or I might just have to run off with a fine-looking young man like yourself," she teased good-naturedly before turning back to the book she was reading.

Moore was surprised to see her reading a mystery adventure written by a Lake Erie Island author. It was an author who he knew well.

Moore turned back to Duncan who was eyeing the crowded pool area. "Any sign of Mitch?"

"No. We'll just relax. Want something to drink?" Duncan asked as he stood.

"Sure. Sweet tea."

"What, no alcohol?"

"Not yet," Moore smiled as his friend walked away.

He returned a few minutes later and handed Moore his sweet tea while he sipped on a beer. "That guy playing the guitar by the bar is from Ohio. You know him?"

"Like I know every entertainer in Ohio?" Moore teased as he craned his neck around.

He spotted the dark-haired, bearded entertainer and recognized him right away. "That's Pat Shepard. He lives in the Cleveland area and plays at Frosty's in Put-in-Bay."

"Small world," Duncan commented. "He's good."

"He is very good," Moore agreed as he joined Duncan in enjoying the scantily-clad females splashing in the pool and walking by.

A dark-haired woman with an olive complexion was emerging from the pool. Her barely-there, hot pink bikini struggled to contain her ample bosom and captured Moore's attention. As she exited the pool, she noticed Moore watching her. She then threw him a welcoming smile as she reached for her beach towel and started to dry off.

Moore noticed that Duncan had spotted her, too. His eyes were laser-focused on watching her.

Out of the corner of his eye, Moore noticed a man wearing dark sunglasses and street clothes approaching them. Must be Salimbeni, Moore thought as he returned his gaze to the attractive woman. She was still smiling at him.

Distracted as he sensed the man nearing him, he watched as the woman sashayed toward him. He'd have to delay any conversation with Salimbeni until he had a chance to introduce himself to the woman.

Suddenly the woman launched herself through the air as she yelled, "Gun!"

Duncan rolled out of his chair, withdrawing a concealed weapon as he hit the concrete patio. He saw the would-be assassin taking aim at him and fired off a quick shot that caught the assassin in the shoulder, causing him to drop his weapon as he recoiled from the wound.

Screams from the confused and alarmed people around the pool filled the air. Before Duncan could jump to his feet to give chase, the assassin had disappeared through the doors to the casino.

When Duncan turned back to Moore, he saw that the bikinied woman had knocked Moore to the ground and was laying on top of him.

"You can take your face out of my chest now," the woman said in a serious tone.

"I'm sorry," Moore said as he moved away, and they both stood up. Moore's face was red with embarrassment. "I am really sorry. That's not the way I wanted to meet you," he stammered at the attractive woman.

Duncan inserted himself in the conversation. "Emerson, meet Mitch Salimbeni."

Moore was stunned. "I didn't expect a female."

"Neither did my father," Salimbeni replied firmly as she extended her hand. "Mother couldn't talk him out of naming me 'Mitch' when she wanted 'Michele'."

Shaking her hand, Moore was surprised by the strength of her grip. "Nice to meet you, Mitch." Turning to Duncan, he asked, "What was that all about?"

"My trip here must have been discovered. Hang on a second. Looks like I have some explaining to do," Duncan said as he saw two of the casino security officers approaching him. He stepped aside to talk to them about the incident.

Moore sensed someone approaching him and turned to see that it was the lady who had been seated next to him.

"Are you okay? What was that all about? I didn't know it could be so dangerous here," Kocias started.

"I'm fine, thank you. I don't know. I'm trying to figure that out myself," Moore answered.

"I wanted you to meet my husband. Emerson, this is Dale," Kocias said as she introduced her husband.

Moore nodded to the tall, bearded man as he noticed that

Salimbeni had walked away to get her beach tote.

"I think we're all going to leave. We don't want to be around all of this ruckus," she said. She wanted to ask Moore several questions but decided against it. "We'll get changed and go to the early bird buffet. You can meet us there if you like."

As her gang of fellow seniors quickly filed by, Moore answered, "I'd love to, but I already have plans. Enjoy your stay. Hopefully it will be calmer than the last five minutes."

Feeling a tap on his shoulder, Moore turned to find Duncan had returned. "I think I've got things under control with security. We need to go back to your room. Mitch, can you join us?" Duncan asked as Salimbeni, carrying her beach tote, joined them.

"I was counting on it," she said as the three began walking.

CHAPTER 7

Moore's Room
Cote d'Azur Casino

The three of them were the only ones to enter the elevator for the ride to Moore's floor.

"Do you know your attacker?" Moore asked.

"No. That's the first time I've seen him," Duncan replied.

"How did he know you'd be here?" Moore asked.

"I don't know. I thought I did a pretty good job of covering my travel plans," Duncan groused. He cast a wary eye at Salimbeni, wondering if he made a mistake in including her.

"Good thing I was there," Salimbeni stated proudly.

"Your timing was impeccable," Moore added.

"Yeah. Impeccable," Duncan answered with a touch of skepticism.

Moore picked up on it right away and started to comment but decided to hold off.

When they reached Moore's room, Salimbeni excused herself to change in the bathroom. While she changed, Moore turned to Duncan.

"Are you having second thoughts about her? I heard your comment in the elevator, Sam," Moore said with concern.

"I just don't know who I can trust any more, other than you, Emerson. I keep my circle small and my wall high," Duncan offered.

Moore nodded before commenting, "For a stunning lady, she seems pretty tough."

"Inspector Salimbeni is. You don't want to mess around with her," Duncan warned as he dismissed his skepticism.

"Why is that, Sam?"

"Her inner strength parallels her outer beauty. That mind of hers whirls. For example, her now ex-boyfriend cheated on her. When she found out, she took her revenge in a unique way."

"What did she do?"

"Painted a message on the side of his car," Duncan said with a mysterious air.

"What was it?"

"Hope she was worth it, cheater!"

"Wow!"

"That's not the worst part."

"What do you mean?" Moore asked eagerly as he fell for Duncan's baited tale.

"It was a brand new Corvette."

"Yikes!" Moore exclaimed. "I'll be sure to do the right thing by her."

"That would be very wise," Duncan agreed. "By the way, Mitch pees standing up," he added.

"What?" Moore asked, confused.

"Not really," Duncan laughed. "She can be a real hard ass. It may take awhile for her to warm up to you. But when she does, she'll go to the wall for you."

"You've worked with her before?"

"Yep. In Canada, she was on my team. We were on a raid. I cornered the terrorist. He was taking aim at me, and I fired first. Or so I thought. My gun jammed. The next thing I knew, there was an explosion next to my ear as Mitch ran into the room and fired. She saved my bacon."

"You bet I did," Salimbeni said as she reentered the room. She was dressed in a gray t-shirt and black jogging pants. She had dried her hair which now hung shoulder length.

"You look stunning," Moore said with admiration as he saw that she had applied some makeup and fresh pink lipstick.

"It's not about looks, Emerson. It's about getting the job done," she countered in a serious tone as she dismissed his compliment.

Duncan laughed. "See what I mean. Tough lady. Very focused."

"Sam told me about you, so you don't need to go over your background," Salimbeni commented as she eyed Moore suspiciously. "Are you able to step it up for this mission?" she asked, skeptically.

Hard-assed and hard-nosed, Moore thought before replying. "Yes. This isn't my first foray into dangerous waters. Good fortune does favor the bold."

"That's for sure, Emerson," Duncan interjected as he began to focus them on the task at hand. "You've had a lot of close calls. But this operation is more serious than any others you've helped me with in the past. As I said, I need you to get close to Lee. And he's dangerous."

"Ruthless, is what you told me," Salimbeni added.

"That's right. The guy won't hesitate to take you out in the blink of an eye. He's focused on exacting revenge and on a real power trip. I think he's a megalomaniac bent on controlling the world like Alexander the Great, Genghis Khan, and Napoleon Bonaparte. They have a tendency to exaggerate their virtues and never see their faults."

"A real nut case," Salimbeni summed it up.

"Exactly. And he has a tough bunch of thugs working for him that are as bad or violent as he is. They're led by a guy named Arsalan Mangus. I mentioned him earlier. He could give terrorists lessons in brutality," Duncan warned.

"How am I supposed to get close to this guy?" Moore asked.

"Since our undercover attempts haven't been successful, you'll go in as yourself. Play to his ego and tell him something that would make him want to meet you in person. Something like you stumbled across his father's work and want to write a story about it because you're suspicious that the real story about his father has been hidden for years. That will grab his attention.

"He'll check you out and see that you're a successful, award-winning journalist. That approach should get you inside his mansion and, with your winning ways, you'll have him eating out of the palm of your hand," Duncan concluded with a wry smile.

"I hope your winning ways are better than what you've shown me," Salimbeni said, arrogantly.

Moore allowed a smile to cross his face. "One should be wise to master his circumstances, lest he become mastered by them. You haven't seen anything, darling," he teased.

"My name isn't darling. It's Mitch and don't forget it!" she countered quickly with a stern look.

Duncan guffawed. "I see you two are going to get along famously."

Salimbeni was frowning as she asked, "And how do you see me fitting into this plan of yours, Sam?"

"You're going to be Emerson's attractive and loving assistant." Duncan couldn't contain himself as he chortled at the thought of the two of them playing their respective roles.

Salimbeni rolled her eyes with disdain. "I'm not a babysitter, Sam," she grumbled.

"I know, and Emerson doesn't need one," Duncan grinned. "I have someone else who I'd like you to meet." He glanced at his watch. "I need to get back to my place and clean up. Mitch, can you pick up Emerson in about an hour and bring him to Smith and Wolensky restaurant for dinner?"

Before she could answer, Moore commented, "They have great steaks there."

Duncan nodded in confirmation as Salimbeni answered, "Yes. I can do that."

"Are you staying here?" Moore asked.

"On the budget I have? No way," Salimbeni scoffed. "I'll go back to my place and freshen up. Meet me in front in an hour."

"Got it," Moore replied as the two left his room.

CHAPTER 8

Lee House
London, England

Lee House was located on Cromwell Terrace in the Regent's Park area, one of the city's most exclusive residential areas. The red-brick mansion entranceway provided a stunning view down the main hall through large patio doors to a well-manicured garden. The hallway with its large floor-to-ceiling windows gave access to the large living, dining and kitchen areas. Stairs to a wine cellar were located off the kitchen. A small reception area was located to the left of the entrance. It led to a first-floor office that was paneled in tulipwood.

The two floors above contained six spacious bedrooms and bathrooms with exquisite furnishings from around the world. Off the master suite was a study next to a solid oak, winding staircase and a lift that serviced the three levels. Each room had tailor-made tulipwood cabinetry, and the bathrooms were complete with Italian marble.

To the rear of the manor were the landscaped garden and brick building that housed a four-car garage, fully-equipped gym, steam room and housing for the manor staff. The property was surrounded by a ten-foot steel fence and a gate with two imposing henchmen guarding it.

A six-foot tall, robust man with rough-looking features and gelled hair walked up to the office door and knocked. Arsalan Mangan was Lee's right-hand man. He had just finished a phone call that didn't provide good news, and he had to tell Lee.

"Yes?" Lee asked.

"Boss. I've got bad news," Mangan reported as he opened

the door.

"What is it?" Lee had been pouring himself a gin and tonic before calling it a night. He slowly turned to face Mangan.

Lee was tall and thin with skin the color of cheddar cheese. He had dark, sunken eyes with dark shadows that stared like a cobra seeking its prey. When he moved, it was like he had no bones at all, slinking like a snake, ready to strike without warning. His face was gaunt with protruding cheekbones and a crooked smile beneath a pencil-thin mustache. He wore his hair slicked back.

Mangan eyed his boss before speaking. He knew how that immobile face with a glint of evil in its eyes could turn on the charm. What he had to share wouldn't be turning on any charm this evening.

"Sam Duncan is still alive. The hit on him was foiled," the hulking Hungarian reported.

"A shame," Lee spoke in a low tone. "And what are you going to do about it?" Lee didn't have to raise his voice. Mangan and Lee's employees knew that Lee maintained a deadly, cool demeanor no matter what the circumstance. Failure to complete covert assignments usually resulted in some very unpleasant results, many times, death.

"I've already ordered another hit. He won't get away from us now," Mangan said confidently.

"I'm pleased that you were able to discover his location after he disappeared. My congratulations to you. Now, let's finish him."

"You can count on that," Mangan said as he turned and left the office.

Lee casually stood in front of his fireplace, sipping his drink as he thought about Duncan. Lee knew, from his mole inside

Duncan's agency, that Duncan was trying to get solid evidence connecting his organization to the deaths of the dairy cows and the Boylens – Carl, Tammy and Tom.

He was aware that members of Duncan's team earlier had gained access to some of his pharmaceutical manufacturing operations under a variety of pretenses. They were trying to unearth what Lee's team was secretly developing and how it would impact worldwide animal health as well as human health.

So far, no one had uncovered what his plan was. He chuckled softly because they were looking in the wrong places. How stupid did they think he was? He had two clandestine manufacturing sites that would be difficult to find.

Lee set the glass down and headed for his bedroom. He was very pleased with his accomplishments and wealth accumulation. He would soon reveal to the world how he was going to terrorize it. He padded up the stairs where he heard a female voice calling his name.

He smiled.

CHAPTER 9

Outside the Main Entrance
Cote d'Azur Casino

A little over an hour later, Moore walked through the lobby to the main entrance. Time had escaped him and he was tardy. He saw a pacing Salimbeni near the entranceway. She was obviously irritated with him being tardy.

"Hi Mitch," Moore greeted her. He was awestruck by how well she cleaned up. She had reapplied her makeup, and her eyes were highlighted by a dark eyeliner. Her hair looked luxuriant. She was dressed to kill with four-inch heels and a mint green dress that ended above her knee. She looked striking.

"You're late," she fumed. "Come on," she ordered as she turned and strode out the entranceway.

Moore quickly caught up to her. "Sorry I'm running behind," he said as he stepped over to a Toyota Roadrunner, the only vehicle that was parked there.

"That's not mine," she laughed as she disappeared on the other side of the Toyota.

Moore raced around the vehicle and spotted her sitting atop a 1998 Harley-Davidson Heritage Softail Classic motorcycle with a 1340 cc, V-twin, four-stroke motor. It had custom paint - black with blue and purple flames - Revtech Billet Inferno wheels and shift linkage in a flame design. It was loaded with chrome.

Moore's eyes widened at the sight of her, sitting on the solo seat with her skirt dangerously high on her thighs. "That's yours?" he asked in amazement.

"No. I rented it from a custom shop here. I know the owner," she grinned triumphantly as she slipped blue reflective glasses on her face.

"We're going to ride through the traffic on the Strip on this?" Moore had a worried look on his face. It was bumper-to-bumper traffic on the Strip.

"Don't worry. They'll get out of the way for us. Climb aboard."

Moore saw a detachable pillion seat attached to the rear fender and deposited himself carefully on it.

"Hang on!" she said as she got her motor running and it roared to life with a throaty rumble.

Moore slipped his arms around her slender waist. "I guess I can do this," he smiled, wistfully.

Within a moment, they headed down the exit ramp to the Strip. When they reached the street, Salimbeni turned on a flashing blue light and siren. As traffic pulled to the side, she drove out into the open lane.

"Aren't you going to get into trouble for doing this?" Moore shouted in her ear.

Salimbeni laughed as she yelled back. "Only if they catch me."

Within five minutes, she spotted The Venetian Resort where the famed New York-style steakhouse was located. She switched off the siren and flashing blue light as she pulled into the parking lot and shut off the engine.

"Emerson, would you kindly remove your arms from around my waist?" she asked as she looked down at his hands.

"Oh yeah. Sure," Moore said, embarrassed that he had gotten very comfortable with them there. He hopped off the bike and she followed, adjusting her skirt as they walked inside.

When they entered Smith and Wolensky, they saw Duncan

seated in a secluded corner with a slightly built man in his fifties with balding white hair and a pair of wire-framed glasses. The man wore a confident smile. Duncan waved them over to his table and introduced them to his guest, Mike VanBlaricum, before they sat.

"Mike is part of our team. He heads up logistics and has technical equipment that we will find useful to have for our operation. Mike, tell them a little about yourself," Duncan urged.

"Sure. Sam and I have worked together a number of times on operations. Whenever he needed special technology, he'd give me a call. I always seemed to be able to connect him with the latest," VanBlaricum said as he ended his explanation and looked at Duncan.

"Mike is being modest. He's a technical genius when it comes to unique gadgets and weapons. He's an engineer by training and does a lot of contract work for Interpol and MI6 as well as several other covert agencies around the world."

"Mr. Gadget," Moore offered with admiration.

"I'd say he's our answer to James Bond's "Q". In fact, we should call you 'V'. Are you okay with that Mike?" Duncan asked.

VanBlaricum smiled. "I've always relished the part of "Q" in the Bond series. 'V' sounds perfect to me."

"V it is from now on," Duncan announced.

"Where are you based?" Moore asked.

"The Netherlands, but I have offsite locations located strategically around the world. I have a small warehouse here in Vegas that I thought we might visit after dinner."

"Splendid!" Moore said as a server arrived to take their drink and food orders.

Throughout the dinner, the four enjoyed a congenial conversation, but Moore was anxious to see some of the toys that V had at his warehouse. When they finished, Moore rode with Duncan and V in Duncan's vehicle to the warehouse as Salimbeni followed on her Harley.

Ten minutes later, they pulled up to a warehouse on the outskirts of town. As they approached, V pressed a key on his cell phone and the giant garage door opened so that the two vehicles could park inside. It closed shut after them as the men stepped out of the car.

V motioned for everyone to follow him to a large table that had several devices on it.

"This is a USB-activated polygraph machine," he said as he picked up a small box with wires attached. "You can question anyone anywhere using its artificial intelligence to analyze a person's statements. You hook up the pulse finger clip, finger wraps and breathing apparatus as part of the process."

"Amazing," Moore commented.

V next picked up two bags. "These are faraday bags. They have the highest level of military-grade RFID blocking to ensure the embedded radio frequency identification chips in your credit cards, passports and driver's license stay private. You also should keep your cell phones in here because they emit radio waves that can reveal your location."

"And that fits right in with a gift I have for you both," Duncan said as he opened a bag that he was holding. "I've got two burner phones for you both so that you can communicate with me. They're preprogrammed with my burner phone number and your numbers," he said, handing the phones to Moore and Salimbeni who dropped them in their faraday bags. "I've got one for you, too, V," Duncan said as he handed a phone to V.

"Good," Moore said. "I wondered how we were going to

communicate with each other."

Duncan nodded.

"And to go with your burner phones, I have a goTenna Mesh Pro-X2 for you," V said as he handed Moore and Salimbeni a small device about the size of a flash drive.

"What's this about?" Moore asked, confused as he examined the device.

"You pair it with your burner phone when there's no cell phone service and it allows you to send texts and your GPS location."

"Cool," Salimbeni commented as she placed it in her faraday bag.

"I've got another gift for you," V said as he grabbed two eyeglass cases from the shelf and handed them to Moore and Salimbeni. "Open it. They're rearview mirror sunglasses so that no one can sneak up behind you or you can casually check to see if you're being tailed."

Moore and Salimbeni opened their glass cases and tried them on. They both marveled at how they worked.

"These are a few things that I thought you'd need to get started. You may or may not use them," V said as he pointed to several nearby cabinets. "I've all kinds of devices here and my other locations, but we can get them if we need them."

Moore turned to Duncan. "This is all fine and dandy, but how am I going to connect with Lee after I get in to interview him?"

"You're going to have to get in close with him by telling him how you two share a common interest."

"What's that?" Moore asked.

"Do you play any games of chance?"

"I play chess," Moore answered.

Duncan allowed a groan to escape his mouth. "Don't you gamble? Play cards?"

"Not really."

Duncan groaned again. "Lee likes to play high-stakes poker. You tell him that you love the game, too. That's how you get close to him. He'd invite you to join him in a game."

"But I don't know how to play very well," Moore said as he dreaded how this was going to work out.

V intervened. "Sam, we could introduce him to Johnny Vegas."

"That's a great idea."

"Who's Johnny Vegas?" Moore asked, concerned with how things were going.

"His real name is John Adams. He's a gambling whiz from Cleveland. He moved out here about 20 years ago. He lived in a mobile home next to Sam's Town Casino and learned his trade at some of the old outlaw bars and casinos. He was a quick study and has a winning track record. The casinos don't get really excited when he walks in because they know he's going to walk out with a ton of cash."

"He can teach me high-stakes poker?" Moore asked with trepidation. He couldn't understand how this guru would be able to transform him into that caliber of player in a few days.

"He can try or train you enough so that you're not a green rookie." Duncan picked up his cell phone and keyed in a number. He then walked to a corner of the room to have a private conversation with Johnny Vegas. When he returned to the group, he handed Moore a note. "He's all in. Here's his address. You need to be there at 10:00 tomorrow for your lesson."

Moore looked at the address. "Sure, I can do that."

The group talked a little longer before breaking up. Salimbeni gave Moore a ride back to his hotel on the Harley.

Rather than going straight to his room, he wandered around the casino, taking time to watch several poker games. After two hours, he returned to his room. He was concerned about getting up to speed on gambling.

CHAPTER 10

The Next Morning
Johnny Vegas' Home

The taxi pulled to a stop in the driveway of a two-story house on Mesa Ridge, overlooking Las Vegas. After paying the driver, Moore walked up to the stunning covered entry to the 4,100 square-foot home and rang the doorbell.

A minute later, the massive double door opened to reveal the immaculately-attired, sixty-five-year-old owner who was wearing a red brocade smoking jacket. He had gray hair and a waxed mustache. His teeth clenched a cigar.

"I'm looking for Johnny Vegas," Moore announced.

"Well, you found him, bucko. You must be Emerson," Vegas responded with a twinkle in his blue eyes. "Come in. Come in."

Moore walked through the well-decorated home and followed the man into the kitchen.

"Beer? Drink? Snack? I was just cutting up a cantaloupe. Want some?" he asked in a gregarious tone.

Moore smiled. "No. I'm fine."

"So, you're going to be my student?"

"That's what Sam told me," Moore said, skeptically.

"I've taught a lot of people how to gamble and how to do it well." He paused as a serious look appeared on his face. "But I had more time with those people. I understand we have about 24 hours?"

"That's what Sam said," Moore replied.

"Hope you're a quick learner," Vegas commented as he eyed Moore.

"Usually, I am."

Vegas picked up the plate of cantaloupe pieces and a beer. "Follow me to the learning center," he said as he walked out of the kitchen.

Moore trailed him to the rear of the house to a large room. It was equipped with a gambling table, a roulette wheel and several slot machines.

"Sit yourself down here," Vegas said as he dropped into a chair on one side of the gambling table. "Tell me what you know about high-stakes poker."

"Other than what I saw last night in the casino and looked up online this morning in my hotel business center, I don't know anything." Moore then added, "I've played some poker, but that was years ago."

Vegas frowned, then smiled as he tried to be encouraging. "Good. No bad habits to break. We're starting with a clean slate."

Vegas opened a fresh deck of cards and began to explain. "When you play, you have to buy in for $200,000 to $300,000, and you better have a bankroll of at least $500,000."

"Sam is taking care of my funding so that shouldn't be a problem."

"I've played in a lot of them, and I've won a lot. But you need to have that big bankroll to get started. You've got to be highly confident and have next level thinking. Out of the box thinking to win," Vegas explained.

Moore chuckled nervously. "I don't even have first level thinking," he spoke honestly. "Will I be playing with cash or chips?" Moore asked.

"Chips. Do you know the reason for that?"

"No."

"Chips on the table look better than cash," said the savvy cardplayer. "Plus, they make for a livelier game. People are quicker to bet a $100 chip than a $100 bill."

Vegas peered under narrowed eyebrows at Moore. He was going to have his hands full. He began explaining the rules of the game and strategies to use.

"There are so many subtle nuances involved with poker that it's mind-boggling to even consider. Then you have the bluffing and the tells," Vegas mentioned.

"Tells are like unconscious signals about the hand the player has," Moore offered.

"Right, but you have to be careful in case you're being set up," Vegas answered. "You need to be cool when you play and don't jump up and fist pump when you win a big pot. You don't do that in high-stakes poker. Be cool," he advised as they continued their conversation.

After a couple of hours and many practice hands, they broke for lunch. As Vegas prepared grilled cheese with avocado on the stove and Moore sipped a sweet tea, Moore asked, "How am I doing?"

Moore was trying to determine if the grilled cheese was giving off more smoke than the cigar that Vegas puffed on. It appeared that Vegas was burning the grilled cheese. Moore had a massive migraine from everything he was trying to learn.

Vegas was slow to answer. When he did, he pointed the spatula at Moore. "You need to think deeper than what I'm seeing. Let's see how this afternoon goes," he said as he turned back to the smoking stovetop.

An hour later, they took another break. Both men were becoming frustrated with the lack of progress Moore was showing. While Moore grabbed a soft drink from the fridge, Vegas went upstairs to call Duncan.

"How's our student doing?" Duncan asked.

"Not well enough to play in a high-stakes poker game. I need about a month to get him ready," Vegas answered.

"You have less than 24 hours."

Vegas frowned. "Then I'll teach him roulette."

"That's not what the other player likes. It's high-stakes poker, Johnny. I've got to get him into that game. It's really important."

"You want him to look like a real schmuck? You want to do that to him?" Vegas snapped.

"No."

"What about blackjack?" Vegas proposed as an alternative. "There's high-stakes blackjack."

Duncan thought back to what he had read about Lee's gambling habits. He smiled as he recalled that Lee did enjoy blackjack. He had forgotten it.

"Yes. That might work, but the target prefers poker."

"What's this really all about, Sam?"

"I can't go into a lot of detail, Johnny. All I can tell you is that I need to get him in a private game with a lot of cash at the host's home. I don't care if he loses, but he can't look like a rookie," Duncan partially explained. "I can probably tell you more once this project is over with."

"You and your secret stuff," Vegas grumbled. He had helped Duncan in the past. They spoke for another minute and ended the call.

Vegas rejoined Moore in the kitchen. "Come with me," he said as he led Moore out of the room. They walked out to a large stone patio surrounding a swimming pool that provided a spectacular view of Las Vegas.

"What a view!" Moore said.

"You should see it at night, and you probably will at the rate we're going," Vegas stated, seriously.

"I'm not doing so well, am I?"

"I called Sam and we're going to try a different approach. Ever play blackjack?" he asked.

"A little, in college. That was a long time ago."

"Good. Sam wants me to focus on poker, but we will throw in some blackjack because whoever you are going to play knows blackjack, too."

He pulled a marijuana joint out of his shirt pocket and lit it. He clenched it between his lips as he took a deep drag on it. He smiled as he slowly exhaled. "Want a hit?" Vegas asked as he held out the joint to Moore.

"No. That smells terrible. What do you have in there? Sawdust?"

"Now that's ironic."

"What?"

"A sawdust joint," Vegas laughed.

"Why?"

"Let me explain what a sawdust joint is. It's typically an unpretentious, illegal gambling venue aimed at the lower end of the gambling market. There are some that only cater to high-stakes players like the game you're going to be in. Sometimes those joints are called rug joints, but the terms are interchangeable."

"I get joint, but why sawdust?"

"Illegal casino owners use to spread sawdust on casino floors to absorb spilled liquids and muffle the sound of people walking on hard wooden floors," Vegas explained. "And based on what Sam told me, he'd like your target, whoever that is, to invite you to play at a sawdust joint because it's a real signal about what he thinks about you."

Moore nodded with understanding.

"Let's start your education on playing blackjack for a bit. Then, we'll go back to poker," Vegas suggested as he led the way inside to the table.

When they sat, Moore offered, "I know the basic strategy is not to go over 21 and you want to avoid busting out."

"Right. Let's say you have 14 showing and the dealer's up card is eight, what do you do?"

"I take a hit."

"Good start." Quickly, Vegas went over the basic strategy to playing and was pleased that Moore was showing a quick understanding of the basic game. It was a much better start than with the poker.

Over the next hour, Vegas taught Moore card counting as a tool to use in winning at blackjack. He also warned him about dealers watching for card counters and how to avoid getting caught.

"It's illegal then?" Moore asked.

"No, but it swings the odds away from the house and dealers can kick you out of a game if they catch you. Another tool you can use is shuffle tracking." Vegas went on to explain how one tracks high cards.

They played several hands and Moore's proficiency increased as the night wore on. Vegas gave him a brief break and showed him how to play the roulette wheel before returning to blackjack for another hour. They next switched back to poker. By morning, Moore was red-eyed and ready to return to his hotel. Vegas called a taxi for him and walked him to the door when it arrived.

"You've done well, Emerson. Not an expert player, but well enough to hold your own," he offered.

"Thanks, Johnny. I appreciate everything you taught me," Moore said.

"I just hope that you're playing with someone else's money."

"Why?"

"Because you're going to lose a lot," Vegas responded with a wink.

"Probably," Moore agreed as he walked down to the waiting taxi. He was looking forward to catching up on his sleep.

As the taxi pulled away, Vegas called Duncan. "He's good to go."

"At what level?"

"Above average. Not an expert by any means," Vegas answered. "At least, he won't look like a rookie."

"Good. Thanks, Johnny."

"Just make that wire transfer for my services," Vegas reminded Duncan.

"Of course. You'll see it in a few minutes."

After ending the call, Duncan sent a text message to Moore and Salimbeni requesting them for an evening meeting.

CHAPTER 11

That Evening
Cote d'Azur Casino

"Sounds like you made some progress, based on what Johnny told me," Duncan commented as he met with Moore and Salimbeni in Moore's hotel room.

"I figured he'd give you an update, but I'm no expert."

"And I wouldn't expect you to be. Neither will Lee. He can see that you'd be an easy target," Duncan suggested. "And that is a good thing."

"And you're going to front me the cash I need, right?"

"We'll get you what you need," Duncan answered.

"Isn't he going to wonder where I got my money?" Moore asked uneasily.

"Probably. Tell him you took it out of your 401K," Duncan chuckled.

"Right," Moore replied stoically. "How am I going to connect with him?"

Duncan turned to Salimbeni. "Mitch has been doing some homework for us. Would you like to update Emerson?"

"Sure," she began. "When he's in London, Lee frequents the Sunrise Casino on Knightsbridge, not too far from his home. He can be found there three times a week playing high-stakes poker or blackjack."

"Our plan will be for you to meet him there during a game of blackjack. Mitch will be there to keep an eye on you," informed Duncan.

"Where will you be?" Moore asked.

"V and I will be nearby in one of V's locations."

Moore nodded. "And what if I lose everything?" he asked.

"No problem. Lee will see you as an easy mark and that should help you in getting close to him," Duncan assured.

They talked over their plans, including flying to London, for the next hour before breaking for a late dinner in one of the hotel restaurants. When they finished, Duncan asked the server to contact the valet to bring his car to the front entrance.

As the three walked to the entrance, Duncan suggested, "Emerson, you haven't had any time with Mitch to get to know her better. I'd like to suggest that you two have a drink together and chat. Okay with you two?" he asked as they walked out the doors to the covered entranceway.

"Fine with me," Salimbeni said. "I'm in no hurry to go anywhere."

"Sure," Moore agreed as the valet handed Duncan the keys to his car. It was parked on the far end of the covered entranceway. In front of Duncan's car sat a black van with its engine idling.

Duncan tipped the valet. "I'll call you tomorrow Emerson, and we can finalize our travel arrangements," he said as he gave them a brief wave. Duncan glanced at the black van before stepping inside his car.

The two returned the wave and walked toward the casino entrance as a large truck drove between them and Duncan's vehicle. After the truck passed, they were suddenly thrown to the ground by the force of an explosion and the sound of wrenching metal. The shock wave shattered the glass entrance door and the windows of two cars that were parked nearby.

Moore and Salimbeni nervously rolled to look back at the fire and smoke that filled the air. Where Duncan's car was parked seconds earlier, now was a large crater. Nothing remained of the car or its occupant. Moore and Salimbeni jumped to their feet and ran with several others to the crater.

"Sam! Sam!" Moore called wide-eyed with fear as a sick emptiness filled his stomach. Moore peered inside the crater in shock and disbelief. The entire vehicle had been disintegrated by the force of the blast. There was no sign of Duncan's remains.

As the sounds of approaching fire engines filled the Strip, Moore sat down on a nearby bench. He bent his head as his eyes teared and his heart filled with sorrow. He sensed someone sitting down next to him, then felt a hand on his shoulder.

"I'm so sorry, Emerson," the voice said softly. It was Salimbeni. Through her tears of grief, she didn't say anything else as the two sat together, staring lifelessly into the parking lot before them. Sam was forever gone. Dead. Blown up. Never coming back. What was happening here?

When Salimbeni noticed fire engines and police cars driving up to the portico, she turned to Moore. "We better go inside. We don't need to answer any questions about Sam. Let's go."

She stood, followed by Moore, and together they walked into the nearby hotel lobby.

"I think I need a drink," Moore commented slowly.

"I could use one, too," Salimbeni agreed. The two went into the bar and sat at a secluded table away from the other patrons.

"What do we do now?" Moore asked. He was filled with anguish at the death of his friend. His grief flowed through him like a river in a mountain valley. He wanted to withdraw from the living world with no thought for the future.

"We honor Sam by completing his mission," she responded. Seeing no reaction from Moore, she continued. "I know you're grieving for your good friend. I grieve for him, too. But we need to move forward. If I had a magic wand, I would wave it to make your pain disappear, Emerson." Salimbeni was a tough woman.

"I don't know," Moore muttered. He was taking Duncan's death very hard.

"He trusted you. He called on you for help. The biggest way you can repay his reliance on you is to go forward. I'll be there to help. I'm reliable. I don't make promises I can't keep. I'll have your back," Salimbeni affirmed.

The server appeared with their drinks. Picking up his rum and Coke, Moore said, "To Sam."

"To Sam," Salimbeni echoed as they toasted and took a big gulp of their drinks. They set their glasses on the table.

"You're right. We need to finish this for Sam. I'll call V to let him know what happened and to set up a meeting with him for tomorrow. It looks like it will be the three of us."

They finished their drinks and Salimbeni left to return to her hotel. Moore went to his room and called V. V was shocked but agreed that they should go forward. They also decided to meet at his place the next afternoon. After they ended the call, Moore texted Salimbeni about the meeting time at V's place. When that was done, he took a couple of aspirin and tried to sleep. He tossed and turned all night as memories about Duncan haunted his dreams.

Meanwhile in London, Mangan ended a phone conversation. He then called Lee who was seated in his dining room, having breakfast.

"Yes?"

"Duncan is dead," Mangan sneered with relish.

"You're sure?"

"Absolutely. You couldn't fill a matchbox with what little remains can be found," Mangan responded with a menacing laugh.

"Good. We won't have him nosing around our plans," Lee said as he reached for his tea and ended the call. "Good job, Arsalan."

CHAPTER 12

The Next Afternoon
V's Place

When Moore awakened from a fitful sleep, he rolled over and sat on the edge of his bed. Waves of grief had swept over him throughout the night as his mind was battered by an emotional storm. He stared aimlessly ahead as he replayed fond memories of his adventures with Duncan. He decided to let his friend's spirit serve as a lighthouse to help him navigate Duncan's mission to a successful conclusion.

He called room service for breakfast before a quick shave and shower. He had slipped into fresh clothes just before his meal arrived. Following the meal, Moore utilized the hotel business center and one of its guest computers for additional research before checking out of the resort.

Several hours later, a taxi dropped Moore off in front of V's place. When Moore called V on his cell phone to let him know that he had arrived, the door buzzed and Moore, carrying his duffel bag, walked inside. He spotted Salimbeni's Harley inside the garage door and saw her talking with V.

"Good morning, Emerson. How are you doing today?" Salimbeni asked.

"Tired. I didn't sleep well."

"Me, too."

Moore noticed a rotund black man with relaxed dreads that seamlessly connected with a close-cropped beard. "Who's your friend?"

Before she could answer, the man spoke enthusiastically. "You must be Emerson. They've been bringing me up to speed about you and our mission."

Moore's forehead furrowed with concern and suspicion at the news.

"I'm Wonderful Israel Nelson. You can call me Wonderful, or Izzy, or Tank," the man replied as he tugged on his bright yellow suspenders that were battling to hold up his trousers.

Moore was surprised Nelson wasn't called Whale. If he was going to be part of any operation, it would be difficult to include him, Moore thought. There was no way that he was going to keep a low profile based on how he looked.

Moore turned to Salimbeni. "I'm not following. What's going on here?"

"I called the agency last night to report Sam's death. They didn't know he was out here and asked what we were working on," she replied.

Moore cringed in recalling that Duncan earlier said he didn't want anyone at the agency to know because he suspected there was a mole embedded there.

"What did you tell them?" Moore asked. He was wondering how far he could trust Salimbeni and especially the new guy – who could be the mole or work for the mole.

"I told them we were following leads to the cause of the cow deaths," Salimbeni explained.

"And how does your new friend Izzy fit in?" Moore asked, skeptically.

"They flew him out this morning to replace Duncan on the team and to act as a liaison," she affirmed.

Nelson was certainly not going to fill Duncan's shoes, Moore thought. He was not happy how things were evolving.

"It all happened so fast that I barely had time to pack my pajamas and catch the flight out here. Good thing they had meal service on the flight because I had to skip breakfast," Nelson piped in as if skipping a meal would harm him.

"Did you mention my involvement, Mitch?" Moore asked.

"No," she replied.

V had been standing in the background listening to the exchange. It was obvious that he, like Moore, wasn't pleased by the newcomer's arrival.

"Izzy, I was wondering how much field experience you have?" V asked, suspiciously.

"None. This is my first assignment. I'm excited about getting away from being a desk jockey. This is my big break. I can't wait to dig in and help you all solve this. Maybe we can get it done by tomorrow. Won't the agency be surprised?" The words gushed out of Nelson's mouth in a torrent with no real thought being given to what he was saying.

V looked at Moore and raised his eyebrows doubtfully. Moore returned the look.

"What did you do before you joined the agency?" Moore asked, doubting the man's capabilities.

"I worked for a funeral home while going to college. I was in charge of arranging the flowers. It didn't pay well, but it sure did smell good," Nelson grinned.

Moore wasn't impressed. He was certain that he'd have to be careful with what information he shared with Nelson. He was very disappointed by Nelson being added to the team without any previous discussion. He was also dismayed that Salimbeni hadn't talked with V or him before contacting the agency.

"Okay guys. What's the next step?" Nelson asked eagerly.

"Do you have a laptop or cell phone?" Moore asked as he remembered how Duncan had cautioned him.

"Yes. I have a cell phone."

"Let me have it, Izzy." Moore handed the phone to V. "Can you destroy this and give him the same phones and gear that you gave Mitch and me the other night?"

"No problem. And I need to take your picture," V spoke to Nelson.

"Why?"

"We're going to give you a new passport, too," V answered.

"Why?" Nelson asked with a lack of understanding.

"We'll be doing some covert work and you'll need a new passport," V explained.

"Covert. Yeah covert. I get it," Nelson said eagerly as he waddled after V to a chair in front of a screen for his photo. They returned after they finished with the photo.

Moore needed some time alone with V. "Mitch, can you take Izzy to a store and get him some not so flashy clothes and necessities," Moore requested. "He's going to need them so he can blend in a little better."

"New clothes. Oh yeah baby. Sounds good to me," Nelson commented enthusiastically.

"Sure. I can do that. Come on Izzy. Let's see if we can find a big men's shop for you." Salimbeni led Izzy to her Harley and climbed aboard. It took a few minutes filled with comical movements by Nelson to get on the back of the bike as the garage door opened. They roared away with Nelson perched precariously on the small pillion seat.

"I hope that's not a sign of how things are going to happen as we go forward," V said with concern.

"I hope not," Moore agreed. "What do you think about this? You think Izzy is the mole or sent here by the mole to report back?"

"I don't believe he's the mole. Not bright enough. I do think you're on to something with the mole perhaps sending Izzy out here. We need to be careful with what we share with him and watch him like a hawk," V surmised.

"I'm with you on that."

"There's one more thing that I wanted to mention to you before they return."

"What's that?" Moore asked.

"After you called me last night, I drove over to your hotel. I wanted to see the bomb crater."

"Did you learn anything?" Moore questioned.

"Yes. Whoever built that explosive was an expert. The force of the blast was directed downward and not outward. That tells me that whoever did it wasn't interested in harming others. The full force was downward. Hardly any fragments were blown anywhere," V observed.

"That's interesting. Directed entirely at Sam."

V nodded his head. "With Sam gone, you're really going to have to step it up," V cautioned Moore. "You're going to have to go feral!"

Moore ginned confidently. "Feral, huh? I can become a wild thing when I need to. Don't worry about me."

"I want you to know that the only role I play is in the background. I do logistics and special technology. I don't do the edgy stuff that you're going to be involved in," V explained.

"That's no problem. Besides, I'll have Mitch to back me up. She seems made for this stuff," Moore replied. "What's next?"

The two spent the next hour going over plans for their flight on V's private jet to London and preparing a passport for Nelson. When Salimbeni and Nelson returned on the Harley, they loaded up V's SUV and headed for the airport.

CHAPTER 13

Sunrise Casino & Hotel
London, England

The towering white facade of the eight-story hotel was lit up by many lights to showcase its opulence and tall English oak trees. Under an awning that jutted out from the front were several cars, unloading their lavishly attired occupants. Valets scurried among the cars to drive them away so that other vehicles could replace them.

Uniformed and plainclothes policemen were stationed strategically near metal barricades to make sure there weren't any problems from unwanted interlopers. The elite guests walked up the two steps into the lavish lobby. It was a spectacle to behold.

After V's jet had landed earlier at a small executive airport north of London, V had driven the four of them to a two-story house on the north side where they went over their plans for the evening. Nelson was disappointed to learn that he would be staying with V at the house as the other two departed separately for the next step.

A London taxi carrying Moore made its way to the casino. As he rode, Moore thought back to his last encounter with a London-style taxi on South Bass Island and how it had played into the disappearance of his aunt. His taxi now pulled to a stop in front of the casino where Moore exited and then walked into the hotel. He was carrying a suitcase and small briefcase.

Moore checked in and took the elevator to his room where he changed into a black tuxedo. He checked the briefcase to make sure the euros that V had provided were still there. Picking it up, he headed for the elevator for the ride back down to the lobby.

Moore quickly noticed a small group of tough-looking Chinese men standing to the left of the stairs near the entrance to the bar. They didn't blend in with the type of people mingling at the casino. They stared at each person as they walked by, and that was not a good sign.

Moore entered the bar with its three open-air entrances and a marble floor that changed to blue-green carpet. There were lounge seats, tables and the bar where two Chinese women served drinks. A cocktail server wandered among the tables, delivering drinks.

Moore spotted an elegantly-attired Salimbeni sitting at the far end of the bar as a man tried to engage her in conversation. Moore smiled as she shot him a frown.

Dropping into a comfortable lounge chair, Moore watched as a stunningly beautiful Asian woman in a bright red dress took a seat at the bar. She crossed her legs as her skirt rode up on her thigh while she placed her drink order. She then swiveled around and stared directly at Moore.

Moore was caught off guard and slowly gazed around to see if she was looking at someone else nearby. Seeing no one engaging with her, he swung his head around to look at her. She was still staring at him as she lifted a stemmed glass to her bright red lips and sipped her drink. When she lowered the glass, she allowed a welcoming smile to appear.

Taking the hint, Moore stood and walked over to her. "Do I know you?" he asked as he approached.

"No, but you should," she smiled, seductively.

Moore returned the smile as he sat on the barstool next to her. "Let me introduce myself," he said with a confident grin.

"Moore. Emerson Moore."

She held out her hand which Moore shook as she spoke with a slight Chinese accent. "I'm Kari Yoki."

Moore chuckled as he heard her name. She was the unpredictable Lee girlfriend that Duncan had mentioned to him.

"I get that reaction from everyone," she said with amusement.

"Your parents must have had a good sense of humor," Moore suggested as he took in her deep brown eyes and long black hair that fell below her shoulders.

"They did, Mr. Moore," a voice spoke coldly behind Moore.

Moore swiveled around to see a tall, Asian with one golden eye. He recognized him right away. "Good evening, Mr. Lee."

"You know my name even though we haven't met, but that shouldn't surprise me should it, Mr. Moore?"

"You can call me Emerson," Moore responded.

"And you can call me, Mr. Lee," Lee countered with an air of indifference before turning to Yoki and speaking in Mandarin Chinese to her.

She nodded in understanding then asked as Lee listened, "What brings a famous reporter like you to the Sunrise Casino?"

"Bjorn Lee in all honesty," Moore answered.

"How's that Mr. Moore?" Lee asked this time.

"My research showed that you frequented this casino, and I thought it would be a way for me to meet you. I'd like to interview you for a story for my newspaper," Moore replied.

"You could have called my office. I have a public relations department that handles interviews," Lee responded with a detached air.

"Gatekeepers. I try to avoid them and get straight to my

target," Moore said without hesitation. "Actually, I've started research on your father and how he was mistreated. The real story about his innovations have been suppressed, and I'd like to tell the truth about him with your help."

"Now you have my attention, Emerson," Lee said as he allowed a slight smile to appear on his otherwise stoic face. "Maybe we could help each other out."

"My boss John Sedler was hoping for that," Moore said as he returned the smile, noticing that Lee had used his first name.

"Do you gamble, Emerson?"

"A little. I'm not very good," Moore answered. When he saw the smile disappear from Lee's face, he quickly added, "I tend to lose often. I cashed in some of my retirement savings for this trip and hope to win big."

The smile returned to Lee's face. He loved winning, especially when he felt he had the upper hand.

"Why don't you come with me to one of the high-roller rooms. You do have at least $200,000 on you, right?"

"I do. Yes, if we can pick a game that I have a good chance at."

"No problem whatsoever. Come with me."

The two, followed by the beautiful Kari Yoki, walked away from the bar into the casino area. Moore nodded imperceptibly at Salimbeni who returned the nod. They went to one of the closed doors where the attendant recognized Lee and opened the door for him.

When Salimbeni saw the three of them enter the room, she walked over to the closed door.

"May I help you?" the door attendant asked.

"Yes. I'd like to go inside," she smiled.

"I'm sorry miss, but only members and their guests are allowed inside," he explained.

Salimbeni batted her bedroom brown eyes at the attendant as she turned on the charm. "Oh, it's okay. I won't be noticed."

The attendant looked at the gorgeous woman in front of him. "Miss, everyone would notice a beautiful woman like you. But I still can't allow you to enter."

Frustrated, Salimbeni returned to her seat at the bar where she kept a close eye on the door.

Inside the high-roller room, which had several gaming tables and a dressed-to-the-heels crowd, Lee asked, "Where would you like to start, Emerson? Roulette perhaps?" He was curious to see how risk adverse Moore was.

"I'd like to try blackjack."

"Follow me." Lee led Moore to the far corner where a table was roped off. The only person there was the dealer.

"Good evening, Mr. Lee."

"Louis," Lee greeted the dealer as he and Moore sat. Yoki stood behind Lee.

"Will it be just the two of you playing this evening?" Louis asked.

"Yes. I'll take 200,000 euros in chips."

Louis slid a note across the table which Lee signed in exchange for the chips that he set in front of Lee.

Lee turned to Moore. "It's this easy when you're a member and they know you're good for any losses."

"I brought my cash with me," Moore said as he set his briefcase on the table and opened it.

"Here's 200,000 in euros from me," Moore confirmed as he withdrew the cash and set it on the table. He glanced down at his shirt pocket where one of V's camera pens resided. V was watching the game and would instruct Moore through the earpiece he had also provided Moore.

While Moore slid the cash with his left hand across the table, he reached with his right hand into his pocket for the earpiece. As he withdrew it, it fell to the floor.

Moore didn't allow his facial expression to change as he glanced at the floor. He remembered learning from his tutor Johnny Vegas the high importance of keeping a straight poker face. There was no way he could pick it up without causing suspicion. Instead, Moore placed his shoe over it and ground it into the floor before sliding its remains farther under the table.

"Shall we open with 10,000?" Lee asked.

"Perfect," Moore replied as he slid chips into the center.

Once Lee pushed his chips into the center, the dealer began distributing the cards. Moore had a king of hearts hole card and eight of diamonds showing. He asked for one more card and went bust when he was dealt a ten of clubs.

Over the next two hours, the two played with Lee winning most of the hands. Yoki had taken a seat next to Lee as the effects of several glasses of wine impacted her. Lee saw the frustration growing on Moore's face.

"You've lost almost everything, Emerson," Lee observed.

"Yes. I better quit while I still have some euros left."

"I thought you had more," Lee said with a furrowed brow.

"I do. They're in a safe in my room," Moore replied.

"I see," Lee said as he stood.

Moore started to stand as he reached for his room key card which he dropped on the floor. "Oops," he said as he bent over to pick it up, along with the crushed earpiece.

"Why don't I send a car over to pick you up tomorrow morning around 10:00? I can have you brought to my office, and we can start that interview."

"Splendid," Moore replied.

"Excellent. I see a few people that I need to talk to before I go. I assume you can find your way out of here," Lee offered.

"Oh yes." Moore shook hands with Lee. "I'm glad we met, and it was nice meeting you too, Kari."

Yoki waved her hand. She was still seated and feeling the effects of the wine.

"I will see you tomorrow," Lee said as he walked away.

Moore departed and saw Salimbeni as he walked past the bar. She had a questioning look on her face, but Moore gave her a slight sideways shake of his head for her to stay where she was. He continued to the elevator, then sensed someone walk up next to him. He turned and saw Yoki. "Going to your room?" he asked innocently to make small talk.

"Yes." Her response was slurred. "What floor are you on?"

"Eighth."

"What a coincidence. So am I."

Moore didn't believe her. He was suspicious as the elevator doors opened and the two entered. As they closed, Yoki fell against the wall, grabbing onto one of the side rails to avoid falling.

Moore stepped over to her and helped steady her on her feet. "Are you okay?"

"I'm just a little lightheaded," she gasped as she grabbed his arm and held tightly. "I may need some help getting to my room," she mumbled as the elevator ascended.

Moore wondered if she was acting or if he was being set up. He decided to proceed cautiously. "I'd be happy to escort you to your room."

"Thank you," she mumbled as she handed Moore her room key card.

"Which room?" Moore asked as the two stepped off the elevator.

"802."

Moore pointed them down the hall and off they went. When they reached the door, Moore unlocked it with the room key and held it open for her.

"I may need some help," she muttered as she fell to the floor.

Moore did not want to go into her room, but he couldn't leave her there. He bent down and helped her to her feet. "Let's just get you over to the bed."

"I'd like that," she said softly.

Moore sat the woman on the edge of the bed. She promptly fell back with her short skirt riding up on her thighs. Without opening her eyes, she pleaded with Moore. "My head. Oh, my head hurts. Could you get me a cold washcloth?"

Moore didn't want to spend any more time in her room, but being a gentleman, he replied, "Sure. One moment."

He walked into the bathroom and turned on the cold water before grabbing a washcloth. He held it under the water, then wrung it out. Carrying the washcloth, he walked out of the bathroom where he was met by a big surprise. Kari Yoki was lying naked on the bed.

"I'm feeling much better." She patted the bed next to her. "Why don't you join me?" she asked seductively with the look of heat in her eyes. Few men could resist the touch of her warm lips on their face and neck. They'd melt to do her bidding as her passionate desires took them to places they had never been.

Now Moore was sure that he was being set up by Lee. He was positive that Lee would love to capture him in a compromising position with Yoki to be sure that he'd write the story the way Lee preferred. Moore's eyes quickly swept the room for cameras, but he couldn't spot any. They must have been well hidden, or someone may be waiting to burst through the room's connecting doorway.

"Kari, you are a very beautiful woman, but you are Lee's lady. I'm not going to get in the middle of your relationship," Moore said firmly.

"I'm nobody's woman. You think I'm property? I'm not!" she retorted strongly as she pulled the coverlet over her naked body.

Moore shook his head. "I better leave," Moore said as he made for the room door.

"You'll be sorry," she called after him.

Ignoring her, he walked out of the room, closing the door behind him. As he headed for the elevator, he thought he heard the door to the adjoining room open. He spun around in time to see it close. He was even more confident that it had been a set up.

He caught the elevator and returned to the lobby where he noticed the Chinese thugs had disappeared. When he walked in the bar, he saw Salimbeni still sitting there. He raised his eyebrows and she nodded.

He walked over and sat next to her.

"That was quick," she observed.

"You saw?"

"Yes. She was playing you."

"I didn't fall for it," Moore said as he ordered a shot of Redbreast Irish whiskey.

"I thought you didn't imbibe," she mentioned with a coy smile.

"I don't really, but I don't like what almost went down. I think there was someone in the adjoining room."

"Danger likes to follow you, Mr. Moore," she said in a muffled tone.

"Mitch, does being alone with me make you nervous," Moore asked after downing the shot.

"Emerson, being alone with any man doesn't make me nervous, but it should make them nervous."

Moore grinned. "Why?"

"Because I can cut their eyes out," she countered, cunningly.

Moore chuckled. "I bet you would."

"And that's a bet you'd win. How did you do gambling in there? I tried to get in, but the doorman wouldn't let me."

"It went well. I lost most of what I had, and Lee seemed to enjoy it."

"Poker?"

"No. Blackjack. But I did make progress with him. He's sending a car around tomorrow to take me to his corporate headquarters for a meeting."

"Nice."

Moore looked around. "I assume Lee has left the building."

"Yes. A few minutes after you and Little Red Riding Hood went upstairs," Salimbeni quipped.

"That's good, and I bet the Big Bad Wolf was next door," Moore laughed. He looked at his watch. "It's getting late. I'm ready to call it a night," he said as he stood.

Salimbeni slid off the bar chair. "Do you need an escort to your room, too?" she teased semi-seriously. "No sweet-talking now."

Moore laughed again. "I'm sure I can make it to my room with no problems."

Salimbeni smiled as she started for the hotel entrance. "Good night."

"Night," Moore replied as he headed to the elevator.

CHAPTER 14

The Next Morning
Lee's Corporate Headquarters

"Arsalan, are you sure?" Lee asked his head of security.

"Positive. This cell phone photo was sent to me from Las Vegas. It leaves no doubt. Emerson Moore was there with Sam Duncan," Mangan said as he walked around Lee's desk and showed him the picture of the two men seated poolside at the Cote d'Azur.

Lee studied the photo. "It certainly is Moore."

Mangan handed Lee a file. "I took the liberty of having my team research Moore. It looks like he and Duncan have worked together in the past."

"Interesting. I thought this Moore fellow was just a reporter," Lee mused as he studied the file.

"According to our research, he is more than a well-known reporter," Mangan stated proudly.

"With Duncan having been eliminated as a threat to our plans, I wonder if Moore is his replacement. Does he work for the agency, too?" Lee asked as he took the file and started browsing through it.

"No. He doesn't." Mangan waited patiently as Lee skimmed the pages. "I checked with our contact at the agency."

"I see here that Moore visited the dairy farm in Tulare and met with local law enforcement," Lee noted keenly.

"Yes. That was before he went to Las Vegas to meet Duncan."

"Did you send the car for him?" Lee asked as he set the file on his desk. He turned and looked out the 20th floor window of his office building at the city.

"Yes."

"Good. We will play his little game and see what he really is up to," Lee said as his countenance darkened like a dangerous storm.

Twenty minutes later, Moore walked into the corporate lobby of the towering white-faced building. After registering at the reception desk, he was directed to the bank of elevators where he took one to the 20th floor. When the door opened, Mangan was waiting for him.

"Good morning Mr. Moore," Mangan said dryly.

"Good morning."

"Follow me." Mangan led Moore to Lee's office where he knocked once before opening it and allowed Moore to enter.

"Emerson, it is so good to see you. I trust you had a good night's sleep," Lee greeted Moore as he sat behind his massive chrome and glass desk. He beckoned Moore to sit across from him.

"Yes, I did."

"I owe you a thank you," Lee said with a sly look.

"Oh?"

"I understand that you escorted Kari to her room," Lee commented foxily as he closed one eye and stared at Moore with his golden eye.

Moore wasn't surprised by the comment. "I'm glad I could help her. I hope she is feeling better today."

"She is." Lee got to the point. "You mentioned doing a story. How can I help?"

"I saw where your father was a leading researcher and developer of formulas to help cows increase their milk production," Moore began. "Then he was blamed when a large herd of dairy cows here in England died after ingesting his feed additives. I'd like to clear his name and write how you, his son, created this biotech company that is helping feed the dairy industry. How you enhanced his legacy," Moore said as he played to Lee's ego. He was anxious to visit Lee's research centers to see what he could discover.

"That is very noble of you," Lee said expressionlessly. It was a proposal he expected to hear if Moore was trying to discover a link between his company and the cow deaths.

"I can have you spend some time with our public relations people. They have quite a bit of information about my father and me as well as the business," Lee answered as he baited Moore with a plain vanilla approach.

Moore bit. "I'd like to do more than that. I'd like to visit your research center and see how you develop the additives."

"I can arrange it, but first you must get background information from my team. Then we can send you to our research center in Cranfield. Have you been to Cranfield?"

"No."

"It's in Bedfordshire, about 50 miles north of London on the M1. There's a research park between Cranfield University and the old RAF airport. That's where my primary lab is located. When you're ready, I can have a car take you there."

"Thank you."

Lee pressed a button on his desktop and Mangan appeared. "Yes."

"Arsalan, please escort our visitor to the public relations department. I'll alert them you're on the way," Lee said as he stood, signaling to Moore that the meeting was over.

"Thank you for your time," Moore said graciously as he stood and walked over to Mangan. He was eager to start his due diligence with the public relations group, but more eager to visit the Cranfield research operations.

"When you're done with your preliminary research, we can meet again to go over any questions you may have."

"Thank you, Mr. Lee," Moore said.

"One more thing Emerson."

"Yes. We must look for another opportunity to gamble together. It would only be fair for me to allow you to try to win back some of your losses," Lee grinned caustically as he picked up the phone to call public relations.

The tone in his voice was not lost on Moore as Mangan escorted him from the office. They took the elevator to the 18th floor where Mangan left Moore with an attractive fifty-year-old blonde. Her name was Pat Breitenstine.

"Mr. Lee called to let us know you were coming. If you would like to follow me into the conference room, you can review several of our press kits and files on Mr. Lee's accomplishments and the contributions that his father had made to the dairy cow industry."

"Perfect, Pat."

Moore followed her as her stiletto heels clicked on the tiled floor. He spent the rest of the day reviewing the information Breitenstine provided. She also assisted in arranging Moore's visit to Cranfield for the next day. When he was finished, he was given a ride back to his hotel.

Arriving at the Sunrise Casino and Hotel, Moore went to his room where the "Do Not Disturb" sign was hanging from his doorknob. He carefully opened the door and stepped inside where he checked for any obvious signs that someone recently had been in the room. He found nothing.

He reached on top of the dresser mirror and found the small

listening device that V had given him the previous day. It was a noise-activated device. He played it and heard someone open the door and walk in. The person had opened and shut several drawers and closets as the room was searched before leaving.

Moore lifted the TV set and withdrew a small pocket-sized scanner which he used to scan his room for listening devices. When he couldn't find any bugs, he replaced it and picked up his burner phone.

"Ten minutes. Pick me up out back," Moore spoke when the phone was answered.

"Right."

Five minutes later, Moore walked out of the elevator and crossed the lobby to the hotel rear entrance where Salimbeni was waiting in a car. The two drove away to V's place on the north side.

"How did your meeting with Lee go?" Salimbeni asked as they rode.

"Plain vanilla as I'd expected."

"Do you think he suspects what you're really up to?"

"I don't know. He's difficult to read. Stoic. Poker face," Moore explained.

"Yeah, but he sounds like a real snake. Dangerous and sometimes hard to tell when it's going to strike," Salimbeni warned.

They continued talking the few remaining miles to V's place. They soon arrived and walked inside where Nelson was the first to greet them.

"Was your visit successful? Did you get anything out of Lee? What's our next step?" A tsunami of questions slammed into Moore from an excitable Nelson.

"Easy. Easy," Moore replied as he held up his hand with his palm facing outward. "Let me give you all a summary, Izzy,"

Moore said as he saw V chuckling softly.

"I want to hear it all. I need to give an update to the agency," Nelson explained with a high sense of urgency.

V interrupted Nelson. "Izzy, we don't want to provide any updates until we have something solid to provide. Right, Emerson?"

"Right V," Moore agreed as he thought of a way to cool Nelson's jets. "Izzy, we want to help you be successful in your efforts. To help your star rise at the agency. When we have concrete news to reveal to your superiors, we can all go over it first so that you present it in the best possible light. How does that sound to you?"

Nelson nodded his head vigorously. "Sounds great. Thank you."

Moore smiled, hoping that his plan to silence Nelson's interaction with any potential mole worked. He then updated V and Nelson on what had transpired during his meeting with Lee.

"Maybe I should go with you next time," Nelson suggested eagerly. "I bet I could pull information out of Lee." Nelson was wide-eyed in anticipation of what he thought he could do.

V saw the look of consternation on Moore's face. "Izzy, we don't want to raise eyebrows by having too many people interacting with Lee."

"That's a good point, V," Nelson replied. "After I spoke, that's the same thought that popped in my mind," Nelson said as he tried to cover up his impetuosity.

"Good. I'm glad you agree," Moore added as Salimbeni nodded her head.

But Nelson couldn't contain himself. "While you're at Lee's research center, maybe I could break into his house and see what I can find in his home office," Nelson said with a hopeful look on his face.

All three of the others were alarmed.

Moore spoke first. "Izzy, you need to mellow out a bit. There will be things you can do when we need you to get involved more."

"Right," Salimbeni agreed as Nelson's face fell.

Moore turned to V. "By the way, someone was in my room. I used that listening device you gave me and heard them going through my drawers."

"Anything missing?" V asked.

"No. I'm not sure what they were looking for, but I didn't have anything there for anyone to find."

"Did they bug your room?" Salimbeni asked.

"No. I checked. It's clean."

"You're being checked out. You better be careful," V warned Moore.

The four of them continued talking for another hour before Salimbeni drove Moore back to his hotel for the evening.

When Moore walked through the lobby, he gazed toward the casino, thinking that he should go and practice his poker. Deciding against it, he instead took the elevator to his floor and walked to his room. He checked his room again for intruders but found none this time.

CHAPTER 15

The Next Morning
Cranfield Research Operations

Lee's driver picked up Moore for the hour drive to Lee's Cranfield Research Operations. The driver was not talkative which allowed Moore to become lost in his thoughts on the drive. He wondered if he would find anything of interest to help identify what was killing the cows or uncover Lee's overall plan. He doubted that he would, but he had to try.

He believed it would be a promising trip, but he did need to play out his hand in researching a story about Lee's father and Lee's subsequent success. Once he arrived, he was escorted inside by the head of operations, Sharon Rose, a tall blonde.

"How was your ride up?" she asked as Moore followed her to her office.

"Uneventful, Sharon."

"Good. We like uneventful around here so that we can concentrate on our work."

Moore spent an hour with her and several of her staff as he went through routine questions. After that, he was given a tour of the various departments. In one department, he observed research scientists running various tests.

"This is where we do most of our development and testing of dairy feed additives," Rose explained as Moore surveyed the room.

"You said most. Is there another site?" Moore asked quickly.

Rose paused for a moment before answering. "Yes," she started hesitantly. "We have another site in Tulare, California."

Moore had to struggle to hide his excitement. He remembered that Tulare was where the death of the cows and Boylens occurred.

"Coincidentally, I was in that area a couple of weeks ago and didn't notice anything there for the Lee operations," Moore mentioned.

"You wouldn't have," Rose replied. "That center is through a subsidiary company of ours."

"Oh. Could I pay it a visit?"

"It's a leading-edge research center with highly restricted access, but I can check. I wouldn't be hopeful of getting a visit there," Rose explained as she led him out of the room and continued the tour. When they were finished, Moore promptly was escorted to the lobby entrance.

"I hope you found this time rewarding," Rose said as she concluded his visit. "If you have any questions, here's my card. Please do call."

"Sharon, I'll give you a call in a couple of days to see if I can visit the Tulare facility. Thank you for your time."

"You are welcome. If you see Mr. Lee in the meantime, you might ask him directly," she suggested before turning away.

Stepping through the entrance, Moore walked outside and immediately realized there had been no prior arrangements made for his return to London. He thus decided to catch a train from Cranfield to the Paddington train station.

It was a short walk to the station where he purchased his ticket and waited an hour for the next train to London. When it arrived, he boarded the second car from the rear and selected a cushioned bench seat with a table between it and the bench seat facing him. He was hoping that no one would sit there and want to chat the entire one-hour trip. He lucked out as the train pulled out of that station with the coach only a quarter-filled.

Moore's concentration on his notes from the day were interrupted when two serious-looking men sat in the seat facing him. They were attired in suits and looked stiff to Moore as he glanced up at them before returning to his notes.

"Emerson Moore?" the one seated next to the window asked.

Surprised, Moore looked up. "Yes?"

"I'm Chief Inspector Scott Manore from Scotland Yard. This is Case Officer Greg Siloy from MI6," Manore said as he introduced the two of them.

Intrigued, Moore sat upright in his seat. "And why are Scotland Yard and MI6 sitting across from me?"

"We wanted to have a little chat with you," Siloy replied.

"About?"

"We noticed that you've been chumming up to Mr. Lee," Siloy replied.

"Yes. I'm an investigative reporter working on a story for my newspaper about his father and Lee's company," Moore answered innocently.

"Is that all?" Manore asked as his eyes drilled into Moore.

"Yes."

"You need to be careful about poking a bear," Manore cautioned.

"What do you mean?" Moore questioned as he feigned innocence.

"We're suspicious that there's more to your inquiries than just writing a newspaper story. Your activities are a bit cheeky in our eyes," Siloy commented.

"Why do you ask?" Moore was wondering why they were getting involved and who may have tipped them off.

"You're going to find yourself in a bloody awful mess," Siloy cautioned.

"You're a little boy trying to play in a man's game," Manore added.

"You're not 007. You're more like 00 stupid," Siloy cracked.

"Stay away from Lee. You may compromise what others are working on," Manore warned as the two men stood.

"Understand?" Siloy glared at Moore.

Moore nodded as he watched the men walk to the end of the coach and disappear through the connecting door. When the train stopped at the next station, he saw the two standing on the platform as the train pulled away.

Moore let his mind process the possibilities as to why and by whom he was confronted. He had no answer, but did have several suspicions. When his train arrived at Paddington Station, he caught a taxi to his hotel. When he reached his room, he routinely checked the listening device for any noises from intruders and scanned the room for bugs. There were none.

An hour later, his hotel room phone rang. It was Lee.

"Emerson, how did your visit go today?"

"Good, although I really would like to visit one of your facilities where you're making the additives and see them being mixed into the dairy feed," Moore replied.

"We'll have to see what we can do about that...and I have an interesting invitation for you although it's on somewhat short notice."

"What's that?" Moore asked.

"It's tomorrow night in Kingston, Jamaica. High-stakes gambling at what we call a sawdust joint. Are you familiar with the term?" Lee probed, expecting a negative response.

"Yes, I am. I'd love to attend. Maybe I can win back some

of the money I lost."

Moore's comment was met with a hearty laugh from Lee. "Maybe, but I doubt it. I'm willing to give you a chance if you have the funds to participate," Lee said slyly.

"That's not a problem. I'll have to see about catching a flight there."

"Do try, old boy. I'm already here, sitting on the balcony enjoying a cool island breeze," Lee smiled as he stroked the side of Yoki's face while the sun began to set on the horizon.

"Here's the address." Lee gave the address of the house where they'd be playing and staying as the nude Yoki stood. She walked across the room to pour Lee another drink. Lee's eyes followed her.

"Do try to make it, Emerson," he said before ending the call.

Immediately Moore reached for his burner phone and called V. He relayed the results of his visit to Cranfield and his encounter with Scotland Yard and MI6.

"That's troubling. I am baffled by why they tracked you down and warned you. It's very disturbing," V said slowly.

"Me, too. And now Lee's invited me to high-stakes gambling in Jamaica for tomorrow night. I don't know if I can catch a flight that quick," Moore grumbled quietly.

"He didn't invite you to fly down with him?" V asked, astonished.

"No. He's already there. I think he's just trying to see how serious I am about this high-stakes poker."

"I should be able to help you with the flight and the cash you'll need. I'll have a car sent for you in the morning at 6:00. Be sure that you're packed for Jamaica," V instructed.

The next morning, Moore checked out of his room and

walked outside to the waiting car. It was a thirty-minute ride to the north of London to the same airport which they previously flown on V's private jet. The driver dopped off Moore in front of a private hangar.

As Moore headed inside, he saw V's plane parked. Greeting the approaching V, Moore asked, "We're going in your plane?"

"Oh no. Come along. I've got something special waiting for you on the other side."

Moore followed V around the plane where he saw Nelson approaching them.

"Isn't that special? Hello Izzy," Moore said, disappointed.

"Oh no. It's not Izzy," V protested.

"But I am special," Nelson countered with a frown.

"This is your wings for today."

Moore found himself staring at an aircraft that resembled Darth Vader's starfighter with its wings folded up.

Moore turned to V. "I'm going gambling. I'm not fighting the dark side, although I do sense a disturbance in the force," Moore quipped.

V chuckled before introducing an approaching, youthful-looking couple. "Meet your hosts for the flight, John and Holly Hall."

Moore shook hands with them before turning to John. "Tell me captain, how does this thing fly?"

John laughed. "I'm not the captain - Holly is. I'm the co-pilot, navigator and flight attendant."

"Chauvinist!" Holly teased.

"I'm sorry. I didn't mean to be demeaning," Moore replied awkwardly.

"Sure. Sure. I get that all of the time," the strawberry blonde responded before continuing. "What you see in front of you is a five-passenger Ranger. It's set for vertical takeoff and landing. Once we're airborne, the wings fold out 75 feet and a pair of turbofan jet engines kick in to provide forward thrust.

"We'll cruise at 510 miles per hour at 10,000 feet altitude. She's got a range of over 11,000 miles and comes complete with a galley and toilet. We can easily set down on the driveway in front of the house you're going to in Jamaica."

"You've checked that out?" Moore asked, amazed.

"I did," John answered.

Moore nodded as he turned to V and Nelson. "Are you two going with me?"

Before they could answer, a feminine voice replied, "I'm going, Emerson."

Moore turned to look behind him and saw Salimbeni approaching. She was carrying a suitcase.

"I wanted to go, but V needs me here," Nelson chimed in, not wanting to be left out of the exchange.

V nodded his head as he rolled his eyes.

"V needs me to help him here," Nelson reiterated with self-importance.

Moore was relieved. He sensed that Nelson on a trip to the sawdust joint would cause an unnecessary distraction.

"Step over here, Emerson," V said as he led Moore to a nearby table. "I have a few things that you may find helpful on your trip."

He picked up a small semi-automatic .38 pistol. "A Walther PPK. This is small and lightweight in case you need it. It holds a single stack magazine with eight rounds," V said. He then handed it with a black leather, concealed carry waist holster to Moore.

"I hope I don't have to use it," Moore confided as he placed it in his suitcase.

"Do you smoke, Emerson?" V asked.

"No."

"I'm still going to give you these." V held up a cigarette lighter. "This appears to be an ordinary lighter, but if you spin the wheel in the opposite direction and throw the lighter, it becomes a smoke bomb so you can cover your escape." V handed the silver lighter to Moore before picking up a cigarette case and opening it.

"This would appear to contain ordinary cigarettes, and they are anything but ordinary except for the first one. That's just in case you do have to light one up. These other are lethal." V extracted one from the case. "If you push on the tip of the filter end, the cigarette fires a lethal dart. It kills instantly," he said as he handed it to Moore.

"I always knew that cigarettes could shorten your life," Moore quipped as he examined it before returning it to V. V placed it back in the case and handed the case to Moore who dropped it and the lighter in his suitcase.

Next V picked up a narrow flashlight. "I'm especially proud of this because it's something I developed."

"A flashlight?" Moore asked in consternation.

"More than that. The housing is manufactured out of indestructible, aircraft grade aluminum. When you depress this switch, it is indeed a very brilliant white-light flashlight. When you push this to expander, it becomes the deadliest handheld laser beam in existence. It's capable of killing a man or destroying a vehicle like a truck at 100 yards."

"What about tanks or armored personnel carriers?" Moore asked with curiosity.

"Not that powerful."

"Good to know. I'll stay away from them," Moore said as he took the laser and dropped it in his suitcase. "How long will it hold a charge?"

"For a full week before starting to fade." V turned to a briefcase on the table. "Here's $500,000 that you'll need for gambling. I'm giving this to Mitch so she can be your banker."

"Don't I get any of the toys, V?" Salimbeni asked as she took the briefcase.

V smiled. "You know how it is – boys and their toys."

"Isn't that the truth? Boys!" she remarked, sarcastically.

"Time's a wasting. Shall we board up?" Holly asked as she led them to the plane entrance. Within a few minutes, the plane had taxied out of the hangar and took off vertically. It then spread its wings and headed for the nine-hour flight to Jamaica.

CHAPTER 16

Sawdust Joint
Kingston, Jamaica

The Ranger approached Kingston on the island's southeastern coast and at the base of the Blue Mountain range. The city faced a natural deep-water harbor that was protected by a long sand spit connecting Port Royal and the Norman Manley International Airport.

As the Ranger slowed and dropped altitude, John gave Holly exact coordinates for landing on the colonial-style mansion's drive on the mountainside. Within minutes, the wings folded in, and the Ranger dropped vertically into the drive near the front of the mansion. It was nestled on five lush, fully-fenced acres with a view of the Caribbean Sea.

Moore and Salimbeni stepped out of the plane as Holly spoke, "We're heading to the airport to refuel, and we'll be standing by for your return flight tomorrow."

As the Ranger departed, the two walked with their luggage to the front of the mansion where they were greeted by Mangan.

"Mr. Moore, welcome to Jamaica."

"Yes, and this is my associate, Mitch Salimbeni," Moore responded as Salimbeni nodded her head.

"I'm Arsalan Mangan, Mr. Lee's chief assistant. We didn't realize there would be two of you. Will you be sharing a room?"

"No," Salimbeni shot back quickly.

Mangan smirked evilly at the response. "Follow me around the house. You'll be staying in two of the villas then."

Mangan escorted them past the pool and the spa cabana to their side-by-side villas. "You should find everything in there to make yourself comfortable," he said as he handed them keys to their respective units. "You have time for a swim before dinner at 8:00."

"Thank you," Moore said as he looked at Salimbeni. "Interested in taking a swim?"

"Yes. I'll get changed," she replied as she unlocked the door to her villa and stepped inside.

Moore found his door unlocked and walked inside where he was met with a surprise.

A blonde with eyes the color of blue seawater stood framed in the open patio doorway. She was watching the enlarging sun turning from yellow to bright orange as it began setting on the watery horizon. A breeze had picked up, toying with the hem of her knee-length turquoise summer dress. As it lifted the light fabric, she unfolded her arms which had been covering her ample bosom. She tossed her head to the side, letting her long blonde hair fly free.

"Well, hello," Moore started. "Am I in the wrong villa?"

"Oh no. You are in the right villa, Emerson. Mr. Lee wanted me to warmly welcome you to Jamaica."

No wonder Mangan smirked when Salimbeni asked for her own villa. He probably knew who was waiting for Moore in his villa, Moore thought.

"I'm Mei Flowers," she said as a way of introduction while she sat on the small sofa.

"Not April Showers!" Moore quipped. He couldn't help himself.

She chuckled softly as she patted the sofa beside her as a signal for Moore to sit down. She lifted her other hand which held a glass. "Come and join me for a drink," she instructed in a seductive tone. Her voice sounded huskier.

Moore saw some bottles of alcohol on a wooden liquor cabinet. He walked over and opened the small fridge. Withdrawing a cola, he walked to the sofa and sat next to her. He decided to play Lee's game to see where it would take him.

Flowers placed one hand on his thigh, then slowly stroked his thigh as Moore set his cola on the end table. She reached up and unfastened two of the buttons on Moore's shirt and slipped her hand underneath, slowly caressing his muscular chest.

"Would you like to get comfier?" she asked as she leaned into him. She then ran her tongue provocatively across her glossy, plump lips as she watched Moore smile helplessly.

The blonde stood and took Moore's hand to help him to his feet. "I don't believe you've seen your bedroom yet," she cooed as she led him toward the bedroom door.

Suddenly, there was a knock on the villa door, and it opened to reveal Salimbeni in her bikini. "Oh! Am I interrupting something? I didn't know you had company," she asked with annoyance at Moore's lack of professionalism.

"Not company. It's room service," Moore explained weakly as he escorted the blonde to the door. "Thank you. I'm sure I'll be seeing you later."

"And a lot more of me. You can count on it," the blonde giggled suggestively as she gave Salimbeni a serious look for interrupting them before walking out.

"What kind of room service was that?" Salimbeni teased.

"Lee's welcoming committee," Moore answered. "I'm sure that you would have had a similar experience had Lee known that you were accompanying me."

Salimbeni frowned as she eyed Moore. "Do you still want to take that swim because you're still dressed?"

"I was just going to get undressed."

"I bet you were and your blonde friend was probably going to help you. I'll be at the pool," she remarked in a disturbed tone as she stepped outside.

In a few minutes Moore joined her, and the two swam and relaxed for an hour before returning to their villas. After showering and changing, they met poolside to walk over to the main house. Moore was clothed in white linen slacks with a light blue, collared shirt.

Salimbeni, who carried the briefcase full of cash, had changed into a simple print dress of a semi-sheer material that lightly snugged her hips and legs when she walked. She added a touch of makeup to highlight her dark brown eyes and had brightened her lips with a soft pink lipstick. Her long black hair hung down past her shoulders.

She looked good, Moore thought. "Very nice," Moore complimented her.

"Don't get any ideas. I'm not that kind of girl," Salimbeni spoke firmly. "Not like your blonde friend at all."

"I would never have thought otherwise," Moore countered. He did like Salimbeni's independent streak. She was indeed a different breed.

As they walked up the steps to the rear of the main house, Lee appeared.

"Good evening. Ready for an exquisite dinner before the game?"

"I am. Let me introduce Mitch Salimbeni," Moore said. "She has my gambling money."

Salimbeni shot him a sharp look at the demeaning comment. Lee noticed it right away but decided to ignore it as he glanced at the briefcase in her hand.

Lee took her other hand and kissed the back of it.

"Charmed," he commented.

"At least someone is a gentleman around here," Salimbeni cracked as she smiled at Lee.

"Welcome to my Jamaica home. It's a place where I hold gambling parties."

"I don't see any other gamblers," Moore observed as he looked around.

"Oh no. Tonight, it will just be you and me," he smiled wickedly. "But first, let me tell you about my home. It was originally built when sugar cane made Jamaica the wealthiest English colony in the West Indies. The architectural style is Georgian with a distinctly Creole character. It's constructed of locally quarried stone and termite-resistant tropical hardwoods. The bricks you see arrived on the island originally as ship ballast."

Lee led them inside as he showed them the first floor. "The main house is surrounded by a veranda and has this large living space, plus the dining room which you will see shortly. Upstairs, there are four bedrooms with balconies overlooking the ocean and Kingston. Did you get a chance to enjoy the view from your villas?"

"Yes," Salimbeni answered.

"I did and the view inside my villa," Moore replied with a wry smile.

Lee snickered. "You mean Mei. I wanted to be sure you felt welcome."

"That I did."

Mangan entered the living area and spoke, "Dinner is ready if it's convenient."

"Splendid. If you'll follow me." Lee led the two into the dining area where reggae music was playing softly in the background. They encountered Yoki who gave Moore a large smile.

Lee introduced her to Salimbeni as they all took seats.

Flowers appeared in the doorway.

"You remember my niece, Mei," Lee remarked.

"Yes, I do," Moore grinned warmly at the blonde who was beaming seductively at Moore.

"Yes," Salimbeni responded coldly. She didn't like the intruder.

"Mei, why don't you sit here next to Emerson, and Mitch, you can sit on the other side of him," Lee said as he and Yoki sat opposite Moore.

"I am amazed that you were able to secure a plane flight on such short notice, Emerson. And what a unique flight. I saw it land in the driveway."

"I have good connections," Moore affirmed proudly.

"Apparently," Lee commented casually as he reached for his wine glass.

"I'm still interested in visiting your feed mill operations to see how they operate," Moore requested.

"That can be arranged," Lee said.

"I also understand that you have another research center. I'd like to visit it too," Moore pushed as he closely watched Lee's face for a reaction.

Lee's face remained stoic. "I don't know whatever gave you that idea, Emerson. Cranfield is the only research center we have," Lee lied.

"I've been in this business long enough for my senses to direct me in the right direction," Moore continued.

"This time your senses have failed you. But enough of this business talk, let's enjoy our meal," Lee said as he redirected the conversation toward the culture of Jamaica for the balance of the meal.

As the dessert was being served, Moore felt a slight pressure on the outer side of his thigh. He looked down and saw that Flowers was trailing her finger sensuously on his leg. He glanced at her, but she stared at her food as if nothing was happening. She, however, ran her tongue provocatively along her lips before replacing it with a coy smile.

Moore returned his gaze to his food as she continued stroking his thigh. Moore did his best to hide any reaction, but he wasn't very good at it as several sensuous waves of pleasurable tremors ran through his body.

"Are you feeling okay, Emerson?" Lee asked.

Moore wondered if Lee knew what Flowers was doing.

"Oh, I am feeling quite fine, perhaps upbeat."

Lee nodded. He knew that seduction was what Flowers did best, and he could see across the table the smoldering heat reflected in her eyes. She was very adept at distracting men who Lee invited to his private gambling games. He snickered quietly at Moore's apparent discomfort.

The under-the-table action was not lost on Salimbeni who had given several sideway glances toward Moore. She frowned at Moore's failure to end the sultry intrusion.

After a few minutes, Lee asked, "Are you ready to let the games begin?"

"Yes," Moore replied although he felt that the games had begun much earlier.

Lee pushed back his chair and stood. "If you would all, please follow me."

Lee led the group down a hallway to a room where there was a green, felt-covered poker table, a roulette wheel and several slot machines. A bar with a mirror behind it lined one wall of the room. The opposite wall was lined with floor-to-ceiling windows that opened to a balcony with a view of the sparkling lights from Kingston below and the Caribbean Sea.

"Kari, could you get our guests a drink? I'll take my usual," Lee said as he sat at the poker table while Moore sat opposite him. "And adjust the lights, Mei."

"Yes," the blonde replied as she dimmed the lights in the room while turning on a stained glass, oblong Tiffany light that hung over the poker table.

"What would you like, Emerson?" Yoki asked.

"I'm not much of a drinker, but I'll take a shot of Jamaican rum with cola," Moore replied.

"And you, Miss Salimbeni?" Yoki asked.

"I'll join you at the bar. Give me a double shot of your best rum," she answered with contempt. "You'll need this, Emerson," she said as she dropped the cash-filled briefcase on the poker table.

"Thank you. I hope to have it stuffed to overflowing by the end of the night," Moore cracked as he noticed her abrupt attitude.

Lee laughed sinisterly. "We shall see, but I wouldn't be too optimistic, Emerson," he said slyly as Mangan entered the room. "Arsalan, would you exchange Emerson's cash for chips?" He looked at Moore. "How much do you have there?"

"$500,000," Salimbeni called from nearby.

"Good. Arsalan, bring me an equal amount in chips," Lee instructed Mangan as he picked up the chips.

Meanwhile, Yoki returned with two drinks. She set them in front of the two seated players before returning to the bar.

"What are you drinking?" Moore asked Lee.

"A martini...well-stirred."

Mangan brought over the stacks of chips and set an equal

amount next to each player before returning to stand by the doorway.

"I believe you prefer playing blackjack, Emerson."

Moore nodded.

"Let's start out playing blackjack then. Shall we start with $10,000?"

"That's fine."

Over the next hour, they played blackjack with Lee losing more than he was winning. He was growing frustrated with Moore's uncanny streak of good luck.

"Another round of drinks, Kari. Is that okay with you, Emerson?"

"Yes." Moore was quite pleased with his card playing and the accumulation of Lee's chips. He had noticed that Lee was becoming frustrated with his losses.

When Yoki returned with the drinks, Lee patted the chair next to him. "Kari, why don't you sit next to me and bring me some luck?"

Yoki did as he requested while Lee looked toward the bar. "Ladies, why don't you join us, too?"

Salimbeni shook her head. "I'm quite fine here," she replied. She had switched to espresso, occasionally walking to the outside balcony to look down on the city below.

Flowers, on the other hand, walked over to Moore and stood next to him as he sipped his drink. Without any pretense of hiding her affection, she crouched beside his chair, reached up and slipped her bare arms around his neck. She gave Moore a provocative smile with flashing eyes. She had the air of a woman with no sexual inhibitions.

Salimbeni rolled her eyes in disgust at the display.

"I feel that I'm at a disadvantage Mr. Lee," Moore said as

he enjoyed the attention. "I may not be able to concentrate as well," he remarked.

"But Emerson, you are such a man of so many talents. I venture to guess that a little distraction is nothing for you to overcome," Lee sneered. "Mei, perhaps you should give Emerson a little space."

"Certainly," she said as she stood, but began to sensuously rub the back of Moore's neck.

"I'd like to suggest we change games. Let's try poker. Would that be permissible?" Lee asked as his snaky eyes stared at Moore as if he were on the verge of striking.

Moore felt an immediate emptiness in his stomach. Poker was not his strong suit, but he needed to play along with Lee if it would give him access to his operations.

"That would be perfect. I need to sharpen my skills."

For the next two hours, they played poker. Lee's luck did change with him winning most of the hands. As night began to change into dawn, Lee suggested, "Why don't we play one final hand with everything pushed into the pot?"

Moore was skeptical the way his luck had been running, but to placate his host, he agreed. "Perfect," he said as he joined Lee in pushing all the chips into the middle of the table.

Lee dealt the cards. His golden eye watched Moore carefully as he picked up his hand. He noticed a slight smile appear for a moment on Moore's face before it disappeared. He didn't know that Moore was holding a flush, five cards of the same suit but not in sequence.

Picking up his cards, Lee wasn't pleased with what he first saw. "Mei, could you close the blinds for me?" he asked. "The early sun is blinding me." He tapped his finger impatiently as he waited.

Flowers stepped away from Moore as Moore turned his head to watch her walk away, then back to his cards.

"Is this better?" she asked as she closed the one blind.

"Quite."

When she returned, she stood next to Moore once again.

"How many cards would you like," Lee asked of his guest.

Moore studied his hand for perhaps a half-minute, then briefly glanced first at Flowers before turning to Lee. "I'm standing pat, no cards needed," Moore said wryly.

Lee was tired and a bit irritated at Moore's exaggerated dramatics. "Very well. I shall follow also in declining any cards," Lee challenged.

"Mr. Lee, what do you have?" Moore asked.

"Four of a kind," Lee said triumphantly as he set his four aces on the table.

"Beats me," Moore revealed as he folded his cards and pushed the chips toward Lee. "Well-played. I enjoyed our evening," he said as he stood.

"And I enjoyed taking your money, Emerson. We will have to play again," Lee said as he stood, placing an arm around Yoki. "And for now, let's call it a night."

"Or a day," Moore countered as he stood, and Flowers slipped her arm around Moore's waist.

"I can show you to your villa," Flowers purred.

Salimbeni strode across the room and took Flowers' arm away. "That is so kind of you, Mei, to want to escort Emerson to his villa, but I'll take care of that," Salimbeni spoke rigidly. She glared at Flowers.

"That's fine, Mitch. Mei, we can catch up later," Moore said as he and Salimbeni started walking toward the door. He was exhausted from the mental stress of the game.

Lee was watching the tension-filled exchange with amusement.

Once outside, Salimbeni turned to Moore. "You better be careful around that trollop! She's no friend of yours."

"Because she helps Lee cheat?"

"You noticed?"

"Couldn't help it. She could see my cards from where she was standing. She'd touch her face when he should fold or put her hand on her hip when he should raise me."

"What about that last hand?" Salimbeni asked. "I thought you were setting him up for the kill."

"No. I let him win. Or I should say cheat. I didn't let her see my cards on that last hand, but I sensed what he was up to."

"What's that?"

Moore told her.

"And you let him get away with it?" she asked in shock.

"I'll confront him later today. It wouldn't be right for me to cause him to lose face in front of everyone in the room although they all may be wise to what he did."

"Do you think that's a good idea? Couldn't it blow your opportunity to visit his sites?" Salimbeni asked with concern.

"It shouldn't be a problem," Moore replied impetuously. Sometimes Moore's actions backfired on him.

They reached Salimbeni's villa.

"We both need to grab a few hours of sleep and then see how Lee can help me with my facility visits," Moore said as Salimbeni walked inside her unit.

Moore walked next door and entered his unit. He looked around to see if Flowers had decided to join him. He was partially disappointed that Flowers had not been there to welcome him, but he needed to rest.

CHAPTER 17

Early That Afternoon
Sawdust Joint

When Moore woke several hours later, he rolled out of bed and spotted a note that had been slipped under his villa door. He walked over and picked it up. It was an invitation from Flowers to join her for a drive up into the mountains to a waterfall. He chuckled when he saw she had scribbled that swimsuits were optional.

Moore shaved, showered and dressed in a polo shirt and khaki shorts before opening his suitcase. He unlatched the hidden compartment and stared at its contents. He withdrew the Walther PPK and held it in his hand as he thought about taking it on the drive. He decided against it but instead took the cigarette lighter, cigarette case and the burner phone.

When he left the villa, he spotted Salimbeni at the pool, relaxing in her usually small bikini. He didn't notice her phone or glass of iced tea on a small table next to her – didn't notice those at all.

"Care to join me?" she asked as she looked over the top of her sunglasses as Moore approached.

"No thanks," Moore replied as he picked up a croissant from a nearby table. "I'm going for a ride up the mountain."

"With your flower child?" Salimbeni taunted.

"As a matter of fact, I am. I'm going to see what I can get from her."

"You want to rephrase that comment?" Salimbeni glared.

Moore laughed. "I want to see if she knows anything about Lee's operations. She could be helpful."

"Be careful. I don't trust her," Salimbeni cautioned.

"Always. I'm always careful," Moore said as he headed for the main house. Once inside he walked to the open front door where he saw Flowers outside, leaning against a car. He also saw Lee in the hallway. "Mr. Lee. Do you have a moment?"

"Yes? What is it?" Lee was on his way to his study to take a call.

"How many aces of hearts are there in a card deck?"

"One. Why?" Lee answered with a confused look.

Moore reached into his pocket and withdrew an ace of hearts. "Apparently our last hand had two - one in your four of a kind and one in my hand. I didn't want to make a scene in front of everyone, but I should have won that last hand," Moore stated assertively.

"You must be mistaken," Lee responded unemotionally, although his eyes seethed with anger.

"I am quite sure. When I folded my hand, I kept this card so I could show you."

"Nonsense!" Lee exclaimed in a cold tone as he turned and walked to his study. Within a minute, he had Mangan standing in front of him. "I've had my fill of Emerson Moore. Kill him. Mei is driving him to the waterfall."

"I'll send a couple of the men up there. It will be a tragic hunting accident," Mangan announced.

Lee waived him along. He was fuming internally at the chance that Moore would cause him to lose face for cheating – even though he was.

Meanwhile, Moore had bounded down the front steps to Flowers who was wearing a soft blue shirtdress. She greeted him with a kiss on the cheek. "What do we have here?" Moore asked as he admired the sleek vehicle.

"It's Mr. Lee's toy," she explained. "I get to drive it from time to time," she added with glee.

Moore walked around the low, white 2015 Koenigsegg One:1 as he admiringly examined the Swedish-built su-percar. It sported a Le Mans-inspired wing, roof-mounted cooling scoop and scissor-hinged doors. Its turbocharged 5.0-liter, V-8 engine created 1,341 horsepower and a top speed of 273 mph. The $2.8 million car was designed for speed and hugging the road. It went from zero to 60 mph in 2.5 seconds and from zero to 100 mph in 4.5 seconds.

"It looks fast, but I wouldn't believe you can open it up on winding mountain roads," Moore guessed as he glanced up at the switchbacks on the mountainside.

"Right. Not where we're going. I'll drive since I know the way. Mr. Lee doesn't allow visitors to drive this one," Flowers said as she opened the driver's door and dropped into the seat. Moore followed suit, sitting into the passenger seat.

"Tight fit," he remarked as he admired the futuristic, cockpit-style layout.

"Like a Le Mans race car," Flowers commented as she snapped her six-point seat belt in place before starting the vehicle. Its engine rumbled with a throaty roar, signaling its overwhelming horsepower.

"Nice," Moore observed as the supercar drove down the circular driveway and began its climb up the mountain roads. After a few minutes, Moore asked, "Mei, do you get involved in Mr. Lee's work?"

Flowers turned her head slightly and allowed a coy smile

to appear. "It depends on what you mean by get involved," she said in an alluring tone.

Moore ignored it and drilled in. "I mean, do you do any work for him like planning for his operations or accounting. Maybe visiting his other operations?" Moore questioned with a raised eyebrow.

"Sometimes, I tag along on trips, but only for social reasons. He likes to have a pretty face nearby for his guests."

I bet, Moore thought. "Where do you go?"

"Wherever he wants. It's not something that I'm at liberty to discuss with anyone. He has strict rules for the ladies to follow," she explained as they entered the first switchback on the mountainside and she turned on the radio to play reggae music.

They drove on the left side of the road as was the norm in Jamaica which gave Moore some relief. He noticed that the only barrier between the other side of the road and the dangerous drop off into steep ravines was a two-foot-high concrete wall. Elsewhere, it was a series of low, steel guardrails. They were not in place for the entire ride up the mountain.

Their side of the road was crowded to the edge with lush vegetation like orchids, palm trees and stands of bamboo, ferns, ebony, mahogany, and rosewood trees. On the other side of the road, rockslides and mudslides from torrential rains had swept away the guardrails in many places, leaving no protection from plummeting into the abyss below.

They crossed numerous bridges over mountain streams as they dodged pedestrians, hitchhikers, traffic and bicycles.

Moore hoped that she was going to open up the powerful car to see how it took the road curves, especially the hairpin turns, but she wasn't a reckless driver.

They drove by a number of ramshackle roadside markets

that were painted in green, yellow and purple. They offered cold drinks, a variety of fresh fruit and jerk chicken. Small homes clung to the mountainside and chickens could be spotted, pecking in the roadway.

Forty-five minutes into the drive, Flowers slowed the car and turned onto a narrow, muddy road that was more of a track with grass growing in the middle and lush vegetation trying to encroach on the rutted lane.

As the car bottomed out a couple of times, Moore commented, "You need a SUV for this road, not a high-powered car like this."

"It's only a short way up here. This lane serves a local coffee plantation, but it has such a beautiful waterfall and grotto toward the end," she said as they bumped along slowly. "Speaking of coffee, did you know that the Japanese import and consume most of Jamaica's Blue Mountain coffee?"

"No," Moore answered at the random comment.

"If I took you to the peak of the Blue Mountains, you can see Cuba on a clear day. Most days the peaks are surrounded by clouds."

"Sounds like quite a view," Moore commented.

Five minutes later, she pulled into an open space and parked. "It's only a little farther. There's a path there," she pointed before grabbing a small cooler and exiting the vehicle.

Moore followed her for the three-minute walk as the path opened to a tree-and-limestone-rock-encircled lagoon fed by a 100-foot, cascading waterfall. The noise from the rushing water was like music accompanied by the chirping of local birds, including yellow-billed parrots.

The lagoon had a shimmery iridescence of an array of unending blues, changing by the minute. It was the perfect setting for an erotic rendezvous, but Moore was focused on getting Flowers to open up about Lee's operations.

"Rum?" she asked as she sat on a limestone ledge next to the lagoon and opened the cooler.

"Only Jamaican rum," Moore spoke as he sat next to her. He couldn't help but notice her fragrant hair.

"Of course," she remarked as she poured a glassful for Moore and herself.

"Do you come here often?" Moore asked before taking a sip.

"Whenever I get a chance. It allows me to step away from the world I live in to be able to enjoy the tranquility of nature," she said as she downed the contents of her glass and poured herself another. "Ready for more?" she asked as she looked at Moore's glass.

He chuckled. "Mei, I'm a slower drinker than you."

"I say you have to enjoy life when you can," she giggled as she downed the newly filled glass.

Moore guessed what she was up to as she worked on unleashing her already loose inhibitions. He hoped that he could draw more information from her as a result of her drinking. He was all business. Well, almost all.

"Isn't this just beautiful, Emerson?"

"Yes. It's almost like being in paradise."

"Want to go for a swim? Did you bring a swimsuit?"

"I didn't bring one," he answered.

"Good. Neither did I." She started to stand, but instead dropped on top of Moore, pushing him onto his back. "Let's get this over with," she purred. In one fluid motion she was astride Moore with her dress riding up her thighs.

She brought her face to Moore's and allowed her soft lips to touch his, causing an exciting, intoxicating moment for the two of them. She moaned as Moore returned the kiss, then groaned when she felt him pushing her up.

"What are you doing?" she asked, confused.

Moore started to sit up. "You've had too much to drink, Mei. I don't take advantage of women who have had too much to drink. Never have. Never will," he started.

Suddenly, she pushed him back down and lowered her head as a shot rang out from the nearby trees. The bullet connected with the back of her skull, killing her instantly as she dropped lifeless atop Moore.

Moore realized quickly that she was gone. He rolled her off of him and felt for a pulse while his eyes searched the trees. Another shot barely missed Moore.

Deciding to take evasive action, Moore grabbed her car keys from the ledge and rolled away as the gunfire continued. He pulled out the cigarette lighter and activated the smoke bomb before throwing it toward the trees. Crouching, he ran toward the path.

"He's coming your way," a man's voice shouted from the trees across from Moore.

He escaped down the path before stepping into the under-brush to hide. As Moore heard approaching footsteps, he with-drew the cigarette case and extracted one of the dart guns. He waited as he saw an armed man carefully striding up the path. He recognized him as one of Lee's henchmen.

The man passed by without seeing Moore who stepped out, aimed and fired the dart gun. The dart struck the man in the back of the neck, and he dropped, shrieking in pain before he died.

Moore sprinted down the path to the supercar as two shots

were fired at him. He jumped in and drove it faster than he should have down the lane as it bottomed several times.

He glanced at his rearview mirror and saw a Land Rover give chase. With its higher ground clearance, it was quickly able to close the distance between the two vehicles.

Thankful that it was a short drive to the main road, Moore accelerated as he pulled onto it and extended his escape. Not being used to the car's power, Moore felt it snap sideways as he drove through the first curve at a too high rate of speed. Wide-eyed, he downshifted as the car held its slide while moving out of the first switchback. He then checked the distance to the trailing pursuer.

As Moore screeched around the bend, the tires engaged in open warfare with the road, and he nearly crashed into the rear of a slow-moving garbage truck. The car skidded as Moore slammed on the brakes. When the road straightened, he rapidly accelerated and careened around the garbage truck.

The Koenigsegg One flew as fast as Moore could safely drive through more curves ahead on the steep mountain road. It was frustrating how the sharp switchbacks limited the car's high-speed capability, allowing the Land Rover again to close the distance between the two vehicles.

Moore quickly swerved into the middle of the road to prevent his pursuer from passing him. The Land Rover faked a pass to the left, then accelerated to the right when Moore again cut it off. Moore centered his car before it was struck from behind by the Land Rover.

Still in escape mode and looking ahead to several S-shaped bends in the road, Moore saw his opportunity. There were several large trucks proceeding slowly up the mountain road. If he could time it right, Moore believed he could squeeze in front of a truck heading down the mountain before the trucks would temporarily block both lanes, thus slowing the Land Rover.

Moore accelerated dangerously to catch up to the truck headed downhill. He pulled out a couple of times as he gauged when the oncoming truck would close the distance. Just before it did, Moore darted out and around the downhill truck, narrowly missing the first uphill truck with its driver yelling angrily and blowing the horn. The Land Rover was temporarily caught behind the downhill truck and blocked from seeing Moore's car as it slowed and waited for the three uphill trucks to go by so it could pass the downhill truck and catch Moore.

After extending his escape, Moore suddenly stood on the brakes and backed into a hidden driveway along the right side of the road. When the Land Rover started to drive by, Moore accelerated onto the roadway, striking the Land Rover broadside. The momentum from Moore's car pushed the Land Rover over the edge of the road where it bounced down the side of the ravine and burst into flames. Moore was able to quickly stop, ensuring that he didn't follow the Land Rover over the edge.

When Moore tried to back up the car to the side of the road, metal screamed against metal. The front end of the car was so damaged that it was undrivable. Moore stepped out of the car as the downhill truck came to a stop.

The driver stepped out and walked over to the side of the road to peer at the burning vehicle below. He saw a sign that read, "Danger. No Guardrail."

"Too bad he couldn't read," Moore quipped when he saw the truck driver looking at the sign. "Can I catch a lift down the road?"

"I'm only going to the next village," the driver explained.

"That will do," Moore said as he walked around the other

side of the truck and climbed in.

When they arrived in the village, Moore found a local to hire for the return drive to Lee's place. Moore followed the man behind his house to his vehicle. When Moore saw it, he gasped.

"Is that safe?"

"*Irie*," the Jamaican replied in their sing-song language. "This will make it to the big city."

"How are the brakes?" Moore wondered.

"They work…most of the time."

Moore was skeptical as he climbed into the worn Suzuki SUV that was missing both doors. The 50-year-old vehicle was long overdue for the scrap heap. It was painted in gray although the paint was faded. The hood had been replaced with a bright green hood. Its engine wheezed when it started.

The dashboard had been painted dark purple and the seats were threadbare. The floorboards had partially rusted away, giving riders an opportunity to see the road below them as they rode. The taillights were broken, and rust served as the vehicle's trim around the base of the vehicle.

"*Irie*. The radio works the best," the driver said as he turned on reggae music that filled the air.

About halfway back, Moore had him turn it off as he made two quick phone calls. He called Salimbeni and briefly gave her a recap of what had transpired. He also asked her to pack her things and his things and to meet him at the front gate.

Next, Moore called Holly Hall and asked her to fly back to Lee's place and pick them up in front of the gate. He didn't want to chance an ugly encounter with Lee or Mangan that could become lethal. After Moore finished his calls, the driver turned the radio volume back up.

Pulling up to the front gate, Moore paid the driver and

walked over to the open gate to Lee's property. A security guard was watching Salimbeni walk toward him as she carried both suitcases.

He began to reach for the phone to alert Lee when he found his arm gripped tightly by Moore. "I wouldn't do that if I were you."

They were distracted by the Ranger's arrival overhead as it set itself down in front of the gate. Moore let go of the guard's arm as he handed him the keys to Lee's car.

"Please tell Mr. Lee that I ran into his friends," he quipped.

Before the guard could react, Moore and Salimbeni had boarded the Ranger and it was ascending.

"Where to, Emerson?" Holly asked from the cockpit.

"Back to London."

"I'll chart a course for us," John added.

"It looks like you pissed on his bonfire when you confronted him about his cheating at cards and he's roaring mad," Salimbeni offered.

"Yeah. I think I made a mistake. I should have thought that move through more. I think that just about closes out my chance to take any approved visits of his facilities," Moore mused.

"I notice your use of approved visits. Are you thinking of unapproved?" Salimbeni queried.

"Maybe if I can find the right one."

"I'm sorry about the death of your friend," Salimbeni said in a sad tone as she changed the topic.

"Yeah. That was unexpected. Mei took the bullet meant for me. I'm sure of it," Moore said. He did feel sorry for the poor woman.

"How was your day?" Moore asked Salimbeni as the plane headed southeast.

"Very interesting," she smiled.

"Oh?" Moore asked.

"It's funny how a bikini and a little cleavage works on men," she grinned.

"How's that?"

"Lee's pool boy became very distracted, and I used that to my advantage to see if he knew anything."

"Did he?"

"Obviously no. But he did ask if I was leaving right away like the others. Then he said that something big had come up and Lee had to catch a flight. I saw a lot of hustle and bustle going on."

"You don't think it was related to the attack on me, do you?" Moore asked inquisitively.

"No. There was something in the air driving this. I couldn't get a handle on it."

"I'm calling V and updating him on what's been going on and to see if he knows anything." Moore pulled out his phone and called V.

After being brought up to speed, V commented, "I'm glad you survived, but that was not a smart move to confront Lee about cheating, Emerson. You jeopardized the entire project."

"I realize that now. It set into motion a number of actions that didn't need to take place, especially with Mei Flowers' death," Moore regretted.

"You sound stressed, Emerson. You need to take a deep breath and relax. Get that tension out of your voice and yourself. You need to slow down and think things through," V cautioned with concern.

"I will. I will," Moore repeated. "Mitch picked up something interesting," he added.

"What's that?"

Mitch leaned forward in her seat. "Something big is going to happen. I got it from the pool boy. It sounds like everyone was scurrying to get Lee to his plane. He had to go somewhere."

"And I know where that somewhere might be," V responded.

"Where's that?" Moore asked.

"While you've been playing cards with him, I've been trying out some new technology. I was able to track his cell phone calls this morning."

"And?" Moore pushed anxiously.

"They were to Morocco. I was able to track it to a building in the Western Sahara Desert that looks like a feed mill."

"A feed mill in the desert? That sounds crazy," Moore said in disbelief.

"When you're mixing ingredients for dairy feed, the most opportune location is in a very dry climate like in California or Morocco. It comes down to limiting moisture content."

"Why is that, V?" Salimbeni asked.

"Moisture in feed causes mold growth and you don't want that. Molds spoil feed by depleting nutrients and making the feed unpalatable. Some molds release toxins that can harm dairy cow health and milk production."

"So that's what's killing the cows and the couple in Tulare!" Moore proclaimed.

"Not unless they found a more deadly mold. I'm pretty sure that it's something that they are adding to the feed mix. I also checked on the toxicology reports from the deaths you mentioned, and they ruled out mold as a probable cause."

"Sounds like we should head to Morocco," Moore surmised.

"But where in Morocco?" Salimbeni asked.

"Let me have Izzy answer that. He's been a whiz on data mining in the last 24 hours," V answered.

"I bet you all will be surprised with what I've come up with," Nelson started excitedly. He was so proud of the results of his research.

Without waiting for the group to comment, he continued eagerly, "The feed mill operation is located in Agafay. It's 22 miles southwest of Marrakesh in a rocky desert area."

"We'll head for Agafay," Moore said without thinking.

"Not a good decision, Emerson," V said. "You just can't drop in even though that Ranger is capable of it. There's more to tell. Go ahead Izzy."

"I used satellite imagery to zoom in on the site. That's when I found a couple of unusual things. It's normal for a site like that to be fenced in, but this one has two fences surrounding the site and it looks like it has security guards patrolling the grounds. There's also a guard at the gated entrance."

"Tell them about the special building," V encouraged Nelson.

"That's what's really weird. There's a building off by itself within the overall site. It has a guarded gate, and I could see images of people going in and out of the building. It looked like they were wearing white coats."

"Probably lab coats," V suggested.

"Right," Nelson agreed exuberantly. "I also was able to identify that Lee's plane landed at Marrakesh several times this year."

"Interesting. Is the feed mill listed under Lee's business name?" Moore asked.

"Lee Biotech Inc.," V replied. "Did you hear about the dairy cow deaths in India?"

"No," Moore replied with a concerned look on his face.

"A herd with 1,000 cows was found with their stomachs eaten from the inside out."

"Oh no!" Salimbeni exclaimed.

"This is getting more serious. India is the world's largest milk producer. They have over 300 million head of dairy cattle," V explained seriously.

Nelson jumped in. "I went back over the last several weeks' worth of satellite images of the feed mill, and it looks like security has been beefed up. Several large trucks arrived yesterday, and I saw containers being wheeled from the small building into the feed mill."

"To mix into the dairy feed?" Moore guessed.

"Could be." V continued, "I'm going to give you an address that is on the southwest outskirts of Marrakesh so the Ranger can drop you two there. There's a local there who can help you. His name is Farid Kadiri."

"You know him?" Moore asked.

"No. But I know of him. He's worked for several intelligence agencies worldwide, giving them tidbits of information."

"Trustworthy?" Moore asked.

"Is anyone?" V countered. "Be careful and keep your eyes open."

"Izzy, great job in discovering all of this," Moore said thankfully.

Nelson beamed. "Maybe you'll find some field work that I can help with," he said eagerly.

"We'll have to see," Moore said before V gave them Kadiri's address and they ended the call. Moore passed along the new destination information to the Halls and the Ranger's course changed. Moore and Salimbeni shared their assessments about the change in events before settling back to get lost in their thoughts.

After a few minutes of silence, Moore glanced at Salimbeni. She had fallen asleep in her seat as Moore turned his mind to reliving the events of the day. The adrenaline rush had left him to be replaced with a sense of grief as he lamented the death of Flowers.

He knew the type of woman that she was and loved her free spirit, her joy for life. He wondered what he could have done to have saved her. If only he had been more alert or hadn't been so foolhardy as to confront Lee with cheating at poker.

Moore's mind switched to thoughts of Duncan's death in Las Vegas. His dreams had been tormented with images of Duncan walking to his car before he and the car vaporized in the explosion. It was just so unexpected. The two of them had been through many adventures together, emerging relatively unscathed. He stared off into space as he recalled those times together.

Moore felt like allowing his moral compass to spin out of control and go after Lee to avenge the deaths of Duncan and Flowers, but he knew better. Lee's time would come. First, he had to discover what was killing the cows and people. He knew that he had to find his inner calm core and center himself if he was going to be successful with his next steps.

"Are you okay, Emerson?" Salimbeni asked as she woke to find Moore's face frozen like a mannequin.

"I am, but I'm going through a hurricane of emotions, swirling at full force," he answered as he snapped out of it.

"We'll get Lee," Salimbeni spoke confidently.

"We better," Moore countered.

"You need to go into bitch mode like I do when I need it. I reach deep inside and unlock a whirling tornado of strength and confidence. No one gets in my way when I'm operating like that. But when it's over, I can switch it off. I'm a strong woman, Emerson. Female strength is a good thing. Knowing who we are still means that we enjoy having doors opened for us," she remarked, all-knowingly.

Moore smiled and nodded his head.

Salimbeni made herself more comfortable in her seat. "You better get some rest, Mr. Moore," she said before closing her eyes for the balance of the flight.

CHAPTER 18

Early That Evening
Marrakesh, Morocco

Marrakesh is Morocco's fourth largest city and known for its red sandstone buildings and palm trees. It's an oasis carved out of the surrounding desert. The old city had walls built from rammed earth, a building method that consisted of combining mud and soil mixed with straw or lime to help adhesion.

The southwest side of the city hosts it airport and retains the distinct old city feel. It has narrow streets and two-story buildings with five-foot-high walled courtyards. The old city is packed with vendors and their stalls.

The Ranger dropped vertically in the parking lot of a grocery store, allowing Moore and Salimbeni to exit before it resumed its flight to London. Moore followed the GPS on his phone along a narrow street where he walked down an even narrower alley to a two-story building with a metal door.

His knock on the door was greeted by a male voice shouting, "Who is it?"

"I'm looking for Farid Kadiri," Moore said through the door.

The door cracked open, revealing two dark, beady eyes staring up at Moore. "And who are you?" the man asked.

"Emerson Moore and Mitch Salimbeni," he replied.

"Why didn't you say so? Come in. Come in. I was expecting you, but I didn't think you'd be here until tomorrow," the man replied as he swung open the door to allow them both to enter. He stuck his head outside and looked up and down the dimly lit street to make sure they hadn't been followed.

When he closed the door, Moore saw Kadiri place a pistol into a nearby cabinet.

"It's dangerous around here?" Moore quizzed Kadiri.

"One can never led his guard down," Kadiri explained. The short, dark-skinned Moroccan had thick white hair, a big moustache and protruding belly. He was wearing a stained white linen shirt and trousers. The air around him was saturated with his cologne.

"Mr. Moore, Mr. VanBlaricum instructed me to help you in any way that I can, and I hope you will give him a good report so he can wire payment to my bank." Kadiri looked up at Moore and flashed a smile with his yellowed teeth.

"I'm sure that he has confidence in your work," Moore responded.

Kadiri, turning to face Salimbeni, took her hand and kissed it. "Miss Salimbeni, I am at your disposal. Your wish is my command," he leered. Kadiri was a womanizer, flirting with and chasing every passing female.

"Thank you, Farid. I'm pretty self-sufficient," she said stiffly as she turned her head away from his foul-smelling breath.

"Come in. You must be hungry and thirsty," he said as he led them through the house and outside to a lush courtyard. "I just made tajines," he said as he pointed to several chairs for them to sit.

"Tajines?" Moore asked a bit nervous about what went into it.

"A little chicken and lamb. Then I add fruit, olives, some spices, turmeric, peppers and vegetables," he explained as he served generous helpings onto their plates from a tajine pot.

Moore and Salimbeni carefully tasted the food, then consumed it with enjoyment. They hadn't eaten in hours.

"It's customary to serve green tea with mint and sugar, but I do have whiskey hidden away." He looked around furtively as if he was afraid that someone was listening. "It's illegal to serve alcohol in places where it's not allowed. But I never let the legality of things get in my way," he roared with a big belly laugh.

"Tea is perfect," Moore suggested as Salimbeni nodded.

"This tajine is delicious," Salimbeni complimented Kadiri who was busy pouring tea from a curved teapot into three small glasses.

"I am very pleased that you like it, Miss Salimbeni," Kadiri responded as he leaned back in his chair. "Mr. VanBlaricum said you needed to quietly inspect a feed mill in Agafay. Is that correct?"

"Yes."

"I know this place. It is heavily guarded and difficult to get on the grounds." He sipped on his tea before looking over the edge of the glass at Moore. "I take it that you want to do this covertly."

"That's correct," Moore responded.

"Let me see what I can do. I have cousins there. They may have some ideas."

Alarmed, Moore sat straight up in his chair. "I don't want to alert anyone that we are here or are interested in getting on the grounds."

Kadiri waved his hands left and right as his head followed suit. "No. No. This is no problem. My cousins there keep their mouths shut. They help me on a variety of clandestine dealings that I do there and other places."

"Black market?" Moore guessed.

Kadiri flashed his yellowed teeth at Moore as he smiled. "I don't tell you my business and you don't tell me your business.

Agreed?"

"That's perfect for us," Moore said.

"We like it that way," Salimbeni added.

"Okay. I will show you your rooms upstairs and then I'll start working on my cousins. Tomorrow, we will take a drive down there so you can see the place in the daylight."

"Sounds like a plan," Moore said as they all stood and followed Kadiri to the second floor.

CHAPTER 19

The Next Afternoon
Agafay, Morocco

Agafay is a remote village of 15,000 people set 40 kilometers southwest of Marrakesh in the foothill desert of the Atlas Mountains. Its towering sandstone buildings, which are set on terraces, remind one of a movie set.

The black Mercedes pulled to a stop in front of one of the homes on the outskirts of the city. Kadiri spoke to his two passengers. "I will get my cousin and then we will drive by the feed mill so you can take a look."

Kadiri returned with his cousin who was medium height and had dark skin stretched across a bony face like a cadaver. It was covered with a dark beard and highlighted by a pointed nose below two bulging eyes. "This is Yusuf Nabil. Yusuf used to work at the feed mill."

Nabil nodded his head suspiciously as he eyed the two visitors. "Why are you interested in the feed mill?" The dark-eyed local wasn't one to waste words.

"Yusuf," Moore started, "We're just interested in how they produce their dairy feed," Moore answered, not wanting to divulge too much.

"I wouldn't think it's different from the way any other feed mill produces feed," he said nonchalantly. "You want me to make introduction so you can take a tour and ask them about it?"

"No. I don't think they would welcome a visit from me," Moore replied.

"They don't like us," Salimbeni added.

Nabil glanced at the woman with skepticism. He didn't like women speaking around men discussing business. No Muslim did as far as he was concerned. Frowning, he asked, "So how do you want to find out this information? You want me to go in and see what I can find?"

"No. I'd like your help in paying a visit to their operations at night," Moore countered. "We can pay for your help."

Nabil looked at his cousin and Kadiri commented as he nodded his head. "They are good to do business with." Kadiri then exchanged words with Nabil in Arabic as Moore and Salimbeni tried to guess what they were discussing. Finally, Nabil's countenance changed.

A contemplative look appeared on Nabil's face. "Let's take a drive out there. Maybe I help you. Maybe I don't." He looked in the back seat. "Tell the woman to cover her head."

Salimbeni began to protest, but Moore shook his head. Deferring to Moore, Salimbeni found a head covering on the back seat and placed it over her head.

"Good. I ride in front next to my cousin," he said to Moore who got out of the passenger seat and took a seat in the rear with Salimbeni. This cousin was a piece of work, Moore thought.

Kadiri, who had returned to the car, started its engine as Nabil plopped into the seat next to him. The car began a ten-minute journey out of Agafay to the feed mill.

The hilly topography was desolate with sand colored in shades of tan and taupe. The dusty sand road was lined intermittently with sparse palm trees.

"We can drive by it and turn off behind one of the sand dunes, then walk up the dune. You should be able to see it from there," Nabil said as they approached the fenced site which sat isolated in the rocky desert. Kadiri did as instructed, parking behind a sand dune.

They exited the dust covered car and made their way to the top of the dune where they dropped to peer at the feed mill across the road.

Nabil began identifying the structures as he pointed to each one. "There are the storage silos and the mill itself. There's a control office inside the mill. That's where they control the mixing of the feed and making the pellets. Next to it is the lab where they test the incoming ingredients.

"Once the grain is mixed or the pellets are made, they are dumped in large totes or bagged. Then they are transported into that warehouse where they are stored until they are shipped. Next to the warehouse is the administrative building," he explained.

"Why are there so many trucks at the warehouse?" Moore asked.

"For shipping."

"And what about that building set off by itself and surrounded by double fencing?" Moore probed.

"I've never been inside of it. The senior lab technicians do secret work there from what I understand. They don't talk to anybody about what they do."

Moore turned his head and looked at Salimbeni with raised eyebrows.

"I'd like to come back here tonight and check it out. Where would be the best place to cut the fence and slip inside?" Moore asked as he scanned the grounds. He saw the manned gate and floodlights on the fence, but he didn't see any cameras.

"You could park behind a sand dune on the other side." He pointed toward it. "Then circle around to the rear corner where you could cut the fence and roll under it."

"You're not coming with us?" Salimbeni asked with a look of surprise.

"No. Farid said that you just wanted me to show you the feed mill. I don't want to be seen there. They'd recognize me right away and I don't need trouble."

Moore's face darkened with concern as he turned to Kadiri. "Are you coming in with us?"

"Oh no, Mr. Moore. That's not part of my agreement. I'll leave you at Yusuf's house where you can get ready for tonight. He will provide you with transportation for your trip back out here."

"How do we get back to Marrakesh when we're done?" Salimbeni asked.

"Tomorrow, I will return to Yusef's house and pick you up. Then we can arrange for your trip back to London," Kadiri clarified as if it were no big deal.

Moore looked grim. "Any cameras on that building that's off limits to just about everybody?"

"I don't think so. There's a guard there who checks the area. He usually stays between the two fences around the building," Nabil offered.

Moore felt a chill run up and down his spine. He didn't like it. Something was amiss.

"Are we finished here? I need to get back to Marrakesh," Kadiri said as he started to scoot down the sand dune before getting an answer.

The others responded by following him down the dune to the car where Moore took a swig of water from his water bottle. It had a gritty taste from the sand dust, and it wasn't washing away very easily.

They stepped into the vehicle and rode back to Agafay with

Kadiri. After they were dropped at Nabil's home, they had dinner with him. Moore and Salimbeni then retreated with their gear to their upstairs bedrooms to rest before starting their evening adventure.

Moore couldn't sleep. He eased himself out of bed and walked to the open window to listen to the quiet night sounds of the village. There was a knock at his door. He turned to see it open and Salimbeni enter the room.

"Can't sleep?" she asked.

"No. The adrenaline is already flowing," he answered.

"Mine, too."

"What were you thinking about Emerson?" She asked as the two walked to the window. It was a moonless night, and the sky was filled with the distant brilliance of twinkling stars.

"Peaceful here, but my mind is racing with thoughts of Mei and Sam. I just wish I could have done something to prevent their deaths," Moore murmured. Their deaths continued to haunt Moore.

"I know. I do, too. Well at least for Sam. He was a good man," she commented quietly.

Moore glanced at his watch. "We better get ready."

The two returned to their respective rooms where they grabbed their gear.

Moore moved to his suitcase and opened the hidden compartment. He withdrew the Walther PPK with its holster and extra clip of ammunition. He affixed the holster to his waist before pulling out the laser and the goTena Mesh Pro X2 tactical communications device earlier provided by V. He dropped them in the faraday bag as he heard a gentle knock at the door.

"Yes?" he asked as the door opened. It was Salimbeni and she was outfitted in dark clothing like him. She had a dark scarf around her head so that she wouldn't offend Nabil.

"I'm ready."

Moore noticed the weapon at her side. It was a Micro Uzi, the Israeli-made submachine gun. "Going to war?" Moore asked.

"Nothing like being prepared," she shot back.

"I guess you had a suitcase like mine," Moore suggested.

"Nothing like them," she smiled as Moore led her down-stairs to where Nabil was waiting.

"Yusef, do you have a vehicle for us?"

"Yes, it's out back," he said with a furtive look. "There's a pair of fence wire cutters on the front seat."

"Good. Thank you."

Nabil walked out the back of his house and led them to the next street where a dusty 2006 Toyota truck was parked. "When you return, leave the truck a few streets over. I don't want it linked to me."

"We'll do that. Thank you, Yusef," Moore said as Nabil dis-appeared into the street shadows. Moore turned to Salimbeni. "You like him?"

"No. He gives me the creeps," she commented solemnly.

"Yeah. Me, too. I just hope he's trustworthy," Moore said as the two climbed into the truck and drove to the feed mill.

CHAPTER 20

Later That Night
The Feed Mill

Misjudging where he was, Moore drove past the feed mill and pulled behind the sand dune that they had parked behind earlier that day. He backed up and drove to the other side of the feed mill where he spotted the turnoff that Nabil had suggested they use. He turned off the lights and parked behind another sand dune.

As they exited the vehicle, Moore started for the top of the sand dune.

"Where are you going?" Salimbeni asked confused.

"I'm just leery. Come on and I'll show you."

When they reached the crest of the dune, Moore ducked down. He withdrew his cell phone and checked it for reception. There wasn't any. He pulled the goTena Mesh Pro X2 communications device and set it up. When he connected his cell phone to it, he had reception and quickly called V in London.

"Hello," a groggy voice answered.

"V, it's Emerson."

V sat straight up in his bed. "Are you okay? Is there something wrong?"

"We're good." Moore quickly explained the events of the day and their current course of action.

"I'm setting this cell phone on video and leaving it here so that you can watch our intrusion. Mitch and I are both a bit wary of this operation and want someone watching in case it goes down bad. Can you do that for us?"

"No problem. You've got my attention," he said as he made

himself comfortable.

Moore positioned his cell phone so that it had a sweeping view of the feed mill. If the floodlights came on, it would give a clear picture to V. Once he was finished, the two made their way down the sand dune and over to the far corner of the fence. The site was relatively quiet as it was shut down for the night. The only movement they saw was a security guard at the front gate.

Moore snipped through the fence and the two crawled through the opening. "So far, so good. Let's split up," Moore suggested. "Why don't you go to the administrative building while I go and check out that secret building?"

"Got it," Salimbeni said as she ran in a low crouch past the parked trucks to the administrative building. When she arrived, she used a hooded flashlight to look around the room and through several file cabinets. She spotted a laptop and tried to access it, but she didn't have a password to use.

Meanwhile, Moore crept carefully toward the other building. He scanned the area for cameras and a guard but couldn't find one. He rolled under a nearby truck and laid there patiently watching. Thirty minutes passed and he didn't see any movement. He decided to ease himself to the fence where he carefully cut through the wire.

Once the final strand was cut, he laid flat and listened. Still silent. He looked around and saw no threats. Carefully he crawled through the first row of fence. As he approached the second fence, he heard a noise. He turned to find himself facing a charging, Chinese-made, robotic attack dog, capable of running 4.5 mph.

The quad-legged, lethal ground drone was equipped with a camera and machine gun mounted on top. It was on perimeter security duty. Moore recalled reading how dangerous these war dogs could be and quickly rolled over on his side. He withdrew his laser and fired two blasts, quickly incapacitating it.

Moore rolled back to his stomach and listened. He heard nothing that concerned him. He resumed cutting the second fence and eased himself under it. He rose to a crouching position and ran to the building where he flattened himself against the wall. He looked around again and saw nothing of concern.

Working his way around to the front of the of the building, he tried the door. As expected, it was locked. He withdrew a lock pick set from his pocket and worked on unlocking the door.

Within a few minutes, the lock clicked, and he was able to open it. He walked inside the windowless room and closed the door behind him. Listening again, he heard nothing but silence. He flipped on the light switch and saw a room without furniture. It was bare.

Spotting a door across the room, he walked over. When he placed his hand on the doorknob, the door was jerked open.

"Mr. Moore, we were expecting you," Mangan said as he and two others grabbed a stunned Moore by the arms and secured them with plastic ties before sitting him in a straight-backed chair.

"Why are you sneaking around here?" Mangan demanded as he towered over Moore.

"I'm doing research on my story," Moore answered as he looked straight into Mangan's eyes, trying to be convincing.

"But why did you break into this old lab?" Mangan pushed, scoffing at the response.

"Curiosity. I just wanted to see what was behind closed doors."

"But there's nothing here. The lab was relocated last week," Mangan explained with a sinister laugh.

Moore reeled at the revelation. He didn't know that Nelson's analysis was based on old satellite photos.

One of the men handed Mangan Moore's weapon and laser. "And you need these for your research?" he questioned defiantly as his eyes bore into Moore.

"You never know what kind of animal you might find in the desert at night," Moore quipped.

"Or robotic dog," another man commented as he entered the room. "The war dog has been destroyed."

"The list of charges against you are mounting. Trespassing, breaking and entering, destruction of property," Mangan glared evilly as he went through the charges.

"Plus, a stolen vehicle," another voice chimed in.

Moore turned his head so that he could see the newcomer. It was a police officer. "My cousin Nabil reported it stolen an hour ago. We found it parked near here."

The officer frisked Moore and found the keys to the truck. He held them up for the others to see. "This confirms that he stole the truck," he gloated.

Traitor, Moore thought. Nabil set them up. He must be playing both sides. Moore was fuming. He wondered if Farid Kadiri was involved although V seemed to be high on his reliability.

"What do you want us to do with him?" the policeman

asked.

"One moment," Mangan said as he held up his finger. He walked into the corner and made a call on his cell phone to Lee. When he finished, he returned to the middle of the room. "Take him to the prison in Marrakesh where he can wait for years for his case to be tried," Mangan roared with a menacing laugh.

The policeman and one of the henchmen lifted Moore out of his chair and started walking him outside to the police vehicle parked under the bright floodlights. It was then that Moore realized they hadn't asked about Salimbeni. He hoped that they weren't aware of her, but his hopes were crushed when he heard three approaching police officers speak.

"Couldn't find Salimbeni," one shouted as Moore was being stuffed into the vehicle's back seat. "Check again. Everyone, look for her. She must still be here."

Moore sat quietly in the vehicle, hoping that she had already escaped. After half an hour, the searchers gave up.

Mangan instructed the police and facility security guards, "Keep watch for her. We'll find her in the daylight. If she did escape, she'll die in the desert," he chortled. "Scorpions and poisonous snakes. No water."

Mangan then turned to the first police officer, "Can you radio in that you're looking for a murder suspect and give them the description of her that Nabil gave you. If she's out there, you'll find her."

"I'll do that right away," he said as he reached into the police vehicle and contacted the police station to put out an alert.

"She didn't kill anyone!" Moore shouted at Mangan.

"The war dog," he sneered even though he knew that Moore was responsible for its destruction.

Moore realized there was no sense in arguing with him. He

kept his thoughts to himself as he contemplated how he would escape and return to help Salimbeni before going after Mangan and Lee.

Mangan had an afterthought. "She probably had a hand in killing your friend Sam Duncan in Las Vegas."

Moore started to react, but a sudden thought crossed his mind. Was this all a charade with them looking for Salimbeni? Was Salimbeni working with them as a sleeper agent of Lee's? Was she Duncan's mole? Moore's mind began analyzing every interaction with her as the vehicle started for the drive to the Marrakesh prison.

CHAPTER 21

Later That Morning
Marrakesh, Morocco

The prison was a traditional mud brick fortress that used the rammed earth reinforcement with cement for construction. It was often used as a site for political dissidents, murderers and terrorists where the prison guards regaled in physically and mentally abusing the inmates. It was also a strategic dumping ground for a number of nefarious reasons. Emerson Moore was dumped there when the police officer left him in the receiving room.

"Strip," a burly guard ordered Moore, who had been freed of his plastic ties and stood in the middle of the room where three beefy guards eyed him. They had the look of men who enjoyed punishing prisoners. Knowing he had no choice, Moore complied, dropping his clothes on the floor as they watched. The lead guard approached him and had Moore bend over while he examined him anally for any contraband.

"You know what to do with this infidel," the lead guard ordered his men after he finished the examination.

"Can I make a phone call?" Moore pleaded, guessing that the answer would be no.

The lead guard laughed wickedly in response.

"What about my trial? When do I go to court? Do I get a lawyer?" Moore cried over his shoulder as he was pushed through the doorway to the cellblock.

"Maybe in a month or two," was the shouted response.

Naked, Moore was led to a concrete cell with no windows and a cold concrete floor where two guards threw him to the floor.

"Don't move," one guard ordered as the other walked away. He returned with a water hose and sprayed Moore with frigid water. Moore curled into a ball as he tried to get warm.

Shortly after the steel door slammed shut, an overhead sprinkler system turned on, drenching Moore with more cold water for the next hour. There was nowhere to stay dry. Moore shivered through the entire ordeal and wondered how he was going to escape.

Two hours after the water had shut off, the steel door opened and the two guards reentered. "Come with us," one of the guards commanded Moore.

Moore tried to stand but was weak from the frigid torture he had undergone. The guards roughly grabbed his arms and jerked him to his feet before dragging him down the hall to the interrogation room. It had a metal table with two chairs on both sides.

He also observed two meat hooks hanging from the ceiling, a chair with a bucket of water and electric wires running to the bucket. There additionally was a large tub filled with water that looked like it could be used for drowning a prisoner. Moore glanced at a long table covered with torture tools like knives, drills, clamps and pliers for pulling out teeth or fingernails.

He was somewhat relieved when he was directed to the first table while the two guards stood behind him. A door across the room opened, and a man in a sharply-pressed uniform entered. He had the bearing of ex-military. His salt and pepper hair was plastic-perfect, highlighting his cold and deliberate appearance. He spoke in a no-nonsense fashion as he extended his hand open-palmed for Moore to sit.

"My name is Haseeb Rahim, Mr. Moore. Welcome to your

home for the rest of your life," he said with an icy stare.

Moore reeled at the comment. "But I thought I was going to have a trial."

Rahim laughed ominously. "Not a trial. Trials. You'll be subjected to daily trials as long as you live."

"But why? I haven't done anything to deserve this," Moore countered.

"Here, you don't have to." Rahim bent forward in his chair. "A friend of yours, if I may describe him that way, has richly paid for your incarceration."

Lee, Moore thought immediately.

"And he has paid extra for us to give you special attention. Something along the lines that he prefers not to get his hands dirty," Rahim snickered with a wicked glint in his eyes.

"Like the ice-cold shower in my cell?" Moore spouted angrily.

Rahim didn't respond. He stood and spoke to the lead guard. "Tariq, I will leave him in your hands. Give him extra today."

Rahim turned to Moore. "Enjoy your stay," he said, then walked out of the room.

Tariq spun around Moore's chair and began beating him with a hard rubber truncheon while the other two restrained Moore. The blows were directed at Moore's rib cage and skull. He soon passed out. After five minutes, they carried a badly beaten Moore to another cell where they deposited him on the floor before leaving.

Moore regained consciousness when he felt a wet cloth being rubbed over his bruised face. He moaned. "Where am I?"

"With your new roommate. Looks like they gave you the customary welcome," he said as Moore's nostrils filled with the smell of the man's pungent breath.

Moore took the cloth and continued rubbing it on his face as he struggled to sit up. "Have you been in here long?"

"Two months so far." The man was in his fifties with thick, dark hair and a sense of bravado. "My name is Abbar."

Moore reached out a hand to shake the man's extended hand. "I'm Emerson Moore. *Salam Alaikum*," Moore said, giving the traditional Arabic greeting of peace on you.

"*Wa Alaykum as-salam*," Abbar replied, wishing peace back to Moore. "I think I like you already. Why are you here?"

"I stole a truck." Moore didn't want to reveal the real reason for his imprisonment.

The heavily-bearded Abbar clapped his hands gleefully. "I knew I liked you," he repeated.

"And why are you here?"

"I steal things. But I am like your English Robin Hood. I steal from the rich and I give to the poor. Everyone loves Abbar," he said jovially.

Moore couldn't understand his positivity.

"Are you an American?" Abbar probed.

"Why?" Moore asked carefully.

"I don't like Americans."

"Do you like Brits?"

"No. They are worse than Americans."

"I'm Irish," Moore explained as he thought back to his Irish heritage.

"That's good. You know any leprechauns?" Abbar asked in a sing-song voice.

Moore chuckled despite himself.

Looking around the cell with its peeling and cracked concrete walls, he saw a small, grated window against the far wall. It was too narrow to escape from but did allow some light into the room. There were two slabs made of concrete which served as beds. They each had a worn and dirty blanket. There was a raised toilet with a wooden seat and the source of a repugnant odor in the room.

"This is terrible," Moore observed.

"It could be worse."

"How's that?"

"Most of the cells here house 75 men. The cells were meant for no more than ten men. They have one toilet and it's just a hole in the ground."

Moore groaned in disgust. "How's the food, Abbar? You do get fed, right?"

"We get two meals per day. Watery beans in the morning and cornmeal with watery soup in the evening." Abbar added, "This is a place of death. There's the overcrowding, tuberculosis, inadequate ventilation and poor medical treatment, if you can call what they provide as medical treatment."

Moore saw a bucket in the corner. "Is that a water bucket for us?"

"Yes. But be sure to pick out the bugs that swim in it before you drink. At night, you can hear the bugs racing across the floor or squishing under your feet when you get up at night."

Moore moaned. "How long are you here?"

"I don't know. They haven't told me. It's up to Allah."

"Do you get beatings every day? It sounds like that's the plan for me."

"Only once in a while," he answered as he eyed Moore suspiciously. "You must have done something more than steal a truck if you are going to get daily beatings."

Moore thought a moment before answering. He did like his cellmate but didn't want to share more with him. He was leery.

"I made the wrong person mad. Now I am paying for it."

"You went to bed with his wife?" Abbar asked with a wink. "Was she worth it?" His face beamed with an all-knowing smile.

"No. No. It was nothing like that. I broke into his business," Moore replied.

"A thief like me. I knew that I liked you. You and I are going to get along just fine unless we get selected."

"Selected?" Moore asked. "What do you mean?"

"You know about the gladiators?"

"They have gladiator fights here?" Moore asked, astounded.

"Cock fights they call them. Have you been to a cock fight where roosters fight against each other?"

"No, but I've heard about them."

"They have them here. It's a small ring where the roosters are fighting at the same time as two naked prisoners fight to the death, using knives or swords. The guards bet on both fights. It gives them entertainment."

Moore was wide-eyed. "Have you fought?"

"No, but I've heard about them."

"I don't like this one bit." Moore surveyed the room again. "Is there any way to escape from here?"

"In a coffin," Abbar laughed seriously.

"That's not what I was thinking. What about the guards? Can they be bribed?"

"You have money to bribe them with?" Abbar asked as he stared at the naked man in front of him.

"No."

"For information and extra food, yes. Escape, no. They would be killed for helping someone escape. Did you meet Rahim?"

"Yes. Nasty character."

"Not only would he kill the guard, but he would kill the guard's family in front of him before killing the guard. He's dangerous."

Moore nodded. "I gathered that."

The two spoke quietly for several more minutes, then crawled onto their individual slabs of concrete for the night. Moore pulled the worn blanket over himself as he tried to sleep. They were awakened the next morning when the steel door opened and the bright light overhead was turned on. Tariq and two guards walked into the room.

"Breakfast in bed?" Moore asked sarcastically as he raised himself up on one elbow.

His question was ignored as the guards grabbed Abbar and jerked him to his feet. Tariq began pummeling Abbar's midsection with blows.

"It's more like a beating in bed," Tariq grinned with cruelty-filled eyes.

Impetuously, Moore jumped to his feet and ran to Abbar's side. He turned and struck Tariq in the throat causing Tariq to gasp in pain and surprise. His eyes narrowed as he croaked, "Drop Abbar. Get Moore."

The guards grabbed Moore who was about to run out the open cell door. Tariq lashed out at Moore's chest with several blows from the truncheon he carried, causing Moore to twist in pain.

"That's only the beginning," Tariq raged. "Take him down the hall," he ordered the guards, who dragged Moore away. When they reached the interrogation room, they strapped him to the chair next to the long table with torture tools.

Tariq walked in front of the seated Moore. "I take pleasure

in controlling and hurting people. Hurting them very bad," he sneered as he pointed to some of the tools on the table.

"Perhaps I'll start with putting your head in a vise." Tariq held up a drill. "Then I could drill through your ear to the other side," he said with an evil smile as he held the drill in front of Moore's shocked eyes.

"But that would be too easy. Instead, we are going to slowly drive a steel spike through your ear," he said as he displayed the spike to the horrified man.

"Each tap of my hammer will slowly drive the spike into you." Tariq set down the spike and picked up a spray container of expanding orange foam insulation. "This foam expands to thirty times its size. Maybe I should spray it up your rectum. Imagine what it would do to you!" he said with evil glee.

"Tariq, stop!" a voice directed. They all turned to see that Rahim had entered the room. "He just got here. We are not to kill him immediately."

"But he struck me!" Tariq protested.

"Then I blame you for not being on your guard." Rahim focused his steely eyes on Moore. "No, our guest's death will not be for some time. There's nothing like taking one to the edge of death, then bringing him back, knowing that it will be a daily journey," Rahim taunted the reality of Moore's desperate situation.

Tariq was chagrined. "We will work him over then. He'll still be alive, but just barely."

"Make sure of it," Rahim cautioned before he turned and left the room.

Tariq led his guards in beating Moore until he escaped by passing out. The guards dragged the unconscious man back to his cell where they deposited him on the concrete floor. Moore was a bloody mess with scarlet blood flowing from a cut above his eyebrow. His eyes were swollen over, and bloody spit drooled from his slack jaws.

When he regained consciousness, he could barely move. Every muscle had seized up. There were great purple welts on each arm. His body struggled to recover. Once again, Abbar was kneeling over him, using a wet cloth to wash away the blood.

"You shouldn't have done that," Abbar advised. "They beat me when they want to. You just make it worse for yourself. In here, you have to think about yourself first if you are to have any chance to survive."

Moore allowed a low moan to emit from between his bruised lips.

Leaning close to Moore's right ear, Abbar whispered, "Now that I know you're not a plant or informant, I can tell you something. I'm going to escape. And because of your sacrifice to step in to protect me, I will take you with me. You rest now and we will talk later."

Moore barely heard the comment.

Abbar helped Moore to his sleeping spot and placed his blanket on the cold slab before Moore rolled onto it. He then covered Moore with the second blanket and began praying for the foolish Irishman.

An hour later, one of the guards swung open the door and threw in a worn shirt and trousers for Moore. "Help him into these. We need to keep him alive," he instructed Abbar. Then, the door slammed shut.

Abbar picked up the clothes and put them on the weakened Moore.

Twenty-four hours later, Moore woke when the cell door opened, and the guard delivered their morning breakfast of watery beans. Moore saw Abbar talking briefly with the guard as the guard handed Abbar a few pieces of cornbread. The door slammed shut and Abbar brought the watery beans to Moore.

"Sit up," he instructed Moore as he set the two meals down and helped Moore to a sitting position.

Moore groaned with pain as he moved and reached for the bowl of beans.

"Take these," Abbar said as he handed the cornbread to Moore.

"*Shukran*," Moore said as he thanked Abbar. "How did you get these?" Moore asked as he wolfed down the bread.

"The guard is my cousin. He takes care of me as best as he can and my family helps his family on the outside," Abbar explained. "You shouldn't have interfered when they started to beat me."

"I couldn't stand by and not do anything," Moore protested.

"Not a good idea as you found out. They made you pay for striking Tariq. Now you have made him into your enemy. Not a good thing for you in here."

Moore nodded as he ate the putrid beans. He needed nourishment to help him recover. "Did I hear you say you were going to escape, or was I dreaming?"

"*Inshallah*, if Allah wills it. But you must not say anything even if they torture you" he cautioned.

"I won't."

"I was deciding if I was going to ask for your help or kill you because you would see what I was doing to escape," he whispered in a low voice.

"I'm glad that you didn't decide to kill me," Moore smiled weakly as his body pain made him grimace. "How are you going to do it? Is your cousin going to let you out?"

"No. No. That would be the death of him and his family. But he told me a way I can escape."

"How."

Abbar turned and pointed to the toilet. "This toilet has big metal grids in the bottom. I'm using the file blades my cousin sneaked to me to file through them. Below the toilet is a big trough that runs at an angle downward to the sewer system. Every night, its flushed with a powerful surge of water to wash the waste down it."

"Must not get it all the way it smells," Moore observed in a weakened voice.

Nodding, Abbar continued. "Since our cell is against the outer wall, there are vent windows with screens facing the street. They are about two feet above the trough and can be easily shoved aside, according to my brother who has examined it from the outside. He got word to me through my cousin."

Moore wasn't excited about wading through the human waste in the trough. "Where you planning on breaking out after the water flushed the trough?" he asked hopefully.

"Yes. My brother will be outside the wall with his box truck parked below the vent. If everything goes according to plan, we drop from the vent window to the top of his truck and drive away."

Moore smiled at the glimmer of hope. "When are you planning on breaking out?"

"In a couple of days. I'm almost finished with sawing through the bars." Abbar looked at Moore. "You need to rest so that you will be up to going with me."

Moore nodded in agreement.

"And don't do anything to aggravate them. You don't

need them to get so mad that they break your arm or leg. You wouldn't be able to come with me. If they found you here when they discover I'm gone, they could kill you," he warned.

"I understand. I will do my best."

"They may leave you alone for today, but I'm sure they will be back for you tomorrow."

"What can I do to help?" Moore asked.

Looking at the steel door, Abbar suggested, "If you feel up to it, you could scoot over to the door and place your ear to it. Let me know if you hear anyone approaching and I will stop sawing. I usually only saw at night."

"I can do that," Moore said as he placed his empty bowl on the floor and crawled to the door. He placed his ear against it and listened. "I don't hear anything."

"Good." Abbar walked over to the toilet and raised the wooden seat that set on the raised concrete supports. He picked up one of the file blades that he had hidden between the wood and top of the concrete. He then reached down the inside of the toilet to continue sawing the bars.

CHAPTER 22

The Next Morning
Marrakesh Prison

The steel door swung open, and the two guards stormed into the room. Moore and Abbar wondered which of them would be targeted that day. That was answered when they walked over to Moore and dragged him to his feet.

"You're coming with us," one barked.

As Moore looked back over his shoulder at Abbar, he saw Abbar mouth, "Stay strong."

A few minutes later, Moore was sitting on the metal chair across from the interrogation table. He was surprised that the guards had not restrained him although they were standing behind him. The door on the other side of the room opened, and a glowering Tariq entered. It was obvious that he was in a foul mood.

"Have you recovered from your beating?" he snarled.

"No," Moore responded in a subdued tone as he constrained his usual confident approach. He would be better to play the part of the vanquished.

A victorious smile crossed Tariq's face as his demeanor changed when he noticed Moore's subdued reaction. "Not the cocky fighter today? Learned a lesson or two?" he reacted triumphantly. He was very pleased with his newly submissive prisoner.

"Today, I will skip punishing you, but here's what I'm going to do." He walked over to the table containing his torture tools. Picking up a pair of pliers, he turned to face Moore.

"Tomorrow will be a different story. I want to give you

something to think about over the next 24 hours. Will I be pulling out your fingernails or toenails with these? Or perhaps I'll be clamping your mouth open and pulling out your front teeth?" His eyes widened in depraved excitement as he played with Moore's mind.

Moore didn't want to incur any of the torture Tariq was planning. He had to escape that night.

"Try to get some sleep tonight as you contemplate what is in store for you tomorrow," Tariq encouraged with beastly delight. "Take him back to his cell."

The guards stood Moore to his feet and half-dragged him back to his cell where they dumped him in the middle of the room. After they left, Moore looked at Abbar.

"We must leave tonight. Tariq has promised to work me over in the most depraved way tomorrow."

Abbar saw the fear on Moore's face. "We can do that. I'm close to finishing sawing through. My brother will be watching for the vent screen to be pushed out over the next few nights, so he should be there tonight."

"Thank you," Moore said as he crawled across the room. Abbar removed the toilet seat to resume sawing through the bars. Moore hoped that Abbar's information about the trough and the vent windows were correct. He did not want to face the next day's torture.

The rest of the day passed quickly as Abbar finished cutting through the bars. He returned the toilet seat to its support and the two waited patiently for the evening, although Moore fell into a fitful sleep.

Later that night, Moore was awakened by Abbar shaking his shoulder. "It is almost time."

Moore sat up, realizing that he hadn't planned any next

steps after they escaped. "Abbar, I haven't been thinking clearly. What am I going to do after I escape?"

Abbar smiled. "I wondered when you were going to bring that up. First, my brother will drive us to the old city and drop us at one of my cousin's homes. You can rest and get cleaned up. Where do you want to go?"

Moore thought for a moment. "Probably London, but I don't want to contact my friends while I'm in Marrakesh in case anything can be traced to them. It would just be better for me to make my way as quietly as possible out of Morocco."

"Once we escape, they will be watching the roads, airports, buses and trains leaving the area. But I think your best option will be to catch the train to Casablanca on the north coast. You can board it at the Marrakesh railway station," Abbar suggested.

"But you said they would be watching the trains, right?" Moore asked in confusion.

"Yes, but I have a cousin there who can help."

"Is there anywhere that you don't have a cousin? How many cousins do you have?" Moore asked incredulously.

Abbar laughed. "In Morocco, we are all related in some way or other."

"What about you? How will you survive if they'll be looking for you?" Moore asked.

"Money buys a lot of people looking the wrong way. Besides, I'm just a common thief. No one will be as interested in me as they are in you. You, for some reason, have high interest from somebody that you did wrong," Abbar suggested.

"And I know who that somebody probably is."

"I hope the day comes when Allah allows you to resolve your issue with that someone."

"I'm counting on it," Moore said with a determined look.

"Listen. There it is. The water," Abbar said excitedly as he lifted the toilet seat as the powerful flow of water surged through the trough. "It's time to go," he said as he cast one final look around the cell before dropping through the open toilet to the concrete trough below.

Moore didn't move as quickly as Abbar since he hadn't fully recovered from his beating. Gingerly, he eased himself through the opening and dropped on the dark trough. It was slippery. He didn't want to think what the slime consisted of as he slowly walked barefooted through it. The vent windows along the outside wall allowed the streetlights to partially light the slanted trough.

"How do we know which vent to push out?" Moore whispered as he followed closely behind Abbar.

"My brother has a red laser beam pointed at the vent that will be at the right level above his truck. That's the one we will push out," Abbar explained.

Ten minutes passed before they saw a red laser light come through a vent striking the interior wall across from it.

"That's it," Abbar said as he moved to the vent. He peered out and saw his brother's truck across the street. Gripping the vent, he was able to pull it out of its bracket and waved it outside the opening so that his brother would notice.

The truck drove across the street and parked below the open vent window.

"You first. I can help you," Abbar said as he assisted Moore through the window and onto the box truck roof. Once Moore was seated on the roof, Abbar dropped out and sat next to him. He pounded twice on the roof and the two men flattened themselves out as the truck drove around the corner.

A mile away, it pulled into a side street, and the driver placed a ladder against the side of the truck. Abbar and Moore climbed down where Abbar and his brother embraced before introducing Moore. The three men climbed into the truck cab and drove to the old city.

When they arrived in front of his cousin's home, Abbar ushered Moore inside to meet his cousin and his family. Moore next went upstairs to shave, shower and change into clean clothes. He was anxious to wash off the slimy residue from the trough that had dried on his feet.

Moore joined Abbar for a quick meal before returning to his room and dropping in his bed. He was exhausted and his body was screaming in pain from his beating and escape. After sleeping for twenty-four hours, Moore was awakened by Abbar's voice. "We have breakfast for you, my friend."

Moore opened his eyes to see Abbar standing next to a dark-haired girl around the age of fourteen. She had a heart-shaped face; a simple, sweet smile; bright, almond-shaped eyes and a tiny voice.

"This my daughter, Azara. She will be helping take care of you and has brought you fish and rice."

"*Shukran*," Moore replied appreciatively with a smile as he sat up on the edge of the bed and took the plate of food. Between bites, he said, "Abbar, I need to get out of here today."

Resting his hand on Moore's arm, Abbar advised, "Not today, my friend. You must be very important to someone. There are many people trying to find you. Rahim is in a violent rage because of our escape, and he has many people out searching for you."

He looked to the open window. "This is worse than I expected," he added.

"I'm sorry. I don't want to bring any harm to you or your family."

"This is life in Morocco. Do not worry about it. It should quiet down in a couple of days and then we will get you out of here. Meanwhile you rest," Abbar suggested. "Azara will get you anything you need," he said before leaving the room.

Over the next forty-eight hours Moore rested and planned his next moves. On several occasions, Azara accompanied him downstairs to the small outside courtyard where piglets nosed around, and chickens scuttled back and forth. He'd sit in a wooden chair with Azara on a straw mat near his feet. Between teenage girlish giggles, she'd ask him questions about life in the United States.

On occasion, Abbar or one of the women in the house, would stop by to make sure everything was well. The women wore hijabs, the headscarf, and long robes as was the custom of modesty in Morocco.

On the afternoon of the second day, Abbar walked into the courtyard and dismissed Azara. He pulled up a chair near Moore and dropped into it. "You and Azara seem to get a long very well," he observed.

"She is very attentive," Moore agreed.

"She like you. Too bad you are not a Muslim. I could marry her to you," Abbar said. "It would be an honor to have you in my family, but very dangerous, too."

Moore was stunned by the comment. He knew that many in the Arab world would marry off their young daughters to men three times older than them. It was a tradition which Moore did not like, but he wanted to be careful not to offend his protector.

"Thank you. I am honored by your gracious thought," Moore suggested. "And with my situation, it would be very dangerous." Changing the focus of the discussion, Moore asked, "Can I leave on the next leg of my escape?"

Nodding, Abbar spoke, "Yes. We are not that far from the railway station. You will have to be very careful not to be followed."

"When can I leave?"

"This afternoon. Here's some cash, your ticket for the train to Casablanca and the address for another of my cousin's there. You can stay with him until you can plan how you are going to leave there for London."

Moore took the ticket as Abbar explained how Moore was going to get safely to the railway station.

That afternoon, the two men walked out of the courtyard toward the front entrance.

As they passed Azara, Moore stopped. "Thank you little one for taking care of me," he said graciously. "May Allah bless you."

Azara smiled and blushed as the two men walked away. When they reached the front door, Abbar stepped out and looked both ways for any potential threats. Seeing none, he turned to Moore and embraced him. "May Allah be with you. I will look forward to the day when our paths cross again."

Moore returned the embrace. "Thank you for everything you've done for me." Moore slipped on the bright yellow windbreaker that Abbar handed him.

"Be careful of being followed. They are still looking for you."

"I will."

Moore walked down two narrow alleys to the old city's main marketplace, the Medina. Its buildings had rooftop cafes, and first floor shops offered carpets, ceramics, handicrafts and spices as they lined the open-air central market.

The market was filled with locals, tourists and motor bikers who haggled with the owners of fish, meat, vegetable, orange juice and fruit stalls as well as stalls with other types of goods. The stalls consisted of four poles with canvas offering protection from the bright sun.

As Moore walked past a group of jugglers, he sensed he was being followed. He turned slightly and saw two men whispering as they stared at him. Moore casually took several steps before stopping to watch a snake charmer and his three deadly cobras perform.

The two men moved up to Moore, one on each side. Sensing their arrival, Moore swung and knocked one of the men to the ground in front of the cobras. One cobra immediately struck the man as onlookers screamed in fear. The other man released Moore and grabbed his friend's feet to pull him to safety.

Moore walked briskly away as the man picked up his cell phone and called Rahim with a description of the American reporter in the bright yellow jacket and the direction he was headed.

Moore crossed the Medina and entered a small shop. He cut through the shop to its rear where he paused and reversed the jacket inside out to its beige lining. He slipped on a shemagh, a man's headscarf, and exited the shop. He then made his way to the street as Abbar had directed him where a driver was waiting.

Moore was whisked away to the railway station as Rahim ordered his men to concentrate on searching the Medina for Moore. With his men pulled away from the nearby railway station, Moore would have an easier time boarding the train without further incidents. Abbar's plan had been a good plan.

Within minutes, Moore was deposited in front of the railway station across from the Royal Theater. Moore entered the station and boarded the train with time to spare. He settled back in his seat with the shemagh pulled low over his forehead.

CHAPTER 23

Later That Day
Casablanca, Morocco

The high-speed train traveled the distance to Casablanca in two hours as Moore relaxed and planned his next steps. After he reached Casablanca, he caught a taxi that dropped him a block away from the home of Abbar's cousin. He walked the short distance to his home where Malik Hadid answered the knock on his front door.

He escorted Moore inside and provided him with a burner cell phone to use. Moore excused himself to go to his room to call V. He was anxious to talk to him and let him know what had happened and to find out if Salimbeni was okay.

"Hello," V answered.

"V, it's Emerson," Moore replied.

"It's good to hear from you. Are you okay? We wondered if you were still alive and have been trying to find you. It was like you disappeared off the face of the earth," V said rapidly.

"Just about." Quickly Moore caught V up to everything that had happened since the night he and Salimbeni had entered the feed mill in Agafay. "What about Mitch? Did she make it?" Moore asked.

"I'm right here," she answered warmly. "Sounds like you've had it really bad."

"Yeah. Pretty tough. How did you get out of there?" Moore inquired.

"When all hell brook loose, I knew the gig was up," Mitch explained. "I scrambled over to one of the big feed trucks and climbed up in the undercarriage. When they searched the grounds, they looked under the trucks, but not up into the undercarriage. I stayed hidden there until the truck drove away the next day.

"When the driver made a stop for gas, I dropped out and called V on my burner phone. He sent Captain Holly to pick me up in the Ranger. She and John brought me back to London. I, of course, didn't go through anything as bad as you."

"That Nabil sold us out, V," Moore said with disgust.

"That's what we guessed," V agreed. "We passed that along to Kadiri."

"Are you sure you can trust Kadiri?" Moore asked skeptically.

"I think so. I'll send you a video of what he sent me. He called Nabil the black sheep of his family and took him out," V assured.

"Okay, but I'm not sure that I still trust Kadiri. What about getting me out of here? I don't have my passport. Besides they are probably watching the airports for me and the railways," Moore pondered. "Could you send the Ranger down to pick me up. Maybe on some building rooftop?"

"Let me check with Captain Holly and see if they are available. I will get back to you on this number," V responded.

"One more thing."

"What?"

"Tell Izzy that the information he gave us for that feed mill lab was dated. They had moved the lab."

Nelson had been silently listening to the conversation on the speaker phone with V and Salimbeni. He spoke reluctantly. "Yeah. Mitch told me when she got back. I'm sorry about all of this, Emerson. I made a mistake, but I'll make it up to you somehow," he said solemnly.

Moore read the regret in his voice. "These things happen. Just be more careful in the future. You could have cost us our lives," Moore scolded softly before asking, "Any progress on what's causing the cow deaths?"

"Nothing concrete. Izzy and I have been splitting our time between talking to research scientists and tracking Lee. I've had to keep Izzy in check."

"That can be a full-time job," Moore offered.

"Yes. He wants to do field work."

"I could turn up all kinds of intelligence for you," Nelson interjected eagerly.

"I bet you could, but when the timing is right," Moore suggested as he tried to dampen, not crush Nelson's hopes.

"We'll get back to you, Emerson," V said as he ended the call.

"Don't take long," Moore said as he watched for the texted video to appear.

The video started with Kadiri apologizing, then cut to an open doorway to a room where screams were emitting. Nabil was sitting on a chair with his arms bound behind him. His torso was bare. Two men were taking turns beating him. The camera moved away to reveal the muzzle of a gun and its flash as it was fired. When the camera scanned back to Nabil, he was slumped in his chair as blood gushed from the side of his head. Kadiri's voice could be heard saying, "We have taken care of the problem." Then the screen went blank as the video ended.

Moore then rejoined Hadid, who offered a small meal and tea in the courtyard. Hadid was not a conversationalist. He was doing only what he needed to do to meet Abbar's request and disappeared in the next room, leaving Moore to his thoughts.

Two hours later, Moore's phone rang. It was V.

"I've got some bad news, good news and better news, Emerson."

"I'm listening." Moore wondered what kind of news V was getting at.

"The bad news is that the Ranger has a mechanical problem and can't be flown in to get you. But I've made arrangements to have a PBY meet you off the coast of Casablanca in the morning and fly you out of there. The good news is that an old friend of yours will be piloting it."

"Who is this old friend of mine?" Moore asked, puzzled.

"You let that be my surprise. You'll need to go down to the waterfront. I'll text you an address so you can find Red Eyes Rasul and his boat. He'll be watching for you."

"What if I miss him?"

"You won't. I'll text you his cell phone number. And don't say anything about his red eyes. He's real sensitive about it. Gets riled easily and you really need him to take you to sea for the rendezvous."

"Got it," Moore said. "And that's the better news?"

"No, I was just coming to that. We've learned that Lee is going to Nice on the French Riviera for a high-stakes poker game. Are you interested in flying there and surprising him at the casino?" V already knew the answer.

"Interested? There's nothing more that I would relish than walking in there, getting in that game and catching him cheating in front of a crowd. That would absolutely ruin him," Moore gloated.

"Then that's what we will plan. Mitch, Izzy and I will fly down to Monaco. I'll make reservations for you and prepay your room. We'll have the proper attire for you and, of course, new technology for you."

"And a Walther PPK!" Moore added.

"Of course," V replied before ending the call.

Moore returned to his room to get a good night's rest. In the morning, he thanked Hadid, who allowed him to keep the burner phone. He then walked two blocks away where he caught a cab for the waterfront.

The cab dropped Moore off near the bustling old fishing harbor that supplied fresh fish to the local market and popular seafood restaurants. The picturesque harbor was filled with small, bright blue, wooden fishing boats, colorful fishing nets and large trawlers. Their daily catch included spotted eels, crabs, shellfish, sea perch, bonitos, chad, mullet, grouper and crates filled with sardines.

Moore wandered through the harborfront where fish mongers were setting up their stalls. Local women with buckets scooped up any dropped sardines so they too could make a sale on the streets.

Following the directions he was given, he arrived in front of a large blue and white fishing trawler where a deep wrinkle-faced man was standing. He had red eyes, and his lips were tightly clamped around the remaining stub of a cigarette.

"Mr. Rasul?" Moore asked.

Rasul threw the cigarette stub into the water between his trawler and the dock. He turned and gave Moore a small grin, revealing his missing teeth. "You must be my passenger."

"Yes, I'm..."

Rasul held up his hand with his palm facing Moore. "I don't need any names. I've been paid and I'll take you to sea. No questions. No talking. You understand?" His dark eyes drilled into Moore as he waited for a response.

"Yes."

"Come aboard and we'll head out. I have the coordinates to meet your plane," he said as he stepped aboard and walked to the pilothouse to start the engine. When Moore tried to follow him inside the pilothouse, Rasul stopped him. "No. You sit in the stern on the nets."

Moore did as he was told while a young boy, who was on the crew, released the lines to the dock. Within a minute, the blue and white trawler was motoring out of the port with a flock of squawking seagulls as escorts.

An hour later, they had safely reached their destination as the trawler engine was cut back, and they waited in calm seas for the plane. They didn't have to wait long before spotting the PBY Catalina flying boat drop out of the sky. The PBY flew a circle around the trawler as Rasul fired off a red flare, the pre-arranged signal.

Besides looking forward to confronting Lee in Monaco, Moore was excited about flying in the PBY. They were used in World War II for bombing U-boats, flying patrols and rescuing downed airmen.

The PBY made one more low pass as the pilot scanned the sea for debris, then circled back on its approach. The PBY splashed down as it throttled back its twin Pratt & Whitney engines. They were mounted high up on the wing to keep them above the sea spray. The wing was connected to the fuselage by a large central pylon and supported by two large struts on either side. It also had two retractable stabilizing floats on each wing tip.

Moore stared at the pilot. He didn't recognize him until he left his seat and slipped down to the bow hatch, formerly a forward gun turret. The pilot opened the hatch and stepped out onto the narrow bow ledge.

"You going to row over here, or do I need to swim to you and drag you through the water?" a familiar voice shouted.

Moore was stunned. It was Ray Grissett. Moore had first met the quirky ex-pat owner of Miracle Airlines in Egypt where he had flown Moore to Turkey in a plane that had constant engine troubles. Grissett had further surprised Moore when he escaped to the Put-in-Bay airport after being chased out of Egypt by creditors for nonpayment of airplane fuel and hanger use.

"The boy will row you over," Rasul said in a stern voice.

Moore had been so focused on the PBY that he hadn't noticed the small boat being lowered in the water. The boy jumped aboard and waited with the oars ready.

"Thank you, Mr. Rasul," Moore said as he stepped into the waiting boat. "I'll be right there, Ray!" Moore shouted. He was so relieved to see someone he knew and, more importantly, could trust.

"Come on now. We're burning daylight," Grissett yelled impatiently. The slim man wore a soiled Cleveland Indians baseball cap, greasy t-shirt and worn khaki shorts. His long gray hair was sticking straight out from underneath the ball cap. He was overdue for a haircut.

When they reached the PBY, Grissett helped Moore climb aboard, and the small boat returned to the trawler. Before ducking into the bow hatch, Moore looked at the idling port engine. He noticed it was losing oil.

"Ray, you know you have an oil leak, right?"

Grissett cast a quick look at the engine. "It'll be fine," he said with no concern.

"Still flying by the seat of your pants, I see," Moore cracked.

"Always remember that it's Miracle Airlines. Our motto is 'If we land in one piece, it's a miracle'," he chuckled at Moore's uneasiness. "You can sit in the co-pilot seat," he said as Moore eased himself up into the cockpit and Grissett closed the hatch.

When Grissett returned to the pilot seat, he cracked, "Welcome aboard Miracle Airlines Flight 1 to Nice, France. To operate your seat belt, insert the metal tab into the buckle, and pull tight. It works just like every other seat belt, and if you don't know how to operate one, you probably shouldn't be out in public unsupervised. Make sure that seat belt is tight, low and across your hips, like my grandmother wore her bra."

Moore allowed a smile to cross his face. The wise-cracking Grissett hadn't changed at all. He was incorrigible.

Grissett began throttling up, and the PBY surged forward as it gathered speed for takeoff. "That's Charlie back there."

Moore turned in his seat and saw a young Arab in his early twenties. "He's my co-pilot, engineer and navigator," Grissett explained.

Moore waved and returned his attention to Grissett. "What are you doing here? The last time I saw you was at the Put-in-Bay airport. You were running an air service there," Moore said confused.

"I am. Or maybe it was running me. Anyhow, I had a couple of engagements here in the Mideast to take care of."

"Covert?" Moore asked.

Grissett smiled. "There are some things in life that get their claws into you and won't let go. They claw you back and I make some good money. I was just wrapping up an adventure and getting ready to head back to Put-in-Bay when I get this call from some guy named VanBlaricum."

Moore smiled at hearing the name.

"Said he was a friend of yours and that you had your back up against the wall. Well, that man called the right guy. Here I am to your rescue," Grissett grinned.

"Mike can track down just about anybody," Moore smiled with relief.

"I was told to take you to Nice. Is that right?"

"Yes."

"To the casino?"

"Right."

"I'll deposit you right in front of that Rue Massenet Casino and Hotel. On the beach. I'll ramp right up on that beach. You know about that beach?" he continued without waiting for an answer. "It's topless. So, you can take your time getting out of the plane while I scan the beach for trouble," he smiled salaciously.

"Some things just don't change," Moore laughed.

"I had a rough time on my way to the landing strip. I was in Libya before I took off to get you."

"What happened?"

"I rode a donkey up to the landing strip, but it didn't go well."

"Oh?"

"I fell off my ass on my ass!" Grissett chortled.

Moore roared. "It's always interesting flying with you, Ray. When we're on the ground, I'm never quite sure whether we landed or were shot down!" Moore teased back.

"I had one hard landing with some passengers on a twelve-seater. I got on the speaker and told everyone to keep their seat belts fastened while I taxied what was left of the plane over to the gate."

Moore chuckled before quipping, "It's those bouncing landings that make passengers call you 'Captain Kangaroo'!"

The two friends enjoyed their jovial repartees for the rest of the flight to Nice.

CHAPTER 24

Later That Day
Nice, France

Located at the foot of the French Alps on France's south-eastern coast, picturesque Nice was known for its premier hotels and casinos fronting the Mediterranean seacoast. Its pebbly beach on the Bay of Angels was overlooked by a promenade that ran for seven kilometers. On the other side of the palm tree-lined promenade with its numerous pergolas was a heavily-trafficked boulevard.

Outdoor cafes, boutiques, delicious restaurants, open-air markets and colorfully-painted stone tenement buildings lined Nice's labyrinth of narrow streets parallel and perpendicular to the boulevard, *Promenade des Anglais*. From Castle Park with its verdant green trees and shrubs on the city's eastern edge to the old port on the west, Nice provided a magnetic allure to its citizens and visitors.

For the last half hour, Moore's mind had been focused on next steps and how he was going to confront Lee. He was anxious to land.

The PBY dropped altitude as it banked to slowly circle the bay as Grissett checked for any floating debris. Seeing none, he took the plane lower and splashed down on the calm sea.

Cutting back on the throttle, Grissett turned to Moore. "I'll run you up on the beach in front of your hotel. Then you can pop out of the forward hatch on dry ground and I'll check out the female scenery while you deplane," he grinned with a wink.

"Of course, you will," Moore laughed softly. "Where are you headed after this?"

"I've got to return this plane to Libya and see if anybody has any other work for me. If not, I'll be catching a flight back to the States and Put-in-Bay."

The plane's bow edged up on the pebbly beach and Grissett cut back the engines to an idle. "First time that I flew this plane that I didn't have warning bells go off or smoke coming out of the port engine," he confidently noted.

"The safest part of your journey is now over," Grissett announced to his passenger, who was dropping through the front opening of the cockpit to make his way to the forward hatch. "Go ahead and pick your way through the wreckage to the nose."

"You should have been a comedian!" Moore said as he unlatched the hatch.

"Too dangerous in this woke society. I'll stick to flying planes like this Millennial Falcon," he cracked.

Moore turned around to find Grissett right behind him. "Thank you, Ray. You're a lifesaver."

Grissett waved him off. "Okay. Okay. Now, you get out of my way. You're blocking my view of that topless beach. And it's got to be a quick view because I'm sure that the local gendarmes, you know the French police, will be here pretty quick to chase my old plane off this beach. They probably prefer you use the airport," he rattled away as Moore departed.

Moore quickly reached the promenade. As he heard the engines revving, he turned to see the PBY moving back into the water and local police chasing after it. Grissett had the plane airborne in seconds and headed for Libya.

Moore resumed walking. He crossed the wide boulevard and went to the corner of *Rue Massenet* where he entered the lobby of the 5-star hotel/casino with a rooftop restaurant and swimming pool overlooking the beach and bay. He stopped at the reception desk and was pleased to see that V had followed through as promised. He checked in and took the elevator to the fourth floor and his room at the corner.

He inserted his room key card, and there was a loud beep as the door unlocked. What an unusually loud and annoying noise, Moore thought as he entered the room with floor-to-ceiling windows and a balcony.

He saw a suitcase on the king-size bed and walked to it. Opening it, he took out the clothes that had been purchased for him and checked for the false bottom. Finding it, he unlatched it and found a replacement Walther PPK with extra rounds of ammunition. Moore smiled as he briefly hefted the weapon before replacing it in the false bottom.

Moore stepped to the window to observe the tranquil scene below on the beach. When his room phone rang, his silent reverie suddenly vanished.

"Hello."

"Emerson, you're all checked in and in your room?" V inquired.

"Yes. A few minutes ago."

"I'll bring the gang down. See you in a few."

When they arrived, they knocked at his door. Moore walked over and opened it to find V, Salimbeni and Nelson.

"It's been a while," V greeted Moore as the three of them entered and took seats in the room.

"It has. What a journey!" Moore replied as he sat on the edge of the bed. "Thanks for the clothes and the Walther PPK."

"No problem," V responded. "I knew you needed the clothes and hope you won't need the weapon," he added.

"Is Lee here?" Moore asked as he focused right away on

business.

"Yes. I got to do some field work. I spied him arriving and walking through the lobby," Nelson stated proudly.

"Nice job, Izzy."

Nelson beamed broadly.

Moore turned to V. "Do you know the setup for tonight?"

"Yes. We've been able to determine that Lee will be in a high-stakes poker game tonight at 10:00 in one of the private rooms." V handed Moore a card. "Present this card at the door. It's your entrance ticket. I just wish I could be there to see the look on Lee's face when you walk in."

Moore nodded. "And what about the cash I need to join this game, Mitch?"

"I wired the funds to an account we set up for you at the casino. You should be able to draw your chips from there," she replied.

"Good. Thank you, Mitch." Moore turned back to V. "What about Mangan. Is he here? I expect he and some of Lee's henchmen will be trying to take me out when they spot me," Moore surmised.

"I saw Mangan when I was spying in the lobby. He had two Chinese thugs with him," Nelson explained.

"I don't think they will try anything while you're in the casino, Emerson. After you leave is more likely," V suggested.

"I'll be standing by in the casino to keep an eye on things and be your backup," Salimbeni said coolly. "And I'll be armed."

"Me too," Nelson added, too eagerly.

The group met for an hour, discussing the perils encountered in Morocco, the continued search for the cause of the dairy cow deaths and plans for the evening. Then, they left so that Moore could rest and practice his poker for the night. Moore ordered room service for dinner.

Around 9:30, he shaved, showered and changed into a lavender linen long-sleeve shirt, khaki slacks and off-white sport coat. He glanced at the suitcase as he thought about the Walther PPK but decided against it.

Moore left his room and took the elevator to the second floor which housed the casino. When he emerged, he took in the grandiose décor complete with gold walls and chandeliers, their lights reflecting on the black-lacquered furniture and mirrored ceiling.

As he walked past the rows of slot machines, he entered the gaming lounge filled with roulette, baccarat, blackjack and poker tables. He paused next to a roulette table, watching as the croupier waved his hand over the table, saying "no further bets."

Scanning the casino, Moore spotted Salimbeni, sitting at the end of the bar near the doors to the VIP high-stakes rooms. She looked stunning in a sparkling, dark green dress as she sipped on a cocktail. She gave Moore an imperceptible nod as he neared, then pointed toward the door as Moore's eyes moved in that direction. He saw who she was pointing to — Arsalan Mangan. He was standing outside the door.

Moore whirled and crossed to the other side of the room where he spotted Nelson. "Izzy, I need your help."

Nelson jumped up from the nearby chair in which he had been seated. "Yes? What can I do?"

"See that man standing by the door behind me. Look over my shoulder."

"I'm too short. I'll look around your shoulder," Nelson replied anxiously. "Yes. I see him."

"I need you to distract him to get him away from that door.

Think you can do that?"

"Yeah. Yeah. I can do that," Nelson said, hungrily.

He scurried away as Moore sat in the chair so that there would be less of a likelihood of Mangan spotting him. He watched Nelson go to the casino entrance and speak to an attendant while slipping him a tip.

The attendant walked across the casino to Mangan where he whispered that a visitor was waiting for him by the elevator. Mangan was perturbed. He looked around for any potential signs of danger. Seeing none, he left his post.

When he reached the bank of elevators, Mangan couldn't find anyone waiting for him. He turned and briskly walked over to the attendant, grabbing him by the front of his shirt as he lifted him a few inches off the floor.

Hurriedly, the attendant pointed to Nelson, who reacted by heading for the stairs to the main lobby. Mangan glared at the retreating figure as he spoke into his radio to his men downstairs. He then returned to his position outside the VIP room.

Meanwhile, Moore had sprung into action. As soon as Mangan left, Moore headed for the closed door. He presented the privileged entrance card to the casino employee who allowed him to enter. Moore next saw Lee, focused on the cards in his hands. When Lee glanced up to see who had entered, Lee's eyes widened, and his mouth opened in surprise.

"I didn't expect to see you, Mr. Moore," Lee frowned irritably. "Aren't you in the wrong room?"

Moore allowed a triumphant smile to appear on his face and replied, "Not from where I'm standing." Moore pulled back a vacant chair. "May I join you, Mr. Lee?"

"You have the required funds?" Lee asked gruffly.

"They are in my account."

Impatiently tapping his finger on the tabletop, Lee whispered to the dealer to check. The dealer made a call and turned back to Lee. "The funds are there."

"Well then, it sounds like you are ready to lose to me again," Lee said with a curt laugh. "Give him the required number of chips," Lee instructed the dealer.

Moore assessed the players at the table. There was a loud Texan wearing a white cowboy hat. Gibson had made his millions in the oil industry. Next to him sat a thirty-some, thin Frenchman with nerd-like, black-framed glasses who was a social media whiz kid. His name was Genard.

A robust German man sulked in the corner as he tossed back another glass of liquor. He had played himself out of the game, losing everything that he had. Moore sat in his recently vacated chair. The dealer placed several stacks of chips in front of Moore, and the card game commenced with Moore now playing.

Over the next hour, the somewhat friendly mood started to change. It grew more intense and competitive. By the look in Lee's eyes, it became more dangerous. An air of distrust burgeoned as they all took turns losing or raking in their winnings.

Three hours into the game, Moore held the queen and nine of hearts with the jack and ten of hearts showing. He decided to push Lee. He bet big. He slid $200,000 in chips into what was already a large pot.

When he did, he saw Gibson's eyes widen momentarily. Moore then began counting the number of chips he had left in his dwindling stack.

Genard folded. "I'm out." He'd lost most of his chips. He was finished for the night. Like the German earlier, Genard excused himself. He stood and left the room.

Lee had two aces showing. He studied the cards in his hand as he tapped his finger. Moore thought Lee actually drooled on the green felt table as he set his cards down for a moment and stared at Moore.

Before he could speak, Gibson spoke. "You boys are too tough on me tonight. I'm out," he said as he gathered his remaining chips and stood. "Thank you for an interesting evening," he added before he leaned against the wall to watch the end of the hand.

Moore was glad that he hadn't left. He may need a witness if he could catch Lee cheating. Gibson's presence would make it more awkward for Lee to find a way to slip a card into his hand.

"It's just you and me," Lee said as his eyes drilled into Moore.

"It looks that way, Mr. Lee."

"I'll see your $200,000 and raise you $200,000," Lee said as he pushed more chips into the center of the table.

Moore followed his action by pushing an equal number of chips to the center before the dealer dealt the final cards. When he did, he dealt Moore a three of hearts and another ace to Lee.

Lee allowed a smile to momentarily cross his face as he saw the card appear.

The dealer looked to Moore.

"I'm good."

"Let's make this really interesting, Mr. Moore. I'd like to increase the pot by $500,000. Can you cover that?" Lee smirked.

That stung. Moore didn't have the chips. "Let me make a call."

"Go ahead," Lee said coolly as he sat back.

Moore stood and walked over to the far wall, keeping an eye on Lee the entire time. He called Salimbeni.

"Aren't you finished yet?" she asked.

"No. Almost. I need another $500,000. Can you cover that for me?"

She hesitated before answering. "Yes. You're good. If you need it, I can have it wired to your account here. Just let me know. How's it going in there?"

"Good. I have to go," Moore said as he ended the call and returned to the table. He wiped a bead of sweat off his brow which Lee noticed.

"Do you have the funds?" Lee asked in a disciplined, cold tone.

"Yes." Moore wondered what Lee was playing for. With three aces showing, did he have a fourth ace or was he playing for a full house? Either way, he'd beat Moore's flush, but Moore didn't think Lee had the cards to do it. That was his hunch.

Lee turned to the dealer. "I'll accept a note from him, and you know that I'm good."

"Yes, we do, Mr. Lee," the dealer responded as he scribbled a note for the extra $500,000 and passed it to Moore for his signature.

Moore signed it and slid it across the table to the center.

"What do you have, Mr. Moore?" Lee asked as he leaned forward to watch Moore reveal the cards in his hand.

"A queen-high flush," Moore said.

"Hold it right there! Hands on the table!" Gibson stormed from across the room when he saw Lee start to drop his right hand under the table.

Indignant, Lee snapped at Gibson, "What are you trying to say?"

"It's just where I come from, you keep your hands in plain sight, especially when you're playing for money like this. We wouldn't want anyone to question what's going on," the Texan cautioned in a very serious tone. He'd been watching Lee closely all night and had a suspicion that he was cheating but couldn't catch him.

Moore nodded his head gratefully toward the Texan.

"Your cards, sir," the dealer requested of Lee.

Reluctantly, a very disturbed Lee turned over the cards in his hand. He showed a king of spades and a ten of clubs. He had lost with his three aces. He was fuming quietly as he had not been able to reach for the fourth ace that Mangan had hidden earlier underneath the tabletop.

"It appears that you have won, Mr. Moore," Lee said caustically as he stared icily at Moore.

"Yes, it does," Moore smiled as he tipped the dealer with a stack of chips. "Could you cash in the balance of my winnings and put them in my account?" Moore asked.

"Certainly."

Moore stood. He walked over to the Texan as Lee walked brusquely behind him and left the room. "Thank you."

"Not necessary, fella," Gibson drawled. "You don't play poker often, do you?"

"No. I'm really just a beginner."

"I could tell by the way you played. You better count your blessings that your game ended the way it did. Talk about beginner's luck." The Texan let loose with a soft whistle.

The two men walked out of the room where Moore saw Lee had stopped in the casino entrance. Mangan was talking to him. When Mangan saw Moore, he mentioned it to Lee, who then turned and motioned for Moore to join him. Moore obliged.

"Yes?" Moore asked when he walked over.

"I'd like to take you for a little ride around Nice. It's raining outside and Nice in the rain at night is a sight to be seen," Lee commented.

Moore was immediately suspicious, but his curiosity got the best of him as he threw caution to the wind. "I'd like that," he said as the two walked out.

Moore glanced sideways at Salimbeni who had a worried look on her face. She held up one finger for Moore to wait, but Moore shook his head slightly to signal that he couldn't talk to her.

The men walked out of the building and its covered portico. They sat in the rear seat of the waiting Mercedes-Benz. As they settled in, Lee turned to Moore.

"You did well at cards tonight."

"Thank you. It was beginner's luck," Moore said, brushing off the compliment.

The car pulled onto the street and headed for Castle Park, which overlooked Nice from its high point on the eastern edge of the city.

After a few minutes of silence, interrupted only by the sound of the gentle rain falling on the vehicle roof and the swishing of the windshield wipers, Moore asked, "Why the car ride, Mr. Lee? Hospitality is not what I'd expect after you lost so much playing cards."

"Ah Mr. Moore, I'm known for doing the unexpected. That's why I've been able to build my biotechnology empire," Lee answered in a level, calculating tone.

The car drove up the hill to Castle Park on wet streets glistening in the light from the streetlights.

"But what did you want to talk about?" Moore pushed impatiently.

Lee turned his head and raised his right eyebrow. "Would

you care to tell me why you broke into my feed mill in Morocco?" he asked dryly.

Moore wondered how long it would take before Lee brought it up. "Research."

"Research? Breaking in is part of your research?" Lee frowned irritably. "Why didn't you just ask?"

"I'm an investigative reporter. My job is to search out the truth and sometimes I must do the unexpected," Moore explained.

"I assure you in your dealings with me that all you have to do is to ask." Lee paused and studied Moore for a moment. "I must admit that you are very resourceful, Mr. Moore."

"I try to be," Moore said as the car stopped. He waited for Lee to discuss his imprisonment but was disappointed when Lee didn't bring it up.

The chauffer stepped out and opened the door on Moore's side of the vehicle. As Moore stepped out into the rain, the chauffer handed Moore an opened black umbrella. Lee slid across the seat and left the car the same way, taking the open umbrella that the chauffer handed him.

As the light rain fell softly on their umbrellas, Lee pointed to the city below, captured in a fine mist with its twinkling lights. "Beautiful, isn't it?"

"An incredible view," Moore agreed as his eyes took in the picturesque view. He imagined the sound of the rain singing on the rooftops and drumming gently against the windows while covering the streets in a sheer sheen.

Lee pointed to the lampposts descending the hill. "These lampposts are like sentries, protecting us from the evils of darkness. I have sentries too, Mr. Moore. Their job is to protect my business and me."

Moore listened without interrupting as approaching lightning and thunder filled the sky.

"I just want to warn you, Mr. Moore. I believe I know what you are up to, and I don't take kindly to you butting into my business. Further intrusions could result in deadly consequences. Do you understand?" he asked with no sympathy evident in his cold tone.

"Is that a threat?" Moore pushed.

"Take it for what it's worth. This is a good night to die. Goodbye, Mr. Moore," Lee said as he handed the umbrella to the chauffer and returned inside the car. The chauffer closed the umbrella, entered the vehicle and drove away. Moore was left standing in the rain.

Strange, Moore thought as the droplets of rain cooled the night air, sending a chill through him. He watched the taillights of the car fade into the mist as the soft rhythm of raindrops beat against the black fabric of the umbrella.

His attention turned to the raindrops that gleamed in the light from the lamppost. Moore studied the illuminated drops, thinking it was as if the sky was crying. Moore, however, soon noticed that some of the drops were red. Confused, he tilted his umbrella sideways and looked up.

A flash of lightning revealed a horrific sight to Moore. His stomach lurched as a wave of emotional pain enveloped him as he stared at Izzy Nelson's body. It had been hung upside down from the lamppost. His throat had been slit and was still dripping blood. Moore didn't know that Nelson had been killed elsewhere and then moved to this location.

In shock, Moore staggered to the next lamppost where he leaned against it as he tried to compose himself. Poor Izzy, Moore thought as he reached for his cell phone. He called V.

"There you are," V answered. "Mitch was anxious to find you. She can't find Izzy anywhere. Have you seen him?"

"Yes. I'm with him now," Moore muttered.

"Good."

"Not so good, V. He's dead." Moore explained what had happened since he left the casino with Lee and how he found Nelson's body.

"I don't like this one bit," Mitch commented as the revelation struck her like a thunderbolt.

"I'm sure Izzy feels the same way," Moore added caustically. He was in a dark mood, a mood for vengeance."

"I'm reading the tone in your voice, Emerson. Don't do anything irrational," V cautioned while also upset by the news of Nelson's death.

Moore huddled under his umbrella as the rain began to fall in sheets and the sky again lit up with lightning strikes. He glanced toward Nelson's body. "What should I do with Izzy?"

"Nothing. I'll make arrangements to retrieve his body and ship it home. While I'm doing that, I'll have Mitch drive over and pick you up. She can take you to your hotel while I make some phone calls," V advised.

Fifteen minutes later, a black sedan pulled to a stop in front of Moore. The window slid down to reveal Salimbeni at the wheel. "Where is he?" she asked red eyed.

Moore pointed with his hand to the lamppost, and she turned to look. "Lee will pay for this."

Moore walked around the car and entered the passenger side. "He will," he agreed with steely determination.

She turned to stare at Moore as he sat. "I tried to alert you when you were leaving that Izzy had disappeared."

Moore frowned. "I'm responsible. I asked Izzy to distract

Mangan from in front of the door to the VIP room where Lee was at the casino. Mangan probably tracked him down and confronted him."

"Do you think Izzy revealed what we are really up to?"

"I don't know, but I'd say we better assume he did. The stakes in this game just got higher," Moore remarked, acerbically as he thought back to the cryptic conversation with Lee.

They drove in silence through the rain-kissed street, bathed in the headlights of passing traffic and the overhead streetlights. It was like the sky was crying with grief at Nelson's passing.

They arrived at the hotel and a shivering Moore crossed the lobby to take the elevator to his room.

CHAPTER 25

Moore's Hotel Room
Nice, France

Walking into the bathroom, Moore turned on the hot shower before going to his bed. He dropped his wet clothes on the floor and returned to the bathroom, closing the door behind him.

Moore stepped into the steamy shower, pulling the curtain closed behind him. He allowed the hot water to run over his skin as a sensory fog of sadness covered him. His body felt a numbing sense of sorrow and his grief surged with every expelled breath.

As he washed, he replayed what little he knew about Izzy. The enthusiastic cherubin had meant well and now would never fulfill his life's ambition. Moore vowed again to avenge his death just as he vowed to avenge Sam's death. He'd lost two friends on this adventure, something that he was not used to, although he hoped he would never get used to it.

Outside the door to his room, a man, dressed in black, inserted a card key in the door lock. The door loudly beeped as it unlocked. The man waited a moment to listen carefully. When he didn't hear anything, he stealthily entered the room as he held a weapon with a silencer in his right hand.

He scanned the room with his eyes and pointed the weapon as he heard the shower running. He then crossed the room to the bathroom door where he paused to listen. Hearing nothing but the running water, he cracked the door open with a loud click and briefly paused to listen again.

Hearing nothing, he eased the door open and was greeted

by a wave of hot mist from the shower. Smiling, he pushed the door wide open and aimed his weapon. He fired three times through the shower curtain before walking over to pull back the curtain. The shower was empty.

"Looking for me?" a somber voice asked from behind the opened door.

The intruder began to swing around when he found himself tackled as the two bodies dropped to the bathroom floor. Moore was able to dislodge the intruder's weapon after it was fired harmlessly one more time. Moore grabbed a bath towel and was able to twist it tightly around his perpetrator's neck, choking him.

Turning the lifeless body over, Moore noted his assassin was Asian, probably someone in Lee's employ, he surmised. He then got dressed before calling V, who advised Moore to vacate the hotel immediately. He would direct Salimbeni to pick him up at the rear of the hotel.

Moore grabbed a few items including his Walther PPK and cell phone before heading to the room door. The shower was still running. He eased the door open and scanned the hall. Seeing no one other than a late-night housekeeper heading in his direction, Moore stepped out of the room, closing the door behind him. He placed a Do Not Disturb sign on the door handle as the housekeeper stopped in front of him.

"Would you like your room freshened up?" she asked with a helpful smile.

"No. My friend's in the shower and he'll probably be taking a long shower. We don't need to disturb him," Moore said as he held his finger to his lips.

"Of course," she said as she pushed her cart down the hall, disappearing around the corner.

Moore began walking to the exit stairs. Suddenly, the door opened and two armed gunmen appeared. One took aim at Moore and fired his silenced weapon, narrowly missing Moore.

Moore leapt the few feet back to his room door, opened it quickly and dodged inside as another bullet struck the door trim. He slammed the door and locked it. Racing across the room to the large floor-to-ceiling windows, he slid one open. He stepped onto the small balcony as he closed the window behind him. It had stopped raining.

Moore saw a drainpipe within his reach. He grabbed it and shook it. It seemed firm. He swung his body over the edge of the balcony as he tightly grasped the drainpipe. He quickly slid down to the balcony below and swung his body on to it.

Just in time as his pursuers burst into his vacated room and searched for him. They looked over the edge of the balcony but didn't see Moore anywhere. They didn't know that Moore had been able to slip inside the room below and was already racing down the hall to the exit stairs.

The pursuers called Mangan and updated him on Moore's successful escape and the death of their fellow thug. Mangan was enraged as he instructed them to remove the body from the hotel.

Meanwhile, Moore raced outside the rear of the hotel where he found Salimbeni waiting. He jumped into the car, and they sped away.

"This has been an interesting night!" Salimbeni said to Moore in a serious tone.

"That, my dear, is an understatement. I'm just glad that you guys are so close to my hotel," Moore said as he allowed his stressed body to relax in the comfortable seat.

"It's actually a mechanic's garage that V was able to rent.

He wants to go over next steps when we get there."

"Good. I'm bone-tired, but I honestly don't think I can sleep. My adrenaline level has got to be soaring."

When she pulled up to the garage door, Moore stepped out of the car to open it. She drove in and he followed her, closing the door behind him. Moore saw V in the far corner where several tables had been set with an array of technical equipment.

When he saw the two approaching his worktable, V observed with concern, "It sounds like they are taking things up to another level."

"They are," Moore agreed. "What are you working on?" Moore asked as he glanced at the tabletop in front of V.

"Mitch and I have been going through Izzy's files. It looks like he was focused on digging info on Lee. There's a flight plan filed for his private jet. He's flying out before daybreak to Norway."

"Norway?" Moore asked surprised.

"Yes. Izzy discovered Lee has a mountain getaway where his mother was raised. Must be family land."

"Interesting."

"We're going to Norway," V added with a slight smile.

"Why?"

"Interpol is now interested in Lee. They've been in touch with me, and I've set up a meeting for this afternoon in Bergen," V explained. "I've already contacted Captain Holly and John Hall. They will pick us up with the Ranger in two hours and fly us there."

"The Ranger has been repaired?" Moore asked.

"Yes," V responded.

Moore nodded. "Did Izzy leave any other tidbits?"

"I've got his laptop. Mitch and I will go through his files. I wish I had his cell phone, but it's gone," V commented.

"Mangan probably has it," Salimbeni suggested.

"Probably," V agreed. "But there shouldn't be anything on it that would compromise us with them."

Moore spotted a cot in the other corner. "I'm bushed. Mind if I catch some sleep?" he asked.

"Go ahead. Mitch and I have some work to do before we pack up and then we all head to the airport."

Moore walked over to the cot and dropped onto it. It seemed like he had just closed his eyes when he felt someone shaking his shoulder and heard Salimbeni urge, "Emerson, wake up. It's time to go."

Moore rolled over and sat on the edge of the cot for a moment. He was surprised that he had slept. Hopefully, he would sleep on the flight to Norway.

CHAPTER 26

Late Morning
Bergen, Norway

Norway was on the western portion of the Scandinavian Peninsula, facing the North Atlantic Ocean and the Barents Sea. Two-thirds of the country was mountainous with deep fjords, gorges and canyons carved by the scouring action of glaciers tonguing down the V-shaped valleys. The steep-walled, narrow fjords cut deep into the interior mountain region.

Thick forests of spruce and pine covered the Lang Mountains up to 2,800 feet above sea level. The ground was carpeted with leafy mosses and a variety of birch, ash, rowan, and aspen with wild berries growing abundantly.

Bergen, the country's second largest city, was located on the southwestern coast and known as the fjord capital because of the number of fjords in the area. It was surrounded by the mountains and was renowned for its colorfully-painted wooden houses.

After landing, a waiting car transported the three to a downtown hotel where they checked in. At the appointed time, the three walked into a meeting room where Chief Inspector Paulette Grubb with the Norway Police Service was waiting. The slender, dark-haired officer had an air of serious calm, one that denoted she was all business.

"I'm Interpol's liaison here," she said as she introduced herself. "Interpol has been watching Bjorn Lee for some time. The primary interested parties are MI6 and Scotland Yard."

Moore thought back to the two individuals who had confronted him on the train from Cranfield to London. They had warned him to stay away from Lee.

"Why are they interested?" Moore asked although he thought he knew the answer.

"There's a growing concern about his involvement in planning a bio-terrorist attack."

"You mean with the dairy cow deaths?" Moore asked.

"You do your homework," she commented. "Yes, that's correct."

"Are you aware of the deaths in Tulare, California and Wooster, Ohio?" he asked.

"Yes, and several other dairy farms in Germany, France and India. There're also recent reports of similar dairy cow deaths in England and Ireland."

Moore, V and Salimbeni exchanged looks of concern.

"Have you discovered any direct linkage between them and Lee?" V asked.

"No, but we're using our resources. One of the problems is that our agents are turning up dead," she spoke solemnly.

"We know what you mean," Salimbeni commented.

"Lee has to know that he's being investigated," Moore suggested.

"We are sure of it. And that's where you come into play. We understand that you are making inroads in tracking him because of your unconventional approach. You're not from a law enforcement background," Grubb said as she looked directly at Moore.

"Some progress. We're still trying to locate his lab to get proof," Moore said cautiously.

"So are we. Every time we get close, we're exposed. And someone gets killed. Can't tie it to him though."

Moore wondered quietly if Grubb was trustworthy in recalling Sam's earlier words about not trusting anyone echoed in the back of his mind.

"How do we come into play to help you?" Moore pushed.

"It's apparent that you know Lee flew here. He took a helicopter to his mountain lodge after he arrived in Bergen. My guess is that you plan to break into his office at that lodge to see if you can find the location of the lab."

Moore didn't comment. He just listened.

Grubb continued as she slid a photo across the table. "Take a look at this picture."

Moore, V and Salimbeni studied the picture.

"What do you see?" she asked.

"Lee," Moore said, not understanding what she was getting at.

"Try this close up," she said as she slid another photo across the table.

"He's wearing a gold chain," Salimbeni observed.

"Right. What's unusual about these photos is that they show him with his shirt front unbuttoned more than he usually has it. It's usually buttoned up to hide his secret. See what's dangling from that chain? What do you think it is?" Grubb asked.

Moore eyed the photo more closely. "It looks like a gold-covered, mini-flash drive."

"Right. We suspect that he has his secret financial records stored on it, plus one other item," Grubb said mysteriously.

"What's that, Paulette?" V asked as he looked up at her.

"The formulation instructions for his pathogenic bacteria. It could also contain his plans to use his bioweapon worldwide," she suggested.

Moore thought for a moment. "I need to steal that flash drive."

"I knew you'd come to that conclusion," Grubb smiled as she slid a small plastic case toward Moore. "Go ahead and open this."

Moore opened the pocket-size container to reveal three syringes as she continued, "When you break in, you can hide in his study until he appears. Then you use one of the syringes to knock him out and remove the flash drive before you make your escape."

"Sounds simple," Moore said.

"What are the other two syringes for?" Salimbeni asked.

"Extras in case you need them," Grubb answered. "You're going to have a hard time breaking in there and that's where we can help you. Ed," she called as she turned toward the door.

The door opened, and a muscular, dark-haired man, wearing rectangular eyeglasses and a wry smile, entered. He had the same all-business look about him.

"This is Ed Patrick," Grubb said as she introduced everyone in the room. "Ed is part of our special operations team and will lead you to Lee's lodge." She nodded to Patrick to speak.

"More like fortress," Patrick started.

"We have a Ranger that can deliver us there," Salimbeni offered.

"I know that plane and there's no way you can fly in. It's too well guarded and he was able to pay off someone in the government to create a 'no-fly-zone' there. Beside it being a no-fly-zone, Lee has an aerial deterrent system for restricted air space. He'd spot you right away."

Patrick spread a map on the conference table. "Here's Bergen and there's his place in the mountains," he said as he pointed.

"Is there a road that we can take there?" Moore asked as he

looked at the map.

"Yes, but it's too much in the open. Besides, they are always watching the road for approaching vehicles. We wouldn't get close enough and they also have a ground deterrent system."

"It looks like that fjord is below his place. Could we boat up the fjord?" Moore asked.

"Good approach, Emerson. We can go up this far," he pointed. "Beyond that, he has heavily-armed guards. They actually have gun emplacements on both sides of the fjord to catch any approaching boats in a deadly crossfire. And you can't use the night as cover because they have night vision technology."

Patrick moved his finger down the fjord. "There's a spot here. It's a moraine in this long canyon. We'd go ashore here and start driving up the moraine."

"Wait a second," Moore started. "I thought moraines were filled with large rocks. We can't drive anything up there."

"Boulders, large rocks, all kinds of glacial debris. When the glaciers melted and receded, they dropped whatever they were carrying and that's why moraine fields are so chaotic. There can be 16-foot-tall ridges of rocks and angular materials jumbled together. But we have a vehicle that can drive up it."

Patrick pulled up a picture on his cell phone and passed it to Moore. "It's a Ukrainian-built Sherp. It's a UTV designed for rough terrain."

Moore found himself looking at a rectangular box that was 13-feet long and 8-feet wide. It was set on four massive, 6-feet-tall inflatable tires. "And you're not going far before you get a flat," he commented skeptically.

Patrick chuckled. "Those are eight-ply, low pressure tires. They have a low weight per square foot and extremely good traction. There's an onboard system that allows us to inflate or deflate the tires so we can scramble over rocks, and travel through sand, water and ice. It's got a three-cylinder, 55 HP engine that cruises at 25 mph on land or 4 mph in the water."

Moore passed the phone to V and Salimbeni as Patrick provided more details about the vehicle.

"It was designed to work in the extreme conditions in Siberia and named after the Sherpa porters that carry supplies up Mount Everest. The Sherp can easily handle a 35-degree slope."

"I've heard of these, Emerson. And it's all been good," V said all-knowingly to ease Moore's concern as he handed the cell phone back to Patrick.

Patrick pointed at the map again. "There's water rushing through that moraine field. It comes from a lake that is about at the halfway point of our travel. The lake was formed when the rocks and debris created a massive dam. We'll drive across the lake and continue to this point where we can park the Sherp. We'll hike in the last mile."

"Who are the we?" Moore asked.

"Two of my team members, you and me," Patrick answered.

"I'd like to come," Salimbeni interjected.

"I'd like to keep this to as few as possible. Sorry," Patrick replied to a disappointed Salimbeni. "It's going to be a quick smash and grab. Hopefully, we go in unnoticed and out the same way."

"Won't Lee have guards watching the approach from the moraine?" Moore asked as he studied the map.

"It won't be heavily guarded. He has a false sense of security, thinking that no one could come up the moraine, cross the lake and intrude on him," Grubb spoke.

"Any concerns about the legality of what we are about to do?" Moore asked.

Salimbeni looked sharply at Moore. "You didn't have any concern about legality when we broke into the feed mill in Agafay," she commented, confused.

"That was covert and acting independent of law enforcement." Moore smiled as he swung his head to look at Grubb. "This time, we're going in with your police and no search warrant."

"There are some things that we do here very quietly. You just worry about finding information that we all need, and I'll worry about any repercussions with our legal system," Grubb said firmly.

"Okay. What are our next steps?" Moore asked.

"Have you done any cliff face climbing?" Patrick asked as he studied Moore.

"No."

"Willing to give it a try? One slip and you could be dead," he warned.

Moore didn't hesitate. He was doing this for Duncan and Nelson. "I'm willing Ed," he said fearlessly.

Patrick slid a picture of the lodge perched on the mountainside to Moore. "This is an old picture, but it shows the cliff face below the deck. There's a very small ledge that runs across it. It has a few gaps, but you should be able to inch your way to the deck and then climb onto the deck."

Moore studied the picture. "How far of a drop is it?"

Patrick laughed. "Let's just say it's deadly. But the good news is that you'll be wearing a safety harness."

Moore breathed a sigh of relief.

"But a slip off the ledge could send you swinging into the side of the cliff face. That could be deadly. Still willing to give it a go?"

Moore had a thin smile on his face. "Let's do it."

"Emerson, I need to remind you that our involvement is unofficial. We can't be compromised. If you're captured, you are on your own," Grubb cautioned.

"I figured that would be the case. No problem with me. I've been in sticky situations in the past and have been able to escape. I'll take the chance," Moore said as he thought about the danger that Lee's toxic threat posed to the world.

"We need to gear you up. We'll leave Bergen pre-dawn and cruise up the fjord to the moraine. If all goes well, we should be starting our drive up the moraine field before noon," Patrick said.

"Good," Moore replied.

They spent a few more minutes discussing the operation before the meeting broke up. Patrick drove Moore, V and Salimbeni down to the waterfront to meet the other two members of his team. He also wanted to show them the watercraft that would be conveying them up the fjord as well as the Sherp vehicle before returning them to their hotel.

CHAPTER 27

The Fjord
Bergen, Norway

The police boat with the Sherp positioned on its stern deck had departed its berth near the fish market and was cruising up the entrance to the deep fjord in the early pre-dawn. It soon left the busy last light of Bergen to be greeted by small farms and villages that lined the serene, emerald green shores of the fjord.

As the sun rose over the snow-covered mountain tops on the horizon, Moore relaxed near the stern while he marveled at the pine clad peaks and waterfalls that he saw cascading from the sides of the mountains. He was beguiled by Norway's rugged landscape with its deep blue waters contrasting with the brilliant white of the snow on the mountains.

Moore turned his attention to the rest of the team who were huddled with him near the stern. Patrick, Todd Hackbarth and Eric Paul were talking in hushed tones. The three men were all business and focused on checking and rechecking their weapons. Moore followed suit as he checked his AR-15 and .45.

"Coffee?"

Moore looked around and saw the white-bearded captain of the police boat, Ed Pickard. He held a cup of steaming hot coffee in his hand.

Taking the cup, Moore replied, "I love coffee, especially on a day like today."

Pickard gazed at the Sherp and the equipment the men had brought aboard. "It looks like you boys are on a dangerous operation."

Moore nodded. "Yep, but I'm going in with the right team."

"Be safe," Pickard said as he turned to walk back to the wheelhouse.

Two hours later, the police boat stopped its engines as it pulled abreast of the moraine field. Moore stared at the large rocks leading up the incline. "Are we going to really drive over that?"

"Very carefully," Paul answered in a confident tone.

"You'll enjoy the ride. Slow and tortuous," Hackbarth added as the three men began releasing the lines that secured the Sherp.

Within minutes, Patrick was seated at the Sherp controls with Paul next to him. Moore and Hackbarth were seated in the rear.

"Fasten your seatbelts," Patrick called out as he started the vehicle. He and Paul quickly checked the digital readouts before Patrick eased the Sherp off the stern, and its large-treaded tires propelled them toward shore.

When the vehicle climbed ashore, Patrick turned to Moore. "I better warn you that's the end of the smooth ride. It's going to be a really slow and bone-crunching ride as we go carefully over those boulders. Eric is in charge of inflating and deflating the tires for maximum climb efficiency."

"You'll get a break when we drive across the lake. That part should be a smooth ride," Paul called from the front passenger seat.

The rugged vehicle moved forward slowly as it angled upward at a ridiculous angle and carefully crawled over the first boulder. Over the next hour, Patrick carefully guided the vehicle on its circuitous route to its first stop at the lake.

Finally reaching the lake, Patrick stopped the vehicle. "Let's take a quick break and rest our bones," he suggested. He then popped open the front door and exited, followed by Paul. Moore and Hackbarth exited through the rear.

"No steering wheel in this thing?" Moore asked.

Patrick smiled. "It's all handled by the two levers. Pull back on the left lever and go left. Pull back on the right lever and go right."

"Easy-peasy," Paul added.

"I wish the ride was smoother, but beggars can't be choosers," Moore offered.

"The suspension system is wanting," Hackbarth explained.

After five minutes, the men returned to the vehicle and drove across the large lake to where they continued their arduous ascent up the moraine.

Three hours later, they reached the top of the moraine field and Patrick shut down the Sherp engine. "We'll leave the Sherp here. It's too dangerous for us to drive it closer. I don't want it spotted," he explained as the men scrambled out of the vehicle with their gear.

"We'll take five before heading toward the lodge," Patrick advised after they finished covering the Sherp with camouflage netting. He handed the men camouflage jackets since it was much cooler at this elevation in the mountains and provided comms equipment to Hackbarth and Paul.

"Don't I get a set?" Moore asked as he watched the men put on their communication devices.

"Too dangerous for you and us. If you get caught, it's best that they think you are on your own," Patrick confirmed.

Moore frowned at the comment.

Soon, they were on their way as they climbed over the edge of the moraine and entered a thick pine forest with Hackbarth taking the lead.

"We should be okay, but keep your eyes peeled for any surveillance cameras," Hackbarth suggested.

"This shouldn't be heavily guarded. Lee feels very safe and secure here," Patrick added.

Thirty minutes later, the men spotted the lodge through the trees and paused to study it.

Lee's massive, hand-crafted lodge was constructed out of logs and stone and sat on the side of the mountain. Its rear balcony overlooked a sheer cliff and provided a scenic view of the mountainside. The front faced a large lake that was partially surrounded by a dense, pine forest. It had a boathouse and guest house where Lee's mother was born.

A long drive led from the house down to a guarded entrance and the nearby bunkhouse for the guards. There were several outbuildings and a small house that provided living quarters for a couple who acted as groundskeeper and housekeeper. She would also cook meals for everyone although Lee would often fly in a chef when he was in residence.

The lodge had 21 rooms with 8 bedrooms, indoor pool and spa. The 5,500 square-foot lodge had several floor-to-ceiling stone fireplaces, cathedral ceilings and hardwood floors. It was decorated throughout as a hunter's retreat, complete with the wall-mounted heads of moose, bear and other Norwegian big game animals. A Sikorsky X2 helicopter sat on a concrete pad to the side of the house.

"This is not meant to be a shoot 'em up, Emerson. You just need to break into his office and see what you can find," Patrick reminded Moore.

Moore was studying the balcony where he would enter, as they had reviewed the plans back in Bergen. "I think I'm good to go," Moore said after a couple of minutes.

"Eric and Todd will go with you. I'll be watching the front of the house," Patrick confirmed as he pulled out a pair of binoculars. "Eric has spent time mountain climbing around here and can help you find the safest route to the balcony."

"There's all kinds of cracks and ledges that you can use to ease yourself over there," Paul assured Moore.

"We should give him a parachute in case he slips," Hackbarth teased wickedly.

"Not funny," Moore cracked back. He was a bit nervous about climbing on the cliff wall. "But that brings up a point. Why couldn't I have just paraglided in?"

Paul shook his head negatively. "The updrafts and downdrafts could sweep you against the cliff face and down you go. Too dangerous in the night and they also have cameras pointed out from the lodge to capture anyone trying to enter from the sky."

"Be careful. Our job was to deliver you here. The rest is up to you," Patrick stated sternly. "Watch for cameras."

"Right," Moore said as the three men headed through the pines to the cliff face.

"And don't get caught!" Patrick called the warning. "And if you do, don't take life too seriously - nobody gets out alive," he teased darkly.

Moore grinned as he gave Patrick a thumbs-up while they walked away. When they reached the edge of the forest, Hackbarth stayed behind a large pine to keep an eye out for any perimeter patrols.

Moore and Paul dropped to their stomachs and crawled to the edge of the cliff. Moore glanced down the steep cliff face. It was a deadly drop to the rocks below if he had a misstep. The two men scrutinized the cliff face as the wind gusted.

"You be careful of those gusts. They can sweep you off the cliff," Paul cautioned.

"Any more good news you can pass along?" Moore asked sarcastically.

"It looks like there's a ledge that you can creep along. It will take you right under the balcony," Paul said softly.

Moore scanned the area where Paul was pointing. He didn't see anything that looked like a ledge. "Eric, I don't see it," he said with anxiety.

"Right there," Paul said as he eased himself closer to the edge of the cliff and pointed down ten feet.

Moore then spotted a small outcropping. It ran along most of the face of the cliff to the balcony. There were two immediate problems which Moore noted. One was that there was a two-foot gap in the ledge about halfway to the balcony. The second was even more concerning. The so-called ledge that Paul pointed to was only about six inches wide.

"You call that a ledge?" Moore asked, unbelieving as he stared at the small protrusion from the face of the cliff. He would have to creep along 300 feet to get to the balcony support.

Paul chuckled quietly. "I've been on smaller ones."

"Yeah, but you're an experienced climber," Moore countered.

"And when you make it to the balcony, you will be, too," Paul reassured Moore.

"If I make it."

"I'm confident in you."

The two men crawled back into the pines and Paul withdrew a length of climbing rope from his backpack. He secured one end to the pine tree as an anchor and looked at Moore.

"Have you ever used crampons?"

Moore's eyes widened as he misheard what Paul had asked. "What?"

"Crampons." Paul pulled a pair of the 12-spike devices from his backpack and showed Moore. "These clamp on your shoe bottoms, and you can use them to dig into the face of the cliff."

"I don't want to experiment with something new. And I do want to be able to sense where my feet are. Those would take away my ability to do that."

"Your call," Paul said as he placed the crampons back inside the backpack and withdrew a harness. "You'll want to slip this one on," Paul explained. "Then I'll attach the rope to the harness. If you slip, this should keep you from dropping to the bottom, although you'll get pretty banged up when you swing into the rock face."

"A little safety net is greatly appreciated," Moore said as he slipped on the harness and then the helmet that Paul handed him.

Paul secured the end of the rope to the harness. "Ready to go?"

"I guess so. I'll leave my AR-15 here," Moore said as the men dropped back to the ground and crawled over the edge of the cliff. Moore checked his pocket to make sure that he had the container with the syringes. He then confirmed that he had his .45 secured.

Paul sat up and dug his heels into the ground while Moore slowly swung his body over the edge.

"You don't look comfortable," Paul observed.

"I'm not. I should have brought an umbrella," Moore cracked.

"What?" Paul asked confused.

"It's raining stupid out here today. That's how I really feel about doing this," Moore quipped.

Paul smiled as he shook his head. "Good luck. It's all about your feet and your fingers. Be careful how you place them. And watch for the wind gusts. It's picking up."

"Thanks. I'm going to do my best impression of human cling wrap," Moore cracked with bravado as he dropped. Ten feet later, Moore's feet touched the narrow fin of granite while his fingers grasped at the cliff face to begin his treacherous trek. He suddenly became aware of the emptiness around him. He was alone with the rope tether, his sole link to safety. The sensation almost made him dizzy.

He looked up to make sure that he wasn't visible to the lodge inhabitants. Seeing that he was below their sightline, his focus sharpened, and he moved with meaning. His fingertips sought out cracks and crevices in the cliff face as he cautiously inched his way along the narrow ledge.

Gusts of wind tore at his body, threatening to tear him away from the rock face. There were cracks in the wall from which water seeped, making his grips frequently slippery as well as his footing.

Moore's adrenaline surged, and his senses sharpened as he tried to safely cross the rocky precipice. At times, his fingers would dislodge rocks and send them tumbling below. One time, his foot slipped, and he desperately searched for a new handhold to avoid plummeting into the abyss below. He was able to regain his foothold on the ledge and now was more awake than he had ever been in his life.

When he reached the two-foot gap, he stopped. The soles of his feet ached as he studied the wall next to him. His finger joints and knuckles throbbed with pain. He spotted a couple of several possible handholds. He reached out to the first and tested it. The rock didn't hold as a chunk came out and dropped into the yawning void below. His heart was pounding, and his jaw was tight from the tension.

He searched again for another handhold and found one. It tested fine, and he cautiously worked his way across the open gap to make it safely to the other side. He continued clawing at the rock face as he took his next steps on the perilous journey.

When he finally reached the first steel support that went from the cliff wall to the edge of the balcony, he grabbed hold of it and rested. It was his first true break in the dangerous path he was following. He slipped out of the harness and attached his helmet to it. He then secured it to the support for use on his return trip.

After a few minutes, he swung his body on top of the support and began edging himself to the area where the support connected with the balcony so that he could climb onto it.

As he moved along the support, he looked below. Losing his balance would result in a fatal fall. He didn't have a safety line for this portion of the trip. Finally, he reached the junction with the balcony. He paused and listened. Hearing nothing, he climbed over the edge and onto the balcony where he ran to the wall of the lodge. From his recollection of the plans of the lodge, he was outside of Lee's office. He slowly opened the door and entered.

The office had a cathedral ceiling. Two dark, green leather chairs faced a floor-to-ceiling stone fireplace where a crackling fire burned. Moore walked over to the massive oak desk. He tried several of the drawers but found them locked. Frustrated he looked around. That's when he heard what sounded like a whimper.

Moore tiptoed around the desk and approached the fireplace where he saw a body on the floor. It was a woman with long black hair. It was Kari Yoki, and she was crying softly.

Moore saw blood on the carpet she was lying on. Moore knelt beside her to check on her. "Kari, are you okay?"

She turned her head in fright. When she saw it was Moore, she relaxed. "What are you doing here? How did you get here?" she asked with a confused look on her face.

"Don't worry about that. Are you okay?" he asked as his fingers wiped away the blood on her lips.

"We had an argument and Lee slapped me," she explained as she began to compose herself. She looked around the office. "You shouldn't be here. Why are you here?"

"I'm working on my story," Moore explained weakly. He was totally caught off guard by discovering her. He wasn't prepared to answer any questions from her.

"You need to get out of here as fast as you can. He won't like finding you here."

They heard a noise from the direction of the interior office door and both stood. She pushed him toward the balcony. "You need to go. I'll stall him," she said as she scurried to the door. She flung it open as Lee began to enter.

"You have a visitor. Emerson Moore is here!" She whirled around and pointed at Moore who was halfway across the room to the balcony door.

Lee walked into the room. "My, but you are resourceful, Mr. Moore." He glanced at the balcony door. "Is that how you got here? Flew in?" he asked with a quizzed look.

Mangan followed Lee into the room. He immediately withdrew a .45 and aimed it at Moore.

"Arsalan, would you check the balcony? See if he is alone,"

Lee directed.

Mangan walked by Moore and out onto the balcony. Not seeing anything, he walked to the rail and peered over. He spotted the rope and allowed his eyes to follow it to the cliff edge where it disappeared into the pine forest. Mangan reentered the office and reported his findings to Lee.

"Have the grounds searched," Lee ordered calmly as he glared at Moore for intruding into his sanctuary.

Meanwhile, Paul had seen Mangan walk onto the deck and spot the rope. He crawled back to Hackbarth and the two retreated into the thick pine forest to meet up with Patrick.

"I think Emerson has been compromised," Paul said when they found him.

"We'll keep watch from here for as long as we can," he answered as he handed the binoculars to Hackbarth. "Todd, you watch the lodge. I'm calling Paulette on the sat phone," he said as he dug the phone from his backpack and called her to report the development.

A few minutes later, Hackbarth looked through the binoculars. "We've got trouble. There are several teams of armed men on ATVs spreading out from one of the outbuildings."

Patrick nodded and updated Grubb. "Paulette wants us to pull back and wait. We can't be compromised," he told his two teammates.

"But what about Emerson?" Hackbarth worried.

"He knew the risks," Patrick replied hurriedly. "Let's move it."

The men immediately grabbed their gear and headed back to the spot where the Sherp had been hidden.

Inside the lodge, Mangan frisked Moore and found the plastic container with the syringes and disarmed Moore of his .45.

He opened the container and showed Lee.

"What do we have here?"

Moore didn't see any reason to withhold the truth. "I was going to sedate you and take the flash drive from around your neck."

Lee's hand went quickly to the flash drive as he patted the front of his shirt. "What do you know about a flash drive?" Lee queried with surprise. He pointed for Moore to sit on one of the two chairs in front of the fireplace. Lee sat on the other while Mangan stood behind Moore's chair and Yoki left the room.

"Nothing other than it must contain something of interest for my story," Moore replied as he watched Lee's reaction.

"Tell me, Emerson, why are you in the habit of breaking into my properties?" Lee scowled irritably as his eyes glared at Moore.

Moore studied Lee's face. The crow's feet around his eyes and the deep creases in his cheeks seemed to have a heightened sense of evil about him. It was like a dark, ominous cloud of wickedness.

"Like I've told you before, I've been researching my story," Moore offered.

Lee looked at his hands, folded in his lap. He next looked up at Moore. "I'm not a violent man, Mr. Moore. When the pressure in me builds up like a ticking time bomb, I never feel the need to let it explode. Do you know why, Mr. Moore?"

"No."

"It's because I'm always in control. I control the controllables. I learned that as a research scientist. I set controls on my experiments. I don't ever feel the need to explode, to vent my anger. I remain calmly in control," Lee explained emotionlessly.

Lee continued talking in a deadly tone. "There's something

to be said about power and pain. Any moron can cause pain, but to do it artfully is a paramount test of a brilliant man's intelligence. And I have something special planned for you, Mr. Moore."

Lee paused as he stared sinisterly at Moore. He added, "You are within my power now. And I must say, the rush is intoxicating. There isn't anyone more dangerous on this planet than me. You can trust me on that."

"Compelling. And the reason you are telling me this?" Moore asked.

"Because when I need to create lasting damage, I have Arsalan. He is my outlet. He is the vehicle for conducting any violence I need done," Lee said coldly.

Moore pushed. "Like with my friend, Izzy Nelson?"

"The black, chubby fellow?" Lee asked with raised eyebrows.

"You know exactly who I'm talking about," Moore countered firmly.

Lee laughed. "Arsalan is very capable as you will soon find out."

Yoki handed Lee a snifter with brandy. He swirled the liquid in the snifter before sipping it. "This may surprise you, Mr. Moore, but I've been aware of your real mission," he smiled triumphantly.

"What's that?" Moore pushed, wanting to see what Lee knew.

"The dairy cow deaths. You trying to tie my company to the deaths."

"Why do you think that's what I'm doing?"

"I have my sources. Arsalan can tell you how much he learned from your associate before he died." Lee gave a curt laugh as Mangan joined in.

Moore went for the throat. "And you're doing all of this in revenge for what happened to your father!"

Lee smirked. "What are the deaths of a few cows? They are my research mice. Our real target is humanity. I will bring a scourge of death of biblical proportions. Worse than frogs, locusts or plagues."

"How? My guess is that you are telling me all of this as I won't be around to witness it," Moore suggested as he egged on Lee.

Lee raised his eyebrows. "Very insightful. I will tell you. Are you familiar with the mixture that people place in their septic tanks? It's an enzyme that works with the bacteria to maintain a healthy septic system. It comes alive in the tank."

Moore nodded.

"Simply put, I have discovered a process to make bad bacteria dormant. When they are ingested in dairy cows or humans, the stomach enzymes waken them after a very short incubation period. They then begin to quickly colonize before devouring their host from the inside out," Lee gloated. "I call it biolee."

He continued. "Scientifically speaking, I've created hazardous biochemical toxins that are biomolecules produced by bacteria through simple culturing systems. These pathogenic microbes are toxigenic."

"Sounds like bioterrorism to me," Moore stated firmly. "Are you going to kill everyone in the world?"

Lee chuckled perversely. "Biolee is a deadly biological weapons agent. Its use is not to kill, but to strike fear into people's lives. That's the focus of bioterrorism."

"And you're starting with dairy cows?" Moore probed.

Nodding with an evil glint in his eyes, Lee replied, "Yes.

Can you imagine the fear in people when the thought of no more dairy products strikes them?"

"Then, you're going to use your biolee to kill humans, right? Terrorize a few so that the others agree to whatever demands you make?"

"I can, and I will."

"How will you deliver it to humans so that they ingest it?" Moore quizzed.

Lee appeared to be tiring of the exchange. "I've said enough."

"But what's your end game? Money?" Moore guessed.

"No. I am after the power. With this, I can rule the world! When this starts, we will have countries begging for my antidote for their biodefense."

The guy was an egomaniac, Moore thought.

"And you will be one of the first humans to ingest my biolee. The sweet release of death won't be so sweet for you, Mr. Moore. Yours will be more tortured," Lee said with doomful glee and a devilish gleam in his eyes.

"You're going to kill me here?" Moore asked as he looked around the room and evaluated his chances for escape.

Lee stood and walked to a window. "Not here. I don't want to have your death take place on this hallowed ground. This property belonged to my mother and her family. She was born here. It's a very special place that helps remind me from where I started."

Lee walked over to his desk where Mangan had set Moore's plastic container containing the syringes. He picked up a syringe and approached Moore. "Restrain him Arsalan," he ordered Mangan.

Mangan's long, muscular arms swept around Moore, holding him tightly as he squirmed.

"No. We are going to take you on a trip with me. When we arrive, you will die there," Lee said in a highly satisfactory tone as he inserted the needle into the side of Moore's exposed neck.

Moore felt the prick of the needle before blacking out.

CHAPTER 28

The Next Day
Tulare, California

A lot had transpired in the previous 24 hours. Patrick and his men were ordered to return to Bergen with the Sherp. A helicopter left Lee's lodge which resulted in Grubb staking out the Bergen airport where Lee's private jet was parked. The helicopter flew south of Bergen to Norway's third largest city, Stavanger. There, its occupants, carrying a body, transferred to a chartered private jet and took off immediately. After a couple of refueling stops, the private jet touched down in Tulare where a waiting SUV drove the passengers to one of Lee's feed mills.

After analyzing flight departures in the area, V and Salimbeni connected with the Ranger pilots and planned for a transatlantic flight to the U.S. on the heels of Lee.

Moaning as he regained consciousness, Moore slowly opened his eyes to find himself in a darkened laboratory. When he tried to move, he discovered that he was tightly strapped to a table.

As his eyes adjusted to the darkness, he saw that the room was almost empty. He heard people in the next room. They were shouting instructions about moving containers. Moore guessed that they were shipping out the biolee if he was in a production site.

The door swung open, and the overhead lights switched on. Moore blinked at their brightness.

"You're back with us," Lee's voice said in a malicious tone. "Did you sleep well? We had to sedate you several times on our flight."

"Where am I?" Moore asked.

"I'm surprised that you didn't realize that you are in one of my labs," Lee teased sarcastically.

"Are we still in Norway?"

"No, you're back in Tulare."

"Can you unstrap me?" Moore asked although he knew the answer.

"There's no need to unstrap you. You're not meant to be long in this world," Lee said as he stepped over to Moore and relished the moment.

"What's going on here?" Moore asked. He noticed Lee was wearing a white hazmat suit complete with self-contained breathing apparatus and a hood with a clear faceplate. He also wore a pair of protective gloves.

Moore was immediately concerned about what was in the air that he was breathing.

"It's moving time. We've completed the manufacturing on my biolee and we're shipping it to a staging location. Then, we will distribute it around the world to our safe sites where we will put the next step of my plan in action."

"Killing people?" Moore guessed.

Lee then released a throaty, depraved laugh through the faceplate in the hazmat suit hood. "Precisely, you fool. Kill as many as we need to show we mean business."

"Someone is going to stop you."

"Certainly not you, and I have my moles who are telling me who is after me and how close they are. You'd be surprised who they are," Lee glowered with a wicked gleam in his eyes.

Moore twisted again. The straps wouldn't budge.

"Nervous, Mr. Moore? How does it feel knowing that you are about to die?" Lee asked as he walked over to the table. He opened a small red container that held three small vials. Two were red-colored; the third was green-colored.

"Your death will be painful and take some time. You'll cry out in anguish as your stomach is eaten alive from the inside out. I can assure you that no one will hear your tormented screams."

Lee walked to the door and called Mangan. "Arsalan, I need your help."

Mangan entered the room. He was also wearing a hazmat suit.

"Bind his head," Lee ordered as he held up one of the red vials. "This is my biolee. I've two vials of it and one dose of the antidote in the green vial, but we won't need that for you."

He turned back to the table while Moore struggled and saw Lee pour water in a cup. He turned around and approached Moore with the cup of water. "It dissolves so easily. You can't even tell that there's anything here," he laughed as he looked inside the cup.

Mangan placed a strap around Moore's head while Moore tried desperately to avoid it by twisting his head. It was useless.

"Pinch his nostrils closed and open his mouth," Lee instructed.

Mangan complied while Moore's eyes virtually popped out of his head as he tried to keep his mouth shut. Needing air, he had to open it and Lee poured the mixture down Moore's mouth, causing Moore to gag.

"Good. You can let go," Lee spoke to Mangan who stepped aside.

Looking at his watch, Lee spoke in a cold, but triumphant tone. "You may have ten minutes before you start to feel the effect of the biolee. The pain starts slowly and then builds to a crescendo. I'd like to be here for the end, but time is precious."

As the two men started for the door, Lee paused and looked back at Moore who was twisting on the table, trying to break loose. "I may have forgot to mention that no one will find your body. We have set explosives with timers that will go off in an hour."

Mangan walked out of the room.

As he closed the door behind him, Lee parted with a comment. "Goodbye, Mr. Moore."

The door closed shut.

Moore's eyes swept to the clock on the wall. It showed that one minute had passed. He heightened his efforts to twist out of the straps, but it was to no avail. They were too tight.

Moore's eyes turned to the clock again. Another minute had passed. He began to feel beads of sweat appear on his face. Were they the first sign of the biolee taking effect or a result of his mounting anxiety?

Fear began to swallow Moore as he fought to clear his thinking and focus on an escape. His mind raced as if he had overdosed on caffeine. His chest tightened. He willed the good bacteria in his gut to conquer Lee's bad bacteria.

His stomach had a spasm. Was it from his anxiety, or was it a signal that the bacteria were beginning its attack? His fingers clawed at the leather straps, trying to tear them off as he twisted harder on the tabletop. His body ached from the stress as he began perspiring more.

The clock showed ten minutes had passed. The door opened and in walked Lee and Mangan. Both had twisted grins on their faces.

"You look very uncomfortable, Mr. Moore," Lee remarked viciously. "I'm surprised that you are still alive," he added as the two men walked to the table.

"You look very anxious. Knocking at death's door does cause that," he sneered.

"He's worked up a sweat," Mangan snickered, heinously.

"You shouldn't be alive," Lee said as he glanced at the clock on the wall. "But you are. Do you know why you are?"

Moore had been gritting his teeth, not responding until now. "No," he muttered.

"Because I didn't empty the red vial into the cup. Poor me. What was I ever thinking? That was devious of me, wasn't it?" he chortled at the stress he had put Moore through.

Moore grimaced at how Lee had tricked him and made him suffer.

"But now, I'm sad to say, is the time for the real biolee to be ingested." Lee walked over to the table and prepared the mixture, allowing Moore to see him emptying the contents of the red vial into the cup and adding water. When he finished, he returned to Moore's side.

"Pinch his nostrils again Arsalan and open his mouth."

They repeated their earlier process which resulted in forcing the liquid down Moore's throat. Once they finished, the two men stood back.

"I'm finished playing with you, Mr. Moore. You'll feel the effects in ten minutes. Goodbye," he said abruptly as the two men left the room, closing the door behind them.

Moore glanced at the clock. It was counting down his death. He struggled again as he tried desperately to escape his restraints. Nothing was working. He then heard a noise behind him. It was the sound of a door opening at the far wall followed by approaching footsteps. He couldn't see who it was, but then he heard the voice.

"Emerson, I am so sorry."

Moore recognized the voice right away. It was Kari Yoki. "Kari, the antidote. Can you get me the antidote on the table over there?"

Instead, she walked to his table and reached down to stroke his sweaty face. "I'm so sorry," she repeated. She was wearing a hazmat suit, too.

"Kari, you've got to help me. Get me the antidote. It's in the green vial over there! I have only minutes," he urged in terrorized fear.

She hurriedly reached down and released the straps binding his arms so that he could release the remaining straps. While he worked quickly, she went to the table and found the green vial.

"Here it is," she said as he joined her at the table. He took the vial and mixed it with water, then hastily downed the cup of water.

"I just hope I got the antidote in time," he grumbled nervously.

"How long has it been since you were given the biolee?"

"About five minutes."

"You have plenty of time. The biolee takes thirty minutes to act," she said quietly.

"But he said ten minutes," Moore countered, confused.

"He was just playing mind games with you," she explained calmly. "He can be such a manipulator!"

Moore looked at the Chinese woman in front of him. "Thank you, Kari. You saved my life," Moore spoke gratefully.

"At least I've done one thing right," she responded.

"But why did you come to my rescue?" Moore asked.

"I've seen him deal with many people. There was something different about you. You just seem like a good person. You showed that when you didn't try to take advantage of me in my hotel room," she smiled.

"That's not who I am," Moore replied.

"I know. That so impressed me. That's not what usually happens when he wants me to seduce someone to get information out of them. You're different," she commented.

"I try to be," Moore agreed.

"I'll help you this time, but no more," she smiled softly before changing her demeanor. "You need to get out of here and I need to return to Mr. Lee. Follow me out the back."

She stopped at the door and pointed to two hazmat suits. "You better wear one of those," she said. "You don't want to breathe the dust from the biolee. It can kill you," she warned.

After Moore donned one of the suits, the two left the lab rear door and entered the darkened feed mill. "You need to be careful leaving here. He has guards everywhere. If you get caught, he'll know it was me who released you."

"Thank you again, Kari," Moore said with a sense of urgency.

"There's a Chinese proverb that says the dragon flies and the phoenix dances. You are the phoenix rising from the ashes. Lee is the dragon," she said as she walked toward the front of the mill.

Moore made his way to the rear of the mill where he spotted a door. Opening it slowly, he peeked out to see two flatcars on a rail line with an intermodal shipping container on each. They were parked next to the loading dock. A red caboose was attached to the rear of the second flatcar while a switch engine was connected to the front of the first flatcar.

A SUV drove up to the end of the loading dock and its rear window rolled down. Moore saw Lee in the back seat and heard him speak.

"Finished loading?"

"Yes," one of the Chinese guards answered. "We just need to lock them up and head out. We'll be riding in the caboose."

While they talked, Moore walked casually across the loading dock into the first shipping container. He felt comfortable in doing it since he was wearing the hazmat suit like the others wore.

The intermodal shipping container was filled with containers from the feed mill. Moore found a manifest and discovered their destination. Smiling, he slipped out the other side of the intermodal container, sliding the door shut behind him.

"Don't tarry," Lee instructed as he ended his conversation. He rolled up the window and the vehicle departed.

Moore crawled under the first flatcar as he heard the approaching footsteps of the guard. The guard closed and locked the doors of the first intermodal container and then the second before joining the three guards in the caboose. As the guard walked away, Moore slipped out of his hazmat suit and left it on the ground between the train tracks.

Hearing the switch engine whistle blow, Moore rolled back and stood by the coupling. As the train began moving, he jumped up and clung to the ladder for the short ride to the train yard.

When they arrived, the two flatcars and caboose were connected to a train of thirty cars. While the connection process was underway, Moore quickly made his way out of the train yard to the highway and walked to a nearby truck stop as he planned how to fly below the radar. Lee's words about moles echoed in his mind and he needed to sort out who he felt he could trust.

As he walked, an explosion could be heard from two miles away as the feed mill blew up in flames. Moore sighed with relief that he had been able to escape.

As he approached the diesel fueling pumps, he spotted a rough-looking trucker. The man with a shaven head and dark sunglasses had just finished filling up.

"Excuse me."

"Yes?"

"Where you heading?"

"Albuquerque, New Mexico. Why?" the trucker replied.

"Mind if I ride along. I'll pay for all of our meals."

The trucker eyed Moore as he tried to determine if the potential passenger posed any risk. The guy didn't seem like he was a threat. "Sounds like a deal to me. I'm John Bishop."

"Moore. Emerson Moore," he replied as he shook the hand of the gregarious trucker.

"Climb aboard," Bishop said as he jumped up into the cab of the semi-truck. "Ranger, we got company. You need to get off that passenger seat," Bishop said to his liver and white Brittany, who jumped to the floor between the seats.

Moore opened the passenger door and climbed into the cab and reached down to pet Ranger's head.

"She's my bird hunting dog. Best breed around for hunting pheasants," Bishop explained as he started the diesel engine.

"She looks energetic," Moore commented as the dog licked his hand.

"Energetic. I wish I had half her energy when I played linebacker at West Virginia University. I would have had a better chance at tackling Franco Harris when he half dragged me to the goal line," Bishop chuckled.

As the truck pulled out of the truck stop, Bishop pointed to a package between the seats. "You like deer jerky? Help yourself. I made it."

"I'll give it a try," Moore smiled as he helped himself to the jerky. He realized that he hadn't eaten in some time and that his stomach was making noises. Remembering his recent close call, he was thankful that his stomach was hungry and not being eaten from the inside out. Moore relaxed and listened to the talkative trucker tell his tales.

"Did you know that the three hardest things to say in the English language are: I'm wrong, you're right and Worcester-shire sauce?"

"I'd agree to that," Moore replied with a tired sigh.

"You look a bit beat. Tough day, huh? I always say put one foot in front of the other and do the best you can today."

Moore nodded as he settled in the comfortable seat. Before long, he drifted off to sleep.

When the truck reached Bakersfield, it turned onto Inter-state Route 40, which would take it to Albuquerque. Fourteen hours and two stops later, the truck pulled into a truck stop in Albuquerque.

"Thank you for the ride, John," Moore said as the truck pulled up to the fuel pumps.

"Any time. And don't forget my invitation to join me pheas-ant hunting," Bishop remarked.

"I will. I've got your contact info right here," Moore said as he padded his shirt pocket where he had stuffed the note from Bishop.

Moore climbed down from the truck and entered the truck stop to use the restroom. He was able to shower and change into the new clothes he purchased before his shower. He grabbed a cup of coffee and walked out the front entrance where he sat at a picnic table to decide his next steps.

Lee's comments about the moles returned to haunt Moore.

Who could he trust? Was Lee alluding to just the mole in the agency that Sam had tried to uncover or were there more? What about V and Salimbeni? Were they moles? Or was Lee trying to throw him off? No, that wouldn't make sense because Lee thought he was finally killing Moore in Tulare.

The thoughts ricocheted in Moore's brain like balls in a pinball machine. There was a lot of noise and flashing lights, but no clarity.

Moore's attention was distracted by two senior citizens next to a RV at the fuel pump. The man had fallen and was struggling to get to his feet. Moore walked over to them.

"Let me help you," Moore said as he extended a hand to the man and pulled him to his feet.

"I didn't lose my balance. I just slipped and fell," he said defensively.

"No Alan, you lost your balance and fell. You keep denying that you can't maintain your balance," the strawberry blonde in her mid-sixties retorted with a southern drawl.

"I'm just peachy-peachy," Alan commented, not liking the fuss.

"Good thing for you this nice gentleman helped you to your feet. I'm Nancy Kolson," she said as she stuck out her hand to Moore, who shook it while she eyed the handsome stranger.

"Emerson Moore," he offered.

"Alan, where are your manners? Introduce yourself to this nice-looking, young man," she beamed.

With one hand against the RV, Alan gave Moore a wave. "I'm Alan, and I'm the one who caught this southern belle," he said with a sly wink at his wife. He spoke with a similar drawl.

"I see you're looking okay," Moore spoke encouragingly.

"It's good to be seen and not viewed," Alan cracked.

"You two from Texas?" Moore inquired as he smiled.

"No, honey. We're from New Orleans."

"Really?" Moore's eyes light up. "Are you heading back home?"

"Yes, although I may have to do most of the driving for Mr. Fuddle Duddle!" she teased.

"I'm heading in that direction. I could help with the driving and fuel expense," Moore suggested. This would be another way for him to stay off the grid.

Nancy eyed Moore again as she thought about it. Nice eye candy, she thought. "Do you like Patsy Cline?" she asked.

"Yes."

"How about gospel songs?"

"Love them."

"Well, that does it then. Climb aboard." She turned to her husband. "I just expanded my audience for my Patsy Cline and gospel songs."

Alan nodded as he started to walk around the RV.

"Oh no you don't Alan. We're letting Emerson take the wheel. You ride in back and I'll keep him entertained from the passenger seat." She winked provocatively. "With my singing, that is," she teased. "Although, I need a couple of aspirin. This headache is killing me," she said as she dug through her purse for the bottle. Finding them she downed two tablets with a swig from her water bottle.

"And your face is killing me!" Alan joked good-naturedly to his wife.

"Sounds like a plan to me." Moore walked around to the driver's side and climbed into the 28-foot RV. He studied the controls for a minute before starting it. He pulled out on Interstate Route 40 for the 18-hour drive to New Orleans as Nancy fastened her seat belt. She then turned toward Moore before starting her first Patsy Cline song.

When they reached Amarillo, Texas, they turned onto Texas Route 287 headed toward Dallas. Moore found a truck stop to tank up for gas while Nancy and Alan started for the restrooms.

"Nancy, do you have a cell phone I could use for a call?" Moore asked.

"Certainly. It's on the console between the seats," she called without breaking stride.

Moore reached inside the RV and grabbed her cell phone and dialed the number for V that he had memorized.

"Hello?" V answered, not recognizing the number.

"V, it's Emerson."

"Emerson! We wondered where you were. Are you okay?"

"Barely."

"We've been trying to track you."

Moore updated V on what had transpired at the lodge and waking up in Tulare.

"Mitch discovered that Lee rented a different jet out of Norway. We were hoping you were on board. I'll have to let Paulette know that you're okay," V remarked in a serious tone. "Then we heard about the explosion at the Tulare feed mill. Did you do that?"

"No." Moore relayed what he had learned from Lee and his near brush with death.

"Why did that woman free you?" V asked.

"Not quite sure. Maybe her conscience made her help me," Moore surmised. "She's different. Sam warned me that she was mentally unstable, and you never knew what she'd do next."

"I'm glad that she was in the right frame of mind to free you before she went back to the other frame of mind," V commented seriously.

"Me too," Moore agreed.

"So that's Lee's plan. Conquer the world," V muttered.

"Yes. The two intermodal shipping containers are on a train for New Orleans and I'm heading there now while I'm being entertained with Patsy Cline tunes."

"What?"

"I'll explain later," Moore said as he spotted the Kolsons walking out of the truck stop.

"I'll get Mitch checking on what properties Lee owns in New Orleans. Sounds like it could be a central staging area for him."

"Probably," Moore agreed. "I've got to go. I'll call you when we stop for gas."

"When do you think you'll be in New Orleans?" V asked quickly.

"Tomorrow," Moore answered as he ended the call and placed the cell phone on the console.

"I brought you a slushy, honey," Nancy beamed as she handed him a large cup. "I got you cherry. I hope you like cherry," she said demurely.

"Anything will do."

"All gassed up?" she asked.

"Yes."

"Want me to drive and give you a break, honey?"

"I'm good. Just let me run to the men's room real quick and I'm ready for the road."

Ten minutes later, Moore pulled on the highway headed for Dallas. Six hours later, the RV was on the other side of Dallas at a truck stop along Interstate 20 where the Kolsons briefly went inside. Moore called V again on Nancy's cell phone while he refueled.

"V, it's Emerson. We're just east of Dallas. About eight hours away from New Orleans."

"Good. Mitch and I are in New Orleans. You call me when you get in and we'll pick you up and bring you to the warehouse we're using."

"Did Mitch get a chance to search for Lee's property holdings?"

"Yes, she did. She had to dig through various shell companies to identify what he owns. There's one that's of particular interest."

"Oh?"

"Twelve months ago, Lee bought a non-functioning oil platform in the Gulf of Mexico. It would be perfect for use as a secured site."

"That's interesting."

"Mitch is still following up on two other facilities he has here. One is on the riverfront."

"Perfect for placing those containers on a ship with no one watching," Moore suggested.

"Right. One more thing. Lee is also in New Orleans. At least his jet flew from Tulare to New Orleans, according to what Mitch found. He arrived earlier today."

"Interesting. The plot thickens," Moore responded as he saw the Kolsons return. He ended the call and returned the cell phone to the console.

"You ready to let me drive?" Nancy asked as they neared him.

"Sounds like a great idea. I'm getting tired. A quick nap would be good," he answered as they all boarded the RV.

Nancy drove onto the highway for the drive to New Orleans as Moore settled into the passenger seat. He was asleep within minutes.

CHAPTER 29

The Next Day
New Orleans, Louisiana

Before the Kolsons dropped Moore at a gas station on the west side of New Orleans, Nancy let him use her cell phone to make arrangements for V to pick him up.

"I hope you don't mind that I deleted my calls from your call history. My friend is very private and doesn't like the number listed anywhere," Moore explained as he handed the cell phone back to her.

"Or is she married?" Nancy asked with a raised eyebrow.

"It's a he and he does covert government work," Moore whispered conspiratorially.

Nancy's eyes widened at the revelation. "Are you a spy?" she whispered back.

Moore laughed softly. "No, I'm not. Thank you both for the ride and the company. I really enjoyed your singing, Nancy. You have quite a voice."

Moore stepped out of the RV, and it drove away. Ten minutes later, Moore was sitting on a bench in front of the gas station and sipping a sweet tea. A black SUV pulled to a stop in front of him, and the window dropped down.

"It's good to see you, Emerson," V smiled.

"And you," Moore replied as he stood. He opened the door and entered the SUV which headed for a warehouse closer to downtown. As they drove, they caught each other up on the events over the last few days.

When they pulled in front of the warehouse, V depressed the button on the remote, and the door rolled up allowing him to drive inside.

"You certainly have a knack for having access to warehouses around the world," Moore commented as the garage door closed, and V shut off the engine.

"That I do. I have a good network that affords me temporary use of a number of warehouses, almost worldwide. They are good locations for me to stage different pieces of technology," he said as he walked around the front of the vehicle. "Follow me."

The two men walked across the floor to a closed door which V opened and walked through. When Moore followed him, he spotted Salimbeni sitting straight up in a chair. She seemed frozen in place. Moore felt a shiver run up his spine as he heard the door slam shut behind him.

The cold end of a pistol poked into the back of Moore's head. He started to react, but the voice commanded him, "Don't move."

Moore's eyes widened with confusion when V and Mitch smiled. The gun barrel was pulled back and the voice asked, "Emerson, aren't you going to welcome me back from the dead?"

Moore spun around to see Sam Duncan grinning mischievously at him. He reached out and gave his friend a bear hug, saying, "You better be glad that I didn't just take you out!"

"Surprised you, didn't I?" Duncan asked.

"Obviously. Where have you been and how did you survive that bomb blast back in Vegas?" Moore asked quickly.

Duncan grabbed Moore by the arm and pulled him over to where Salimbeni was sitting. "Sit down and rest a spell while I catch you up."

Moore plopped onto one of the chairs as did V.

"Do you remember me saying that I needed to go off the grid?"

"Yes," Moore answered.

"V helped me with the explosive device. Did you notice how barely no other vehicle was damaged by that explosion and most of the force was directed downward?"

"Yes."

"V took care of that. Tell him, V."

"I placed a shaped charge in his vehicle. These are plastic explosives molded into shapes that channel the blast's force into a particular direction," V explained.

"Creative," Moore commented.

"Do you remember seeing a van drive away?" Duncan asked.

Moore thought back and recalled it. "Yes."

"V was sitting in it, waiting for me. You were momentarily distracted by the truck that blocked your view. That's when I ran over to the van and jumped inside. Then V detonated the explosive and we drove away. I was concerned that you might try to track down the van, but you didn't."

"But what about the video surveillance cameras at the hotel?" Moore asked perplexed.

V answered Moore's question. "It seems that they had a momentary recording failure."

"One of V's technical feats," Duncan added.

"So, this entire time, you've been in the background?"

Duncan nodded.

"Did you know, Mitch?" Moore probed at being left out of the secret.

"No. I didn't know anything until Sam showed up here a little while ago. It was all between him and V."

Moore turned back to Duncan. "Sam, why didn't you clue me in? You know you can trust me, or were you concerned?"

"Remember that I told you I was trying to find the mole?"

"Yes."

"To be able to do it, I really needed to disappear and make it very believable. I'm sorry for the anguish I put you and Mitch through, but it helped Lee and the mole believe that I was really dead."

"Did you find the mole? Was it Izzy?"

"I did, and it wasn't Izzy, although he inadvertently played a role in revealing the mole. I didn't anticipate Mitch interacting with the agency and bringing in someone after I disappeared." Duncan looked at Salimbeni. "You outthought me on that one."

"I wish I hadn't. Izzy would still be alive," she said remorsefully.

"I know. In our line of business, we never know when we will take our last breath," Duncan remarked sympathetically.

"So how did Izzy help?" Moore pushed.

"With V's help, we were able to identify who Izzy was communicating with. It was Ken Magyary who worked for me. I flew back to Virginia and began staking out Magyary's home and travel. I was able to install a tracking device on his car and place several listening devices in his home."

"Breaking and entering?" Moore asked.

"It comes with the territory. I was able to listen in on several of his phone calls and observe his meets with Lee's people. I also intercepted some of his communications that he left at unattended drops. I actually changed some of them which caused him quite a bit of distress."

"Has the mole been arrested?" Moore asked.

"No. He died," Duncan acknowledged.

"You killed him?" Moore continued.

"No. Apparently the information I changed on one of Magyary's communications caused Lee so much grief that Lee had him killed. So, the case is closed on that matter," Duncan explained.

"Going back to me and my role, why?" Moore probed.

"Because, Emerson, you weren't part of the agency. I told you that in Las Vegas. You are an outsider who has a knack for getting results. You've always been that way, even when you've had close calls with death," Duncan explained.

"You used me," Moore said sternly.

"Yes, I did," Duncan acknowledged. "I had to. I knew you could discover where Lee was making his lethal bacteria."

"He calls it biolee," Moore inserted.

"We didn't know what he called it. You've been tremendous with your accomplishments, and I'm sorry about the distress that you've gone through. V has done an excellent job in keeping me updated."

"Yeah. I've been pretty beat up and stretched on this operation," Moore agreed.

"I didn't mean for you to go through all of that pain." Duncan paused for a moment. "Emerson, you really outdid yourself. What a survivor you are!"

Moore had a serious look on his face as he glanced at Duncan. "I want to warn you. Don't do this to me again! Understand?"

Duncan nodded his head. "It will never happen again."

Moore studied his wayward friend for a moment. "I don't believe you."

Duncan chuckled at the reality of Moore's comment.

"Has anyone been successful in understanding the components of the biolee or coming up with an antidote, Sam? Lee does have an antidote, but I'm not sure he's willing to share it," Moore admitted. He internally criticized himself for not grabbing the vial of antidote at the Tulare lab before he escaped.

"No," Duncan responded with a grim look on his face.

Moore shook his head from side to side at the lack of progress.

"Which brings us to the next steps. We need to destroy Lee's biolee and catch him," Duncan remarked seriously as he turned to Salimbeni. "We need to obtain the antidote and discover how to replicate it. Mitch, do you have any updates on the location of the freight train with those intermodal shipping containers?"

"Yes, Sam. I just found them a few minutes ago and it looks like we're a bit late," she answered as she looked up from her laptop.

"What do you mean?" Duncan asked.

"They've left the New Orleans train yard."

"Can you find the trucks that pulled them away?"

"They didn't use trucks. They used two helicopters," she answered. "Let me see if I can find flight plans for them." Her fingers flew across the keyboard.

"Helicopters?" Moore asked in surprise.

"A Chinook could do it. They can lift 36,000 pounds," V explained.

Duncan nodded his head. "That's right. They can hoist them up and fly them virtually anywhere."

"Like to an oil platform in the gulf," Moore suggested.

"Yes. It would be a perfect location. Easy to ship from there on small helicopters to connect with larger planes at airports for flights to anywhere in the world. Or, the biolee can be loaded on ships, using the cranes on the oil platform," Duncan affirmed.

"Plus, its easily defendable," Duncan noted. "I'd expect they would have radar to identify anyone approaching from the land or air. Add in some underwater listening devices and they could hear anyone trying to approach through the water." Duncan rattled off his thoughts.

"I've got it," Salimbeni exclaimed from her desk. "The chinooks are delivering the two containers from the New Orleans train yard to the oil platform."

"I guess I know where we are heading," Moore mused as he looked around the group. "What's the plan, Sam? Since you hatched all of this so far, I'd guess you have something in mind."

"I do. We've got some C-4 here. We'll go out to the platform and blow up the containers," Duncan insisted.

"Just like that?" Moore questioned skeptically. "What about the surveillance equipment you mentioned? Won't they see us coming?"

Duncan smiled. "V has an answer for us. Why don't you tell him, V?"

"I'll do better that that. I'll show you." V led the group to the side of the warehouse where he pulled a tarp off a piece of equipment.

"That looks like one of the speeder bikes from the Star Wars movie!" Moore exclaimed as he looked at the bike-like vehicle. It was 12-feet long and 8-feet wide. It looked like a jet ski mounted on two large horizontal propeller blades encased in plastic with four smaller, plastic-encased blades at each corner.

"Good comparison. It's a Japanese-made Xturismo hoverbike. It can fly for 40 minutes at speeds up to 100 miles per hour at an altitude of 1,000 feet," V explained. "I have three of them."

Moore had a confused look on his face as he turned to Duncan. "I don't get it, Sam. I thought you said they had radar to detect incoming craft."

"They do, but we'll fly these at wave top. We'll be too small for them to see us coming."

"What about their surveillance cameras? Won't they see us?" Moore pushed.

"We're going to do it in a storm. And there's one headed this way early evening."

"You have time to get ready. I have C-4 and weapons for you," V commented. "When you're ready. I'll drive you down to the Gulf and you can launch from there."

"What about security guards. Does anyone have an idea how many are out there?" Moore questioned.

"Based on what we saw on satellite imagery, we're guessing that there are a handful. No more than eight," Duncan replied.

"Three against eight?" Moore asked in disbelief.

"Yeah, they probably should have a few more to make it fair," Duncan teased. "Really, it shouldn't be a big deal. And we will have the element of surprise on our side. I'm sure that they are not expecting us. Remember that they think you were blown up in Tulare."

"You sound pretty confident," Moore observed.

"I am, Emerson. We can do this," Duncan confirmed in a confident tone.

"What about Lee? Does anyone know where he is?" Moore asked.

"He's on the oil platform. The guy is quite creative. From

what we discovered in our construction record search, he had a seven-foot-high underwater pipe installed from the shore to the oil platform three miles away. He travels through that pipe on a small four-wheeled vehicle that runs on an electrified rail. It has two seats with a small cargo platform attached to the back of the seats. When it arrives below the oil platform, he takes an elevator up to the platform."

Moore turned to Duncan. "Why can't we go in that way?"

"Too dangerous. He probably has cameras down there and would be waiting for us when we get there."

"I like the hoverbikes better. Remind me of my Harley," Salimbeni chimed in quickly.

Moore turned back to V. "And you sure Lee's out there?"

"Absolutely. We were able to identify that his vehicle traveled out there shortly after Lee arrived at the shoreside building where the entrance to the pipeline is. It has not returned," V answered.

"So, we go out there, Sam. Blow up the containers and capture Lee. That simple?" Moore asked skeptically.

"In a nutshell, yes. We'll eliminate anyone who challenges us. The first priority is to destroy those containers. We're going to do that in two ways. When we arrive, we're going to affix C-4 to the support legs of the platform below the containers. That's our backup plan," Duncan stated.

"Based on what the lab scientists gleaned from the stomachs of the dead dairy cows and the Boylens, they believe sea water will neutralize the effectiveness of the bacteria. Those shipping containers are not waterproof," V interjected.

"Right," Duncan agreed. "But our main objective is to plant the C-4 on the containers so that we are sure they are destroyed."

"How do we trigger the explosions?" Moore asked.

"We have remote devices. We can detonate them while we are still on the platform if we have to or after we capture Lee and are at sea," Duncan responded.

"You'd be surprised at the range of the remotes. We want to be sure that we are a safe distance away," V added.

CHAPTER 30

Early Evening
Gulf of Mexico

On the horizon, the charcoal sky displayed wisps of silver as it indicated the approaching storm. The wind rose as the waves became choppy with chaotic foam crests that struck the beach.

"Storm should be here in a few minutes," V observed as they finished unloading the hoverbikes from the trailer.

Moore looked seaward as he slipped on his goggles. "How long of a ride is it?"

"We'll go flat out. Should be there in under fifteen minutes," Duncan said as he started his hoverbike. He along with the other two had backpacks with C-4 and AR-15s strapped on the backs of their wetsuits. They also carried .45s as sidearms. Each of the hoverbikes had additional backpacks, containing C-4, secured to the seat behind the riders.

"The GPS on each hoverbike is already programmed for the oil platform," V announced as the other two climbed aboard their hoverbikes.

"Try to stay together," Duncan called as he eased his hoverbike three feet into the air.

Moore and Salimbeni started theirs and duplicated Duncan's altitude.

"Ready?" Duncan asked. He accelerated without waiting for an answer.

"Hang on to your walnuts, Emerson!" Salimbeni shouted as she gunned her hoverbike to catch up with Duncan.

Moore followed suit and joined them in racing across the wave tops. Within a minute, the rain began to patter from the dark clouds as thunder boomed overhead. Lightning cracked in the sky as the rain fell harder.

The three hoverbikes sped across the rising and falling waves as the lightning bursts ignited a rapid infusion of adrenaline in the three riders. The thunder overhead acted like a drum roll, announcing upcoming danger while the rain pummeled their exposed skin.

As the waves grew in height, the hoverbikes increased their altitude to stay about the swirling waves. At times, rogue waves threatened to crash on top of the outlying propellers to cause the hoverbikes to slip sideways into the seas. The riders fought to stay in control.

Soon the towering offshore oil platform emerged into view from the dense downpour. The structure reached 500 feet above the stormy sea on four metal legs that were driven into the seabed. Metal cross-bars connected the legs, holding the platform steady in fierce storms. A metal tube, running from the platform along one of the legs below the water, housed the elevator to the large pipe where Lee's vehicle was parked.

The main platform held the crane, former production offices, tool room, living quarters, and a helicopter pad. The two intermodal shipping containers were below the crane on the edge of the platform.

The platform was bathed in light as the three maneuvered to the nearest two legs below the area where the intermodal shipping containers were placed. Moore followed Duncan while Salimbeni went to the next nearest leg. The rise and fall of the waves complicated their attempts to dismount and tie off the legs which had steel ladders running to the platform above.

Duncan was able to loop a line around a ladder rung and tie off his hoverbike before shutting it down. He pulled off the backpack of C-4 and turned to help Moore. After several attempts, they were successful in securing Moore's hoverbike.

"They're going to take a beating," Moore shouted through the downpour.

"Yep. I just hope we don't need them to go back," he said. Moore saw the right front housing of his hoverbike crack open and break off as a wave threw it against the steel platform leg.

"Emerson, climb up and keep watch. I need to fasten this C-4 to the leg," Duncan instructed as he saw Salimbeni fastening her extra backpack of C-4 to the other leg of the oil platform.

Moore's fingers clung to the steel rungs as he climbed. When he reached the edge of the platform, he slowly raised his head over it and saw no one.

As quickly as the storm blew in, it blew out. The rain, thunder and lightning moved westward, giving the three intruders a respite. The seas began to calm as an eerie silence hung over the oil platform. It wouldn't last for long. Moore felt a tap on his leg and looked down. It was Duncan.

"See anything?" Duncan called quietly.

"No. Looks clear, although I did spot several cameras. They'll probably pick us up."

"Not too much we can do about that. V did say he would try jamming them. Hopefully he's effective in doing that," Duncan suggested.

"Hopefully," Moore echoed as he looked at the other platform leg where Salimbeni had been working. "Where's Mitch?"

Duncan looked and didn't see her. He did see a catwalk that was fifteen feet below the platform. It went around the leg. "I don't know," he remarked, exasperated. He regretted that he had pooh-poohed using communication devices on this operation.

"She's supposed to be covering us while we set the C-4 in the containers. Maybe she found a good spot," Duncan suggested. "Let's roll."

The two men crawled up the ladder and scurried in a crouch to the far side of the first container. Duncan pulled a pair of bolt cutters and quickly cut through the lock on the rear door while Moore played lookout with his AR-15 ready.

Before entering, Duncan pulled out a respirator and placed it over his face. He had come prepared after Moore warned about breathing any of the container contents. He stepped inside and placed the C-4 strategically throughout the container. Finished, he stepped out and closed the metal door.

They moved to the second container and repeated the process with the C-4 from Moore's backpack. While Duncan was inside, Salimbeni crawled over to join them.

"Sam, here's my backpack," she called as he returned to the doorway to take it.

"Where have you been?" Duncan asked.

"Checking out a possible backup escape route for us, in case we need it," she replied quickly.

"Okay," Duncan said as he ducked back inside.

When he finished, he stepped out and closed the door. The three of them crouched while they talked about their next step, capturing Lee.

"I hope V cut the camera feed because we will be bathed in light when we run to the buildings," Duncan expressed with concern.

"I'll take the lead," Moore offered as he moved to the end of the container. He stuck his head around the corner to look for danger while Salimbeni took a position between the two containers to provide covering fire if necessary.

"How does it look?" Duncan asked.

"Good," Moore said before he burst around the corner and streaked for the office structure.

He was halfway there when a burst from an AK-47 cut through the air. Moore dived for cover as a firefight erupted. The air was filled with bullets whizzing by like lethal bees in both directions. Several of the guards atop the building exchanged gunfire with Salimbeni and Duncan.

A scream rent the air as two rounds struck Salimbeni, knocking her to the ground. One round grazed her head, causing it to bleed profusely. The other round caught her in the left shoulder.

Duncan rushed to her side, pulling her behind the container. After quickly examining her, he said, "They're not serious." Between returning fire, he pulled out his medical kit and placed a bandage over her wounds. "This should help temporarily."

"Thanks, Sam," she said through gritted teeth.

"Can you shoot?" Duncan asked as the intensity of the gunfire from the guards increased with them spraying the area with rounds. It appeared that several were advancing on their position.

"Yes."

"They've got more ammo than us. Be prudent," Duncan urged as he picked up his AR-15 and returned fire. His weapon flickered flame and death as his round struck the nearest guard in the chest, lifting him off his feet and depositing him on the metal platform.

Salimbeni fired intermittently as Duncan took a defensive position at the end of the first container. He was surprised at the resistance they had encountered.

He couldn't detonate the containers because he and Mitch

were next to them. Duncan was unsure how he safely could lower Salimbeni to the hoverbikes and whether they were in any shape to ride away on. He heard Moore firing from his position as worry confronted him.

Suddenly, the air was filled with the sound of a M230 chain gun firing 625 rounds per minute at the guards. The rounds chewed up the metal platform and exploded when they connected with human tissue. The guards were cut down quickly, and all firing ceased. The air was filled with the noise from whirling blades as Duncan stepped around the container.

To his surprise, he saw the Ranger with Holly and John Hall in the cockpit as it hovered overhead. V was crouched between them as he gave a thumbs up. As they landed on the helicopter pad, Duncan noted that the M230 was mounted on a chin turret on the Ranger nose.

"Are we glad to see you!" Duncan exclaimed as he helped Salimbeni walk toward the Ranger while its occupants deplaned.

"We'll take her," Holly said as she and John helped Salimbeni back to the Ranger.

"You got here in the nick of time," Duncan said, appreciatively.

"I thought I'd surprise you with a little backup. I had them fly in yesterday and got the Ranger fitted with that M230," V smiled.

"Glad you were thinking ahead of us."

"Where's Emerson?" V asked as he looked around the oil platform.

Duncan looked back to the spot where he had last seen Moore. It was empty. "He's probably after Lee. Are you armed?"

V waved a .45. "Yes. Let's go before he uses up his nine

lives."

When the Ranger opened fire, Moore saw his opportunity and sprinted for the first building. When he entered, he was confronted by a guard who was aiming his AK-47 at Moore. Moore promptly fired, killing the man.

He walked across the room to a door while holding his weapon ready. He opened it and found the room empty. It was a lab, and Moore saw there were several small boxes on a table next to the wall.

He additionally observed a black container next to the small boxes, similar to one he saw previously in Tulare. It displayed a biohazard warning sticker and was labeled as biolee. He opened it and withdrew a vial of the deadly biolee. Moore smiled. He had a sample to give V.

While Moore snapped shut the container, the door on the far side of the room opened quietly. Lee and Mangan walked in and they had the drop on Moore.

"Place your weapons on the floor, Mr. Moore," Lee muttered with controlled rage.

"Do as he says, otherwise, you'll be leaving this platform earlier than you expected," Mangan said. He quickly crossed the distance between them and Moore, then kicked aside Moore's weapons.

"I should have known you were involved with this gunfire." Lee glared at Moore with anger-filled eyes. "I must admit that I am truly, truly amazed by your resiliency, Mr. Moore. I thought I'd seen the last of you in Tulare!" His words were filled with vile.

"I am more capable than you expected," Moore remarked with an undefeated tone as he heard the rounds from the M230 firing outside.

Lee glanced at the window and saw the flashes of gunfire. He turned to Mangan. "You have him. Finish him, and make sure he suffers, then join me below."

"It will be my pleasure," Mangan grinned malevolently.

Lee strode across the room and opened the elevator door. As the door closed, Lee muttered coldly, "Goodbye, Mr. Moore." The door shut and the elevator could be heard descending to where his vehicle waited to take him back through the underwater pipe to the mainland.

Moore didn't wait. He bull rushed Mangan, catching him by surprise. Mangan was knocked down as his weapon flew across the floor. As he half-rose to his feet, Moore swung a powerful right cross, connecting with Mangan's left jaw. Spitting out blood, Mangan raged as he jumped to his feet and hurled himself at Moore. The two men fell to the floor as they grappled and pummeled each other.

Mangan was the stronger of the two, and Moore was no match for him in a long-drawn fight. Moore writhed and was able to break free of Mangan's grip. The two men rose to their feet and circled each other. Moore then lunged head-first into Mangan's chest, knocking the wind out of him and dropping him to the floor again.

The big man gasped for breath as he scrambled to his feet. He moved in and caught Moore off-guard with a leg sweep that knocked Moore to the floor. Mangan sent several swift kicks into Moore's rib cage and then connected twice to Moore's head. Fighting through the sharp pain in his ribs and skull, Moore rolled and got back to his feet.

Moore retaliated by leg sweeping Mangan, causing him to fall to the floor. Moore then pounced on him from behind. He was able to slip one arm around Mangan's neck while reaching into his pocket for the vial of biolee. He flipped off the lid and brought the open container around Mangan's head where Mangan was gasping for breath and clawing at Moore's chokehold. Moore emptied the biolee into Mangan's open mouth.

"Enjoy the biolee!" Moore said triumphantly as he released his grip on Mangan. "Mmmm good."

A wide-eyed Mangan roared with fury as he realized what Moore had done. The two men jumped to their feet when unexpectedly the door opened as Duncan and V entered.

Mangan took one look and saw that they blocked his escape path to the elevator. He turned and ran to the table where he snatched the black container from which Moore had extracted the vial of biolee. Mangan then escaped before anyone could react. Within seconds, they heard the enclosed lifeboat rolling down the davit.

Duncan ran out of the room in time to see it splash into the Gulf. He turned and reentered the room where he found Moore collapsed on the floor. "He got away."

"Not really," Moore urged. "He's ingested a healthy dose of the biolee. He won't last long."

Only half-conscious and consumed with pain, Moore was barely aware of his surroundings. He was down on both hands and his knees, struggling to get to his feet. Duncan and V raced to his side.

"Let us help you," Duncan offered as he placed an arm around Moore's waist and hoisted him to his feet. Moore winced in pain as V placed his arm around Moore's shoulder and assisted him to a nearby chair.

"I might have a couple of broken ribs," Moore grimaced as he allowed a small laugh to escape his lips.

"What's so funny?" V asked.

"Mangan grabbed that plastic container that contained the biolee and the antidote. He was probably thinking he'd use the antidote during his getaway, but there's one problem." Moore reached into his other pocket and withdrew the green vial with the antidote. "I have it. This is for you two. You can now save the world," Moore suggested, pleased with his action. "And here is another vial that contains the biolee," Moore said as he produced it from his pocket.

"Good work," V said as he carefully took the vials.

"Amazing that the vials didn't break," Duncan said as he looked at the vials.

"Extremely high-quality vials. Have to be. You wouldn't want to chance one breaking," V commented as he examined the vials.

Catching his breath, Moore remarked, "Where did you come from V? I didn't know you were part of the plan."

V smiled with concern as he looked at Moore's face with purple-colored bruises and bloody lips. "I wasn't." He quickly explained how they had arrived in the Ranger.

"Mitch took a couple of rounds," Duncan added.

"Serious?" Moore asked.

"No. She should be okay."

"I need to get these ribs looked at," Moore winced as he shifted.

"Where's Lee? Did you find him?" Duncan asked.

"He's gone by now. Went down the elevator. He was going to wait for Mangan, but I don't think he'd wait for long."

"It's too bad he got away," Duncan said, disappointed. "But at least we can destroy the containers of biolee."

"That's true," Moore agreed. Duncan and V helped Moore leave the room. They walked to the Ranger where Salimbeni was resting in one of the seats.

"Ready to depart?" Holly asked from the pilot seat.

"Yes. Let's go about a mile toward shore and we'll detonate the C-4," Duncan instructed.

Within a few minutes, they were hovering a mile away as Duncan depressed the remotes — first to explode the containers, then to explode the two legs of the oil platform to allow the exploded containers to sink into the saltwater.

"Too bad Lee got away," Moore lamented.

"I wouldn't be too sure about that," Salimbeni grinned mysteriously.

"What do you mean?" Moore asked.

"Watch," she said as she triggered a remote in her hand.

Suddenly there was an underwater explosion two miles away toward the shore. Water plumed into the sky from below.

"What was that?" Moore questioned with a confused look.

"That was the end of Lee. Remember when I disappeared on that catwalk?"

"Yes."

"I found a door to the elevator shaft to where Lee's vehicle was parked. I climbed down the safety ladder and affixed my extra bag of C-4 to the bottom of his vehicle," she smiled victoriously.

"You got him," Moore said with relief.

"I most certainly did. That was for Izzy!" she cracked seriously.

"Way to go, Mitch!" Moore said amidst the cheers that filled the Ranger as it headed for the shore.

"Mission accomplished," Duncan stated satisfactorily.

CHAPTER 31

Several Hours Later
New Orleans

Salimbeni was laying on her bed in the emergency room. Her wounds had been treated and she was conversing with Duncan and V.

One bed away, Moore was laying after returning from having his chest x-rayed. He was woozy from the painkiller injection he had been given to relieve the pain of his injuries.

"Mr. Moore?" the ER doctor asked through his face mask as he approached Moore's bed.

"Yes," Moore replied through a fog of sedation.

"I've got some good news for you."

Moore wrinkled his forehead as he tried to concentrate on what the doctor was telling him. "Yes?"

"The x-rays showed that your rib injury wasn't serious enough to require surgery. I didn't see any multiple, bicortically-displaced rib fractures that would require surgical stabilization."

Moore struggled to comprehend what the doctor was saying. "No surgery, right?"

"Right. You probably won't need treatment other than rest, ice and breathing exercises. Most people need at least a month to recover," the doctor explained. "I'd suggest you take it easy."

"That's impossible for him," Duncan called good-naturedly from Salimbeni's bedside.

"I'll give you some exercises to do and you can take naproxen or ibuprofen if you have any pain," the doctor continued before he walked away.

"Thanks doctor," Moore responded.

"You're very lucky that nothing more serious happened to you on your adventure, Emerson," Duncan said as he walked to Moore's bed.

"I know," Moore agreed.

Their conversation was interrupted by the arrival of a dark-haired nurse, who also was wearing a face mask.

"I'm so sorry to break up this lovefest, but the doctor wants one more test," she said as she picked up the chart at the end of the bed. "Mr. Emerson Moore?" she asked as she confirmed the patient's name.

"Yes."

"First, what is your date of birth?"

Moore provided the information.

"Secondly, I'm going to take you back down the hall," she said as she looked at Duncan. "I should have your friend back in fifteen minutes."

Duncan returned to Salimbeni's side as Moore asked, "What kind of test am I having?"

The nurse began wheeling Moore's bed out of the emergency room through the hallway. "I'm not quite sure. I just was asked to take you down there."

Moore felt lightheaded and closed his eyes while she pushed his bed into another room. She half-closed the door behind her as she switched on the light and pulled down her face mask. Next, she approached the side of Moore's bed. As she leaned over him, she withdrew a small Berretta from a thigh holster and placed the barrel against Moore's temple.

"Emerson," she called softly. "Remember me?" she asked calmly.

Moore opened his eyes and tried to focus. Was he dreaming

as he looked at the face with almond-shaped eyes? "Kari?" he asked, stunned.

"Yes."

"What are you doing?" he asked, panicked as she dug the business-end of the weapon into his head.

"You killed Bjorn, his plans and my life!" she responded in a deadly tone with narrowed, anger-filled eyes.

"But. But. I don't understand. You saved me from the biol-ee and now you want to kill me?" Moore asked. He struggled through the drug-induced fog to understand the reality of his situation.

"I don't know what I was thinking when I freed you, but it was wrong. I never imagined you would be successful in killing Bjorn," she sneered cynically. Her widened eyes burned with anger and the vein in her neck pulsed as the tension arose.

Moore saw a side of her that he hadn't seen in the past. The trauma of losing Lee had flicked a switch in her inner self, releasing a demon of death.

"Drop it, Kari!" Duncan's voice yelled from the doorway where he stood with a .45 pointed at her.

Yoki turned, aiming her weapon at Duncan. As she fired, Moore struck her arm, causing the bullet to fly harmlessly past Duncan. Duncan fired and caught her in the chest. Her body dropped to the floor as blood flowed from the fatal wound.

"I see you remembered her name," Moore quipped as he recalled the first time that Duncan had mentioned her to him. "I think she got the point."

"Yes, this time I did remember," Duncan said as he walked over and kicked aside her weapon. Two nurses rushed into the room and knelt beside her. One looked at Duncan and shook her head. Duncan nodded.

"I'm taking my friend back to ER," Duncan said before wheeling Moore out of the room.

"Thanks Sam," Moore said, appreciatively.

"That's what I do. Rescue you all of the time."

"What made you come down to find me?" Moore asked.

"You can thank Mitch for that. Remember, I hadn't met Yoki, but Mitch recalled seeing her at the casino and in Jamaica. She thought it was her behind that facemask and urged me to come check on you. Good thing I did."

"I'll say." Moore added as they arrived back in the ER, and Duncan wheeled Moore next to Salimbeni's bed.

"I assume the gunshots involved you two," Mitch commented as she looked from one to the other.

Moore quickly explained what had transpired. "Thank you, Mitch. I'm glad you recognized her."

"We all are," V added.

"Ready to plan another adventure?" Duncan asked. "I have something that I could use some help on."

Moore smiled. "No. I'm going to take it easy. I have a friend down in Holden Beach, North Carolina. I think I'm due for some peace and beach time."

Coming Soon
The Next Emerson Moore Adventure
Holden's Promise

BOB ADAMOV